Books by Jerry Farmer

Jobe Carson Mystery Series

Jobe's Daughter
Jobe's Curse
Jobe's Torment
Jobe's Anguish
Jobe's Vexation
Jobe's Ordeal
Jobe's Affliction
Jobe's Fiasco

Standalone Titles

Jobe's Recipes

Essay Collections

America Ya Gotta Love It # 1
America Ya Gotta Love It # 2
America Ya Gotta Love It # 3
America Ya Gotta Love It # 4
America Ya Gotta Love It # 5
America Ya Gotta Love It # 6
America Ya Gotta Love It # 7
America Ya Gotta Love It # 8
America Ya Gotta Love It # 9
America Ya Gotta Love It # 10
America Ya Gotta Love It # 11
America Ya Gotta Love It # 12

Jobe's Daughter

By

Jerry Farmer

Prologue

Dark.

A faint buzzing noise. Coming from somewhere. Stopping. Starting again. Almost like a dentist's drill. A mumbled curse. Then light, and the sound of a door opening.

Footsteps.

He tried to open his eyes. They wouldn't respond. He wasn't sure where he was. Some drug, fogging his brain.

He smelled a familiar odor. Something cooking. Smoked meat?

A dog barked in the distance.

The footsteps came closer. He heard breathing now. Muffled, as through a mask. Where had he heard that? A painter's mask maybe, or one to keep out pollen.

The breath sounded wet. Ragged from exhaustion—or tension. He could feel the cold. All over. His muscles were paralyzed, deadened to his efforts, but he could feel. Feel the movement of air on his skin as whoever it was came closer. The warmth of breath as someone bent down towards him.

A moist hand grasped his big toe and pinched it hard. He felt the pain but couldn't jerk away. The hand moved up his right leg, then grabbed his genitals, squeezing his testicles together till an autonomic response from his brainstem made tears well from his eyes.

Then laughter. Crazy, maniacal, laughter.

The dog barked again outside. He felt his head being lifted. Felt a rudely-shaped hard object propped beneath it. There was a light ripping noise, then fingers poked into his right eye and opened the eyelid. Roughly sticking it open with tape. He could see his lower body and arms now, but a high intensity lamp left his tormentor obscured in shadow.

He was totally naked.

Then the noise started again. Louder. Closer. Buzzing.

He recognized it now. An electric knife.

Advertising phrases bubbled in his brain on waves of adrenalin. Their insipid declarations suddenly macabre. "Just the thing every family needs." "Make quick work of that holiday turkey." "Catering made easy." "Act now and we'll throw in a set of shish kabob skewers."

He tried to get away, tried to squirm, tried to recoil, but of course that was impossible. He could only watch in horror as the knife lowered and started cutting.

The blood welled up from the first slice into his elbow.

Crazily, that initial cut felt familiar. The shock-like burr of the funny bone.

Then the pain began in earnest...

CHAPTER 1

It all started with the "lump." And as lumps go, this one turned out to be a doozy. If I didn't know better, I'd say God was trying to punish me, making me suffer for being part of an arrogant culture. A culture whose worst example was having a whole cable channel devoted entirely to the preparation and gluttonous consumption of food. While the rest of the world was starving, of course.

Then again, I'm sure God has better things to do than plan my personal torment. For whatever reason. Maybe I'm just not too lucky.

I like to think I'm a pretty ordinary guy. But for some reason extraordinary things keep happening to me. Not like the time an arrow creased my skull, or the time I crashed through that deadfall and nearly busted my head on the river rocks down below. I mean ordinary extraordinary things, like the key busting in the lock of my car, or my shoe full of crane flies because I left them out on the porch all night. Which, by the way, I found out too late for my favorite pair of socks.

So, on the face of it, me being a private investigator is something I really can't explain in logical terms. It's certainly not the sort of profession one would expect to lend itself to uneventful placidity. When people ask me why, I just say it seems to fit. Call it instinct. The hours are flexible. I have a fair amount of people skills. And my philosophy training in college honed my analytical mind to a fine edge. Besides, I love solving problems.

Which was precisely what I was trying to do when the "lump" happened—trying to figure out a way to solve the problem of getting the moss out of my lawn. I was facing the conundrum of every homeowner since Adam was relocated out of Eden; how to remove the obnoxious plants while keeping and nurturing the good ones. The conundrum is intensified where I live, in the great Pacific Northwest,

3

by the fact that lawns don't grow all that well. At least if you define "well" as uniform, single species-type lawns. Competition in our inundated, fertile environment is tremendous. And the chief competition precisely where lawns don't grow well, namely moss, is also green and verdant. Ah, "green and verdant," my favorite subtle repetitive redundancy.

So there I was, pulling up big hanks of hairy brown stuff that my chemical moss killer had caused and noticing with dismay that it left behind big hairless brown patches of bare dirt. That got me cursing the holy hell out of the manufacturers of said travesty who'd failed to warn me in big bold letters of this possible result. Then all of a sudden, I hear this whining truck go zooming down the street, hit the big pothole out in front of my house and with a bomp, a thump, and a bump, out of its rear-end bounces the lump. The lump hits the ground while the truck keeps zooming away. And me, with my reading glasses on because I've also been studying the fine print of the manufacturer's recommended dosage of herbal death lotion, can't squint quick enough to determine the jerk's license plate number. Not only that, but the tears misting my eyes from the rising fog of defoliant emanating from the moss killer package makes it hard to determine even the model of his older midget pickup truck.

Probably one of the local gardeners. Or maybe one of the trash pick-up entrepreneurs that roam through the neighborhoods since the last time garbage rates went up. I hate those guys. Garbage rates may suck, but that's no cause to pay some sleazy bastard under the table to illegally dump your crap out in the woods somewhere.

Or a lump near my driveway for that matter. The lump, as it turned out, was a shapeless green mass of Hefty bag. Now what was I gonna I do with it?

"Sonofabitch," I shouted, as I hurried across my mossy battle zone to the curb. My dog Sparky, ever intrepid when it comes to sticking his nose in other people's (or other dog's) business, was already there, nuzzling it around. I grabbed the lump from him just as

4

he started to carry it off. His hangdog expression told me he was sorely disappointed I'd chosen to relieve him of his newfound trophy before he had the chance to give it a thorough gnawing over.

I tossed the lumpy package over by the garage door, shooed my dumb dog into the back yard and closed the fence gate. My damn kids. When will they ever learn? They weren't born in a barn, but they never fail to try to show the world they're white trash to the core. Gates left open, doors left open, drawers left open, notebooks scattered from hell to the breakfast table. And of course, the obligatory caps left off the toothpaste and empty toilet paper tubes left on the spindle. Messes goddamn everywhere. You'd think my two ex-wives had moved back in.

The only thing the two boys ever obsess about closing is their zippers (for which the rest of us are eternally thankful). It's a wonder they manage to get through the day without their ankles giving out from dodging all the junk they leave around to trip over. And my daughter, I don't even want to go there...

So I needed another shapeless lump of garbage around the place like I needed another hole in my head. My mood, already fermenting from the moss-out debacle, was turning sour as a peeled kumquat. First off, I bitched out the road department: Why is it they build brand shiny new roads to lead in more and more people to fill up the new developments and overfill our already brimming schools, but they still can't budget a hundred bucks to fix a damn pothole in an old residential neighborhood that's been breaking legs, bending bike rims and cracking leaf springs for the last five freaking years?

Maybe it's their idea of a speed bump, to slow down all the idiots driving through our neighborhood. Yeah. That's it, save the little unsupervised kiddies from getting crushed by a giant SUV while they're tootling their razor scooters around the blind corners which our now out-of-state developer built into his illegal plat. Pothole speed bumps, what a concept. Like a passive restraint system from the county roads department.

Oh well. The current administration ran on a "no impact fees for new development" platform, so what do you expect? It's obvious they sure as hell didn't think about the impact fees we shell out every time one of our vehicles gets buried to the fender in a monster pothole. Or the impact fees we pay to the hospital when our kids fly over the handlebars because their mountain bikes bit the big one. Poor kids. Poor adults. Poor me. Blah, blah, blah.

Not that the county's responsible because some idiot in a nondescript pickup is barreling through my neighborhood at top speed. And, truth be told, I kind of liked the pothole at that moment. I hope the bastard busted a hole in his oil pan. Because if there's one thing I hate more than an unresponsive, palms-greased-under-the-table county government it's a freakin' idiot speeding through a slow kids zone like a teenager late for a date. Or a firetruck late for a fire. Screw you buddy, and drop a few letters from "firetruck" and add an "off" while you're at it.

CHAPTER 2

It wasn't long before the boys drove in, oblivious to anything but themselves as always. When they pulled up in the gray Honda Civic, I couldn't help myself from surreptitiously checking it over for what I've come to call MSD's: Mysterious Spontaneous Dents. It seems that ever since my oldest son Kiah—pronounced Ky-ah—started to drive, the oddest little dents appear in the biggest variety of places. As if by "magic." He has an excuse for every one. From it "musta happened when you were driving the car" to "...this big dog jumped against the door." Great. From the dog ate his homework to the dog dented my car. That's Kiah for you, the facts change but the theme remains the same. It's good to know that externalization of responsibility hasn't died in this country because of video games and the Internet.

Kiah and his taller little brother Jack headed for the front door with a muffled "Hi." I assumed the pantry was their goal, there to inhale any starchy substances I'd been stupid enough to buy. Sometimes living with two teenage boys is like being a bacterium surrounded by a couple of giant white blood cells. As the amorphous maws keeping sucking up everything in their path you can't help but think that maybe you're next.

For two boys that had been raised in common they sure were different. Their genetic package included the same dominant genes that gave me my brown eyes and hair, and also determined their slender builds—though mine had finally expressed itself to the pot-bellied side. But Jack was taller, and lankier, while Kiah was more compact, and wiry as a hungry coyote. Much like I had been in my youth before my final collegiate growth spurt shot me up from five six to my terminal five ten. It was in their expressions that they differed most. Jack's facial attitude was as relaxed and broad as his feeling of camaraderie for all and sundry. Kiah's countenance was darker and more intense, as befitted his constant questioning of everything and everyone. Well, almost everything. Caught up as they were in their teenage priorities sometimes they were both blind as bats.

So I wasn't surprised they'd barely given the lump a glance on the way to their afternoon feeding. I also knew that when it was finally discovered by their sister Miranda later, they'd be aggrieved that I hadn't pointed it out to them. By this time, I was only dimly aware of it myself. I'd raked up a pretty big pile of dead moss and was wondering if I should bag it and try to pitch it in the wandering trash truck on its next drive-by or bale it and sell it to the feed store around the corner.

It was then that the school bus pulled up with a screech of brakes and a thwang of its bumper protector thing. Suddenly the air was filled with the cacophony of voices that can only be a vehicle full of elementary schoolers. I admired the poor driver for her ability to both tune out the everyday riot of noise that was kid-generated and tune in the specific traffic sounds she needed to get the little screamers safely to their respective destinations. I'd never be able to pull it off. I'm not sure what would happen first, me dying of an acute burst aneurysm or a busload of machine-gunned children.

Just kidding.

With a swoosh of the door and a crunch of gravel, out came my little angel, Miranda. My salvation. After her mother disappeared, Miranda helped keep me together. There is really no way to describe the depths of agony I felt when my wife disappeared. No way to convey the emptiness, the loss, the gaping, ragged hole that was left behind in a heart that was once so full of joy and love.

When you find the woman you love, and you have children, you embark on a vast uncharted course into the unknown. But you do it together. You plan together; you dream together, you hope together. The track of your life becomes a continuum of two. And as you build a present with each other you also build a past and a future. When that is suddenly and unexpectedly cut off, you find yourself adrift on an ocean of uncertainty. All your anchors are cut loose. You are tossed this and way and that, with no clear direction and nothing to hold on to. It's bad enough when a relationship ends—when a divorce severs your past from your future. But to suddenly have the love of your life disappear. And not know. Not know if she's alive or dead. Not know if she's happy, or in pain. To just not know.

But responsibility to my children was the anchor I was finally able to reset. And slowly, surely, I was able to find a way to at least stabilize. I was in despair over losing the wonderful woman who held my heart, especially under such mysterious circumstances, but somehow, I needed to hold on to my sanity to see the kids through. Especially my little girl. It wouldn't be right for me to collapse. If I'd been alone there's no telling what I would have done, just to end the agony. But Miranda kept me whole. She kept me focused on living each day, one day at a time, and though it may sound trite, it was the love of her mother shining through Miranda's eyes that kept me from going completely over the edge.

Miranda's about what you'd expect of a girl between the ages of nine and twelve. Sunny disposition, positive approach to life, messes drifting in her wake from dawn till dusk. In many ways she's quite neat and organized, but she also has no problem maintaining that important random element to her personality that is nothing if not endearing. A rap sheet would put her at about five feet tall, with brown hair and brown eyes, which are open in a constant state of wonder. Miranda is as nosy as I am curious. That is to say, she's always poking around where she doesn't belong, which has got both her and me into trouble a million times. You might say she's an extraordinary ordinary kid.

We call her Mir, for short, like that Russian satellite. For two reasons: One, she's always in erratic orbit, circling around us like a hummingbird around a trumpet vine; and two, little bits of her are always falling off and crashing to the ground. Bits like hair barrettes, bobby pins, butterfly thingies that she strings to her braids and various other beanie or electronic whatevers she hangs from her backpack. She's never met a fastener she couldn't leave undone, if you know what I mean.

But she's also as observant as a pirate in a crow's nest.

"Lump ho," she called out as she alighted from the bus. "What's that green thing, Dad?"

"That? I don't know. Something that fell out of one of those stupid gypsy trash trucks this afternoon."

"Cool," she said, and started for it, both hands ready to rip.

"Hold up," I shouted, suddenly cautious, "Let's look at this real slow, Mir. Could be something toxic you know."

"Oh Dad, you're always so dramatic."

"Mir, if anything is this world can possibly go wrong it'd be when you're somehow attached to it. Heck with that Murphy guy. I'm inventing a new principle called Mir's Law."

"Hummpf," she muttered. Then, alarmed: "What's that?"

"Jesus! It looks like a finger."

Sure enough, peeking through a hole that Sparky had chewed open earlier was the unmistakable form of a human finger.

Before I could shove her aside, Mir was tearing at the plastic. We both felt a churn in our stomachs as the gruesome vision was exposed. Not just a finger—but an entire human hand and forearm; apparently severed at the elbow.

"Oh my God!" We both yelled simultaneously.

Somehow neither one of us felt the urge to shout jinx. This had been sitting by my garage door all afternoon?

"What is it Dad? How come it looks so shrivelly?"

I didn't have the heart to correct her word usage. Shrivelly it indeed was.

"It looks like it's been dehydrated, Mir."

"Dehydrated? Like that jerky machine on QVC?"

"Yeah," I said, "Like that jerky machine on QVC."

Not only that, it looked like it had been shrink-wrapped too. Whoever disposed of this guy, they sure were trying to prevent any stench from giving him away for a long, long time. If this vacu-pack had made it to the landfill, it would have been centuries before some future anthropologist tried to use it do a doctoral thesis on the embalming practices of the early 21st century.

Funny how things just seem to happen. Money had been getting even scarcer than usual lately. I'd been wondering what I was going to do for a case. And here one had landed near my doorstep like a badly thrown newspaper.

Except this time it looked like the newsboy had thrown his arm out too.

Chapter 3

Now was the time to solve one of those problems I keep saying I'm good at. The dilemma as I saw it was this: How to turn this gruesome godsend into a windfall for my family. I don't mean to sound harsh here. God knows the poor schmuck in the shrink-wrap must have suffered. But he was in the hereafter now. And although, arguably, in his present condition he may have found it hard to roll over in his grave, I'm sure his surprise that I was looking to turn his misfortune into cold hard cash and possibly in the process put some bread on the table for my kids wouldn't make his rest too un-peaceful. If nothing else, it meant bringing his killer—or should I say renderer—to justice. The butcher that did this must be some cold sumbitch indeed. And I intended to use that to my family's advantage. First things first:

"Miranda, we have to have a little talk"

"You want me to keep this a secret, right Dad?"

Ah Miranda, perceptive beyond her years. "Yes Honey, the fewer people that know about this the better chance I have of catching the killer." No need to bore her with the realities of our finances.

"And that's how you make your living right?" That girl, she fired right to the heart.

"Right, Hon. So not a word to anyone. Promise?"

"Promise."

That was good enough for me. Ever since Mir was in kindergarten just the simple word 'promise' had stood as our bond. No elaborate handshakes or vows required. I only hope she wasn't tempted beyond her tender years to let the cat (or arm) out of the bag.

I opened the garage door and tossed the rewrapped package by the freezer. Good. It looked like any other piece of trash scattered on the floor. And there was a lot of that. I'm real neat when it comes to my household; some have even trotted out the epithet "anal retentive" when describing me, but my garage is inevitably a shambles. It's not that I don't put things in special places originally, it's just that I forget sometimes what part of the stack a given thing is in and have to search for it later. So stacks soon turn to piles and sorting soon turns to rummaging. This time tossing my lump on another pile worked just fine. Sometimes the best place to hide something is in plain sight, and if this particular piece of detritus looked like it belonged with all the rest, it stood to reason no one would notice. I once hid Kiah's Easter basket under a pile of dirty laundry in his room. He didn't discover it till the ants led him there.

My next task was to act as if everything was normal tonight and try to divert Miranda from thinking about the horrid member in the garage that had somehow hitchhiked into our life. I made dinner as usual, cleaned up afterwards with the reluctant assistance of the entire motley crew, then settled down to a half hour of reading before retiring for the evening. There's not a lot of private time when you're a single dad of three kids. Thank God for the Internet, WWF wrestling and South Park. The boys would be occupied till 11:00. I hoped they'd keep it quiet when they shuffled into their bunk bed. I was glad I'd at least saved that when we had to sell the big house.

At dinner earlier, I had asked them about their day, Miranda and I exchanging glances every time the conversation turn weird. And it was weird.

"How was your day Kiah?" I asked. Kiah is short for Hezekiah. It's a long story and this isn't the place to tell it.

"Pretty good, Dad," he mumbled, "Trevor asked me to give him a hand on his homework. So I'm gonna call him later."

"I got a burned copy of the new *Armed and Dangerous* computer game," piped up Jack, barely letting Kiah finish his sentence. "It's amazing how much data you can pack on a compact digital CD!"

"Yeah, and I like going to those ATM machines" I grunted, "And using my PIN number." Jack missed my subtle attempt to point out his acronymic redundancy. I looked over at Mir to see if she was catching all the appendage references the boys were eerily making.

"And Jill needed a shoulder to cry on after sixth period today," Kiah continued. "How do you do it, Dad? I mean, I like it when people confide in me, but sometimes I feel so emotionally blackmailed. It's like someone is twisting my arm to give them compassion. I gotta hand it to you, you really juggle things well."

"Thanks, Kiah," I replied.

"We studied the occult in our culture class today," Jack said. "It's cool. All the fundies were totally cranked, especially when we talked about palm reading."

"'Fundies?'"

"Yeah, that's what we call the fundamentalists, Dad. They need to have more fun and act less mental if you ask me."

"You go, Jack," proud to see my son's critical thinking facility developing early. "Give me five."

"Da-ad," he sneered, somehow making two syllables out of one. "Nobody high-fives anymore."

Mir looked on with her eyebrows raised in wonder.

I ruminated about the odd turns of conversation as I turned out the light. Had the boys actually noticed the arm and hand in the trash bag on some subconscious level? Or was fate just trying to hurry me up with a gentle verbal reminder? Hard to say. I don't much believe in all that occult mumbo-jumbo. And being a Virgo I particularly don't subscribe to that astrology crap, but every now and then it's hard not to believe in the power of fate.

The phone rang. Who could be calling at this hour? The boys knew our house was a "no call zone" after nine o'clock. As did their friends. I picked it up.

"Jobe," a voice barked, "This is Nelson Knudson. Heads up. My lab tech said you called her recently. If you're nosing into county business again I'll find a way to shut you and your slimy little P.I.

business down once and for all. You'll be back peddling menswear faster than you can say Tommy Hilfiger."

"In your case mountain figure's more like it," I shot back.

"What's that peewee? Don't push me too far Jobe, or I'll squeeze your skinny little smart ass so hard your eyes'll pop."

"Look Mr. Knudson. I believe I'm what you call a private citizen. And I think that means I have rights, among them the right not to be harassed by popinjays like you. Run your freaking coroner's office any way you see fit, but I can talk to anyone I like, any time I like and there's not a damn thing you can do about it."

"I said don't push me. You... you... you little pipsqueak."

"I'd say 'I-know-you-are-but-what-am-I,' Knudson, but your giant corpulence couldn't fit into any possible permutation of the word pipsqueak. Why don't you go back to your evening bottle and pick a fight with someone your own size? Like my ex-wife. I'm sure she's trying to pull that cheesy wedding ring you gave her off her puffy finger right now."

"Why you—"

"See you Nellie."

I hung up while he was still sputtering. He hates it when I call him Nellie.

CHAPTER 4

For anybody that gives a damn, Nelson Knudson is my nemesis. I guess we all need an adversary in life, from Popeye to God himself, but why the hands of fate incarnated my Bluto/Satan as Nelson Knudson I'll never know. It makes me think I must have done a lot of baby bird killing in my previous life. My karma must really suck if I have to spend most of this time on the wheel turning with the likes of Knudson.

I first met him years ago when I worked in the men's store. I was a men's clothing salesman before circumstances led me to the private investigation profession. And old Nellie, Nels as I called him then, was a frequent customer. His desire was to run for county office and so, naturally, he needed to drape his even then expanding form in the most flattering (read: fat obscuring) clothes he could. I did my best. In fact, I think it was largely (pun intended) because of my fine work and understanding of the psychology of dressing well that he was able to get elected. Let's face it; a fat slob like him wouldn't have gone far in carpenter pencil-holder jeans and a baseball cap. Sometimes a little fashion retouching is necessary on the portrait of personality. And that's what I did for Nellie. Except in his case I used a 54 portly airbrush. In the meantime, he took every opportunity to hit on my then not yet ex-wife. And she, whose latent social climber disease chose that moment to surface, ate up his aspiring politico attentions like a pig eats slop. Eventually they decided to share a wallow. Seems my profession was just not professional enough for the status my soon to be "ex" craved. Why is it we have "ex" wives and "used" cars? Anyhow, it all turned out just fine with me. I hope they're very happy. I know I am.

Needless to say, we've since maintained a certain friction in our relations with one another. And though I swallowed my pride and made sure the tuxedos they rented from me for the wedding fitted perfectly, (why the hell should I hurt my reputation by making him look bad?) the alum powder I dusted on the inside of his pants pockets was more than enough to salve my ego. I wonder if when he reached into his pocket to pull out a little scratch to pay the preacher he was able to stop scratching himself at the same time. Hope they had a nice honeymoon.

It was weird though that he should call on the very night the arm had dropped into our lap. I wondered again whether I should just turn it in to the authorities, but decided I'd probably have more luck if I got a leg up on any official investigation.

As a private investigator, I often work for insurance companies who are looking to "not" pay out their hard-earned money. I'm sure from their point of view that makes a lot of sense. If all a person had to do was off somebody, bury the body in the back yard and get instant cash, we'd have a real backyard landscaping problem across this great land of ours. A whole new industry would have to emerge. Something like: "What to do with those unsightly shallow grave mounds" a la Martha Stewart. So it's in the insurance companies' and society's best interest to make it tough for people to collect that kind of cash.

The police, fortunately for carrion pickers like me, are also quite overworked, especially in the missing persons department, so if no leads turn up fairly quickly in an investigation, they feel it's a better allocation of resources to go back to closing down meth labs and crack houses. Hey. Who can blame 'em? Steady work is steady work. That leaves an open field for people like me. Not good enough to support a lot of us, but with the occasional fat fee, good enough to scrape by.

And the hours are pretty flexible. Which is important to a single dad that has to take this kid to school and that kid to band and that kid to basketball and that kid to feed her horse and so on and etc.

Unfortunately, my current choice of profession put me on a more or less constant collision course with the honorable Nelson Knudson, coroner and cuckolder. And competition it was, not just for vanity, but for my bottom line. The insurance companies don't pay one cent without results, and if a case is solved through official channels, even if in the process of that solving I do most of the legwork, the companies won't pay me a dime. Nelson, because he loves getting credit for everything, and because he's got the only good forensic facilities closer than the FBI lab in Seattle, had more than once yanked the rug out from under one of my investigations. And in the process doomed my children to another week of lentils, rice, and Costco pack generic chili.

Bastard.

CHAPTER 5

I woke up at 4:30 to start the shower cycle; me, then Kiah, Jack, and Miranda. Getting us all off to our various morning obligations is often a cluster of major proportions. It was 8:30 by the time I put Miranda on the bus—with a final look to insure her secrecy—and headed down to the police station. My first job was to make sure I wasn't stepping on any official investigations. Threats from Knudson notwithstanding, I like to keep on a pretty good basis with the professional law enforcement community. You never know what kind of bone they're going to throw you, and since I don't really pack heat in my daily rousts of debt-skippers and missing-person-claimers, it doesn't hurt to have a uniformed menace to trot out when needed.

I beelined right past the receptionist and headed for the messy desk of Officer Greg Miller. In this case the description "beeline" was accurate, as I had to circle around any number of desks, piles of evidence, and bustling cops on my way to the final flower of my destination. Like a true bee, going straight to my target was out of the question. Greg looked up from rummaging around on his desk with the bleary-eyed expression of one who has spent way too much time the previous night watching television, or in his case I'm sure, dirty movies. Pay-perv-view, as it were.

"Jobe," he called out boisterously, "How the hell are you?"

"Pretty good, Officer Greg. Been stroking the cable again I see."

"Ha ha. Nah. Just my insomnia rearing up."

"Yeah, right. I wouldn't touch that line with a ten-foot remote. What's new?"

"If by 'what's new' you mean what tidy tidbits can I give you that might make me lose my job, the answer is nothing."

"Now Officer Greg," I soothed, "you know I've never asked you to do anything illegal."

"Tell that to my boss."

"Oh yeah. Sorry about the flak from your chief. It's not my fault he and Knudson were frat buddies in college. But hey, schmucks like you and me gotta stick together. I always try to remember one thing; the Greek system didn't work very well for the Greeks. People ending up at the top of the socio-political ladder 'cause they once greased pigs together has got to have ramifications on world leadership status eventually."

"You're full of crap Jobe. Whatever you just said."

"Up yours too, Officer," I replied graciously. "What do you think? Any hot missing person investigations I should not mess around in? Murders perhaps, official business I should steer clear of?"

"Nah, nothing actually hot. In fact, the department could probably use your nosy sniffer to turn up a tasty mushroom or two. We got four cold missing person cases right now and no leads. Four different people reported loved ones missing. It looks like all four of 'em are clean as a whistle. The only thing they have in common is they're trying to cash in policies from the same insurance company."

"Let me guess. Megapolitan Life and Indemnity."

"You nailed it. You private dicks shoot straight to the target don't you?"

"Yup, like a bee to a flower." Private dick? What kind of reference was that? When he wasn't watching porno, Officer Greg must have been reading too many old detective novels. Nobody called anybody a private dick anymore.

He did some rummaging on his desk and gave me a bunch of files he'd collected on the various cases. We high-fived each other and I headed out towards the street.

As I went through the foyer I heard a big booming voice saying: "... so she returned the M&M's to the store because she thought they were all W's" and a huge burst of raucous laughter. Damn. I recognized that bombast. Knudson. Oops. He saw me.

"Hey Jobe, I thought I told you to stay away from the building."

"Well actually, Sir, you told me to stay away from your lab tech, and as I recall I told you to mind your own business. Which, come to think of it, is not spending taxpayers' money threatening members of the public. Or, for that matter, telling sexist blond jokes at the water cooler."

"Screw you, pipsqueak." He seemed to have settled on an epithet for me he felt comfortable with. That's nice. I decided to kill him with kindness.

"Just a friendly word of advice, your honor. If some enterprising young intern out to save the world from sexist pigs like you wanted to tape-record your little jokefest and play it back to the public on your next reelection run, you'd have a pretty hard time playing it down. No matter how well I dressed you."

He swallowed hard, glancing around to see if any such intern was lurking in the corridor. Then he looked at his watch, muttered an unintelligible exclamation and headed back in the direction of his office. The panting engendered by his strenuous movement was quite audible after only a couple of strides. "Strenuous," in his case, being any movement of his incredible bulk.

I felt a little smug. Don't get me wrong here. I'm not a feminist. I'm an anti-sexist. I think every gender's got a right to respect. And every hair color within that gender. People used to look at my missing wife and say; "You'll like this. This is a blond joke." My wife, who was both blond and smart as a tack, would grimace in expectation. As if telling her that it was a "blond" joke somehow made it better. Like saying to a Polish person, "You'll like this. This is a Polack joke." Yeah, right.

Then again, my cynicism cuts both ways. I'm also against the more sentimental members of any gender spinning webs of romance around essentially craven acts. I admit, I'm about as romantic as a diaphragm. But my spin on, say, the Bridges of Madison County movie was that it wasn't romantic at all. Infidelity was the dissonant keynote. It wasn't about one woman and one man finding true love in a brief but poignant moment. It was about a horny cornhusker humping it up with a rutting shutterbug. National Geographic or no, the guy was developing the wrong kind of negative. He should have been working with a little less exposure if you catch my drift. It's a good thing he finally realized that although he was in the field, he was definitely out of his depth.

Nonetheless, I knew Knudson wouldn't let me forget I had embarrassed him in front of his water cooler cronies. He'd find some way to get back at me. Me, I was just glad I didn't have to sell him a new set of clothes every year anymore. It was certainly lucrative for me at the time, picking up a fat commission every time I completely replaced his wardrobe, but there was something mildly disgusting about the whole enterprise. Like I was an active participant in a snake shedding his old skin. Or a crab molting.

CHAPTER 6

I got in my dirty CRV and headed for the bright new offices of the Megapolitan Life and Indemnity Company. Who says the insurance business is lousy? They may not make as much money in the short term on stocks and bonds as other big corporations, but the truth is, the combined real estate assets of the biggest domestic life insurance companies make up a good third of the marketable property in America. And, as a big bonus to them, there is absolutely no federal regulation of life, health or auto insurance policies. That difficult job is left entirely up to the puny little states. Must be one of those state's rights we're always hearing about; that local control that always seems to give the public the pole. Except in this case it was a double-edged sword, the sharp side positioned right against the neck of any state insurance commissioner that tried to take them on. The reality is no single state, save perhaps New York or California, has the political and financial muscle to take on the big national insurance boys. Because all those boys have to do is accidentally get together at a party in Mazatlán and agree to pull out of any such state that gives them trouble. Pretty soon the paying public is screaming for the well-meaning anti-rate-gouging insurance commissioner's political head. Bye, bye commissioner, hello high insurance rates.

But that's only occasionally, most of the time the free spirit of competition is enough to keep rates marginally okay and though the new insurance building is the nicest on the block, it's not like it's the Taj Mahal.

My experience with Megapolitan goes back to the disappearance of my own dear wife. The beautiful, intelligent blond I mentioned earlier.

One day she just disappeared. She didn't come home from work. She didn't come home the next morning, or the next. And the downward spiral began. As things went along and my wife didn't return, as all the investigations didn't pan out and all the leads dried up, as we lost hope and then despaired and then even lost despair, as the uncertainty eventually turned us all numb, we finally had to give up looking and try to go on. Because the world did. The bills were stacking up and the bankcards were maxing out.

We'd been, like most people, accustomed to living on two incomes, and also like most people, had been obligating ourselves to bills that two incomes could manage. Then, suddenly, no second income. You try to plan for the worst. You have savings. You have life insurance. But the savings were gone. And life insurance only pays when someone is dead. And no one was dead. At least legally.

It was about then that our renters decided to move out. Years back, we'd held on to our first home when we'd built a new one. With renters covering its house payment every month it seemed like the perfect investment. But having the extra seven hundred dollars a month going out on a vacant house finally put me over the edge. Not that I could afford the payment on the big house anyhow. I had to sell it, and we all moved back to the little one. The kids were crushed. And so was I. All we had worked for, my lovely wife and I, all the struggles of our family to get ahead, all our common dreams, lost for no reason.

I tried to get something from my own insurance company after six months had passed, but nothing doing. They told me, essentially, no body, no booty. To add insult to injury, if I stopped paying the premiums on her policy and let it lapse, and she did eventually end up being dead, I couldn't collect then either. In the course of my struggles I heard about Megapolitan. Seems Megapolitan was the only company that, in a burst of competitive fervor, had offered a policy for a few years that paid a death benefit when the insured had disappeared.

Of course, there were qualifications. You still had to wait three months. And no foul play could be involved between the insured and the beneficiary. How did they prove that? They hired private investigators to do the legwork. Of course, cheapskates that they were, they didn't just hire investigators to do the work on an hourly basis. They hired them on a contingency/commission basis. Prove foul play and you get one-tenth the face amount that would have gone to the beneficiary. Find no foul play, you get nothing. Enter Jobe Carson, ex-clothing salesman, single dad and starving not quite widower. I'd found a career.

As I pushed through the smoky glass door in the fancy slate facade of Megapolitan's entrance, I was greeted by a tepid breath of perfectly controlled air. I thought I even detected a hint of eucalyptus, or perhaps chamomile. The comforting gurgle of the waterfall directly across from the entrance lulled my senses into a welcome feeling of placidity, the indirect lighting inviting me to relax and ease my tensions, as if I was about to enter a sanctuary from the hectic pace of the outside world, a haven for the weary and the lost. I could barely hear the hypnotizing drone of Gregorian monks rising over the waterfall's steady rhythm.

Jesus, I thought, and shook my head. I've been feng shui-ed.

Chapter 7

Not that my epiphany mattered. The tranquility didn't last long. It was too bad really, here Megapolitan had spent piles of money creating an atmosphere of peace, solace and comfort and it was completely shattered by the first person you encountered—the receptionist.

"Help you?" A voice shorthanded with biting lips. In those short two words all the expensive feng shui was pulverized like a student under a Tiananmen Square tank. Talk about annoying. She had one of those voices that can only be compared in attention grabbing quality to the shriek of an infant passing his first formula-impacted bowel movement.

"Yeah, I'd like to see Mr. Swinson, please." I always try to be formal with her.

"Oh, it's you Carson, I didn't see you. Damn ophthalmologist dilated my eyes this morning. Go right in." She waved with one splinted wrist in the direction of a green wooden door. I was glad to see the specter of the carpal tunnel didn't ignore cranky witches. I went through the door and made my way back through the maze of cubicles in the inner office.

This was the hub of Megapolitan's work force; hundreds of drones crunching numbers for the actuaries and rendering arcane sentences for the policy writers. And tortured advice for claims managers to deliver unctuously to unpaid beneficiaries. Pay this, don't pay that, collect here, deduct there, cancel this rider, deny that waiver, add some fine print to page 475 of the cancellation of policy for whatever reason disclaimer. A day in the life of the insurance business. This area was strangely lacking in the posh and comfortable luxury of the sales offices. Here was where the real business got done. Once the money was collected, this was the place that made sure the company held on to it.

By now I'd more or less got used to the impersonal nature of it all, though occasionally some mild resentment over my own callous treatment would bubble up to the surface of my consciousness like an acrid burp. I headed across the cubicle-strewn floor to Swinson's office. I mused for the jillionth time about his name. These Nordic types always make me wonder. If the ancestor of my enemy Knudson got his name in the old country because he was the son of Knud, then what had Swinson's father looked like? Oh well. At least he had found a job with a company suited to his genetics.

I knocked on his door. A real door. He had worked his porcine way out of the cubicle pen and into a real office. He responded quickly, "Come in, Jobe."

"I see Sunshine told you I was coming," I said, as I came through the door.

"I wish you wouldn't call our receptionist Sunshine, Jobe, it makes me not want to wake up in the morning. To what do we owe the pleasure of your presence?"

"I'll be happy to ignore the sarcasm, Swinson, since you indirectly pay my bills. Officer Greg tells me the police, and presumably you, are having trouble with four missing person cases. I figured you and the big boys'd be getting desperate about now."

"Teh," he made a noise of frustration. "I was against those disappearance policies from the start, Jobe. And now that it turns out I have to deal with you every time I turn around, I'm against them even more."

"Thanks for the vote of confidence Swindle, I mean Swinson. One would think you'd just as soon pay the murderers. What is it with you Swedes? I thought you were a friendly people. Got a little tension built up 'cause you haven't raided a coastline or pillaged a village lately?"

He had to laugh. "All right Jobe, I do appreciate your help. But it doesn't make me any happier that we have to do these investigations in the first place."

"I'm with you, Swinson. If it wasn't for having to feed my family and all, I'd much rather not have to deal with people who think the road to financial security means driving over their loved one's body. Whatever happened to the simple straightforward honesty of Amway? Enough hand wringing. What's the poop?"

"Four missing policyholders. And four people who stand to gain from 200,000 to 500,000 dollars."

"Let's hope the murderer has expensive taste in face amounts."

"Glad to see you English types are craven too. But you may not want to be so lucky. At least for the one with the half-million dollar policy, because face amount is an accurate description. If she has one more plastic surgery she'll be somebody else. But the other ones certainly aren't off the hook either. You'll earn your money with this bunch, Jobe."

I hoped he was right. I needed to earn some money soon. Even if it was from an old pirate like him.

He handed me his files on the four people. Names, addresses, pictures of the presumed deceased and pictures of the purported perpetrators. As I glanced through them I searched for some common thread, in the cast to their eyes maybe, or the set of their shoulders, some clues as to what would move them to kill the one they supposedly loved solely for financial gain. Nothing. Psychic I'm not, and phrenology was never my strong suit. Heck, even if I was allowed to probe the bumps of their heads I doubted whether it would reveal the churning emotions underneath that led them to kill. Much less butcher, dry and shrink-wrap.

I had negotiated the Rubik's cubicle puzzle and instinctively found my way out while perusing the files. I was remembering again my feelings of loss when my own loved one had disappeared, and I couldn't for the life of me fathom why someone would want to do away with their partner voluntarily.

A fingernail screeched down the blackboard of my reverie. "Good Bye Mr. Carson."

Then again, I hadn't been married to Ms. Sunshine...

CHAPTER 8

I looked at my watch as I hit the street and noticed that its numbers were getting more and more unreadable. Maybe it was time I saw an optometrist, or ophthalmologist, or whatever. It was then I was forcibly reminded that sometimes our disabilities turn out for the good. Just as I was leaning back to try to focus on the dial I felt a searing rush of concentrated wind right in front of my nose. I involuntarily ducked as splinters shot out from the bark of the tree to my right. Jesus! A bullet! I saw a car speeding down Capitol Way. It slipped in front of a big bus before I had a chance to identify it. Damn.

I could just see myself trying to report it to the police now. "Yeah Officer... It was medium gray, like a used bar of soap, some version of an H-like logo on the rounded gray bumper."

Let's face it; aerodynamic engineering and gas efficiency have played hell with snap identifications of automobiles. I stayed low as I glanced around to see if this was just a single drive-by or a whole convoy. Seeing nothing suspicious, I turned to look at the damaged tree. Whatever it was, caliber-wise, it was buried pretty deep, and the little penknife I carried since my Leatherman tool was confiscated at the airport couldn't reach deep enough to dig it out. Not that ballistics would help anyhow. There are more hot guns on the street than at a flea market these days.

Strange. It seemed a little early in the investigation for someone to be taking potshots at me. Probably just some hopped up crankhead thinking I was his abusive father. People are always thinking I'm someone else—like they've seen me on a milk carton somewhere, or at the post office. I'm the man with the generic face. Medium everything. Lucky thing too, if I had an extra-long nose the tip of it would be buried on the front side of that bullet halfway through the tree. Nonetheless, I made a mental note to look out for gray cars. Yeah, right.

I got into my own car, glanced at my watch again and made out that it was about noon. Time flies when your whole life flashes before you. Might as well try to check out the first suspect on my list. She had an office downtown. Well, a store really, a decorating business off Capitol Way that catered to the more affluent in our community; for planning parties and such like, interior decor, special events, that sort of thing. "Elizabeth's Environments." It was the real deal. Want to change your drab old chintzy slipcovers for something bold and seasonal? Add some flowers and wall hangings to the sitting room to entertain an important client? Throw a big adult Halloween bash with fog and silken spider webs drifting through the room and all the pumpkins and cornucopias you can carve and stuff? Elizabeth would do it all, and make it look like you did it yourself. She could make you look like your neighborhood's own Martha Stewart. And be the only one in on the secret. She was nothing if not discreet.

I drove over to Fifth Avenue, parallel parked with three swift movements and got out of my car on the sidewalk side. People always think parallel parking is hard, but with four-wheel drive and those great low concrete planter boxes on so many of the new "beautified" downtown streets, I find it's pretty much a straight shot in. I kicked some of the ferns in the planter back over to cover my tire marks and headed down the block to "Elizabeth's Environments." The tiny little bell on the top of the door announced my presence as I entered. The lady behind the counter looked up over her half-moon reading glasses and smiled one of those stormy ocean smiles. There were white caps everywhere. This must be the plastic person whom Swinson had referred to.

"How can I help?" she breathed huskily.

"Um," I stalled, "Just browsing for ideas." Never hurts to be at least marginally truthful.

She took off her reading glasses and opened her eyes real wide. Or, then again, maybe they were just stuck that way. Her face had that stretched look, like her original brow line was tucked somewhere behind her temple. Even if she wasn't a murderer, it must be tough to sleep at night.

"Excuse me for noticing," she said, "you seem to have something in your hair. Is it... beauty bark?"

I ran my fingers through my hair and pulled loose a couple of pieces of wood. In the old days, with the natural chestnut mane of my youth, no one would have noticed, but with my current hair turned mostly silver, brown chunks stick out like pepper in a salt dish.

As if reading my mind, she murmured, "I always liked George Peppard in his Banacek days. Gray hair is such a turn on."

"Yeah, well, um," I squirmed, "I, uh, just had a frosting cap accident."

"You know what they say," she was cooing now, "if there's smoke in the chimney..."

"It's a cold day?" I offered.

She blinked. Sort of. Then she tried to frown. The lines that dug into the lower part of her face made her look like a ventriloquist's dummy, or one of those wooden German nutcrackers. Meanwhile her upper face maintained its featureless porcelain immobility.

She must have been attractive at one time, before the scalpel boys got hold of her and carved her into a living china doll. But now, with her imprisoned beauty fixed on her features like a decoupaged rose petal, I couldn't help but think there must be a portrait of her growing old in a closet somewhere. Dorian Gray meet Elizabeth Greene. You four have so much in common.

Her confusion was only momentary. "How can I help you?" she ventured again, this time more businesslike.

"I'm supposed to do a party for some mucky-mucks at my company this spring, but I'd really like to be contrary and have a fall theme. Is there any way we can plan ahead?"

"Well," she considered, "you could use dried flowers and foliage."

"Is that real expensive?"

"We don't talk about expense here, Mister—?"

"Carson."

"Mr. Carson. If you mean is it difficult, the answer is no. We just pick what we need now and dehydrate it."

This was going to be easy. "Where does one get a dehydrator?"

"About twenty steps away in my back room. I don't know what you've heard about 'Elizabeth's Environments,' Mr. Carson, but we're set up to do most anything."

"Bet you can't make gourmet 'Lunchables.'" I challenged.

"Hmm," she considered. She was seriously intrigued. "Find some plastic trays, pack in some brie and some Carr's crackers, add some thinly sliced prosciutto, some caviar perhaps, or goat cheese, shrink-wrap the whole package. Yes, I think it could be done."

"Don't tell me you have a shrink-wrapper?"

"Shrink-wrapper, vacu-packer, I even have a German nutcracker." She must have thought my sudden look of surprise was skepticism. "I told you Mr. Carson, we're set up to do most any kind of soiree."

"Soiree, wow."

She looked at me questioningly again. Enough for now. I better beat feet. "Well, thank you, Ms. Greene. You've been very helpful. I'm afraid I have to get to another appointment now. But if you don't mind, I'd like to come back real soon." I reached out to shake her hand.

She lifted her immaculately manicured fingers like a queen and placed them delicately in mine. "Call me Elizabeth," she was cooing again, "and come anytime you like…"

CHAPTER 9

As the bell tinkled behind me I couldn't help from gulping in big breaths of sweet autumn air. For one who prided herself on creating the perfect atmosphere for any occasion, the inside of her store sure was hot and sticky. Or maybe it was just me. I felt my shirt plaster against my back when I sat down in my car and put the key in the ignition. As I drove off I mentally replayed my impressions. Places like that always make me feel like I'm up to my armpits in pretentiousness. Is it really necessary to cover every square inch of space with something frilly and useless? How does she ever clean the joint? I've never seen so many tea cozies, doilies and antimacassars in one room in my life.

Call me unsentimental, but my experience with those things at my Grandma's house was that they were nothing more than perfect repositories for dust. All the little holes, curlicues and delicate interweavings were eventually clotted with dust bunnies and hairballs. And they all had to be washed by hand. Unless, of course, they were the new-fangled plastic ones from the fifties. Those just turned yellow, except in the places where they weren't exposed to light. You'd lift up a lamp during your allowance-earning weekly cleaning and there was an inner white circle of pristine plastic where the lamp base had been; surrounded by the dirty beige of the sun-damaged outer edge. At least I knew exactly where to put back the lamp.

And talk about the persistence of cultural artifacts. When I asked my grandmother what an antimacassar was, she just said it was a head protector for the couch and chairs. Which made a kind of sense, except the top of the couch and chairs was a good five inches below normal head height. "Protection from what?" I would persist.

"Dirty hair," she would reply.

I went through most of my early adulthood thinking my grandmother was obsessed by a fear of tall people with filthy hair ruining her furniture. It wasn't until much later that I found out the "Macassar" that the antimacassar was anti-ing was a type of oil that turn-of-the-last-century folk put on their hair to slick it down. These same people had inordinately erect posture and a lot of high-backed stuffed chairs, with hard to clean velvet upholstery. Enter the hand-tatted antimacassar. Victorian times were so civilized.

All of which is to say the chief distinguishing feature of the human race is that we are creatures of habit. And a good thing too. Because habits were often the main clues that led me to my quarry. People intent on malfeasance don't normally screw up in the big things; murdering someone in cold blood takes planning and foresight. You would expect the obvious stuff to be arranged perfectly. It's the little things we take for granted in normal life that lead to the criminal's undoing. The place the victim set their comb perhaps, or whether their toothbrush is still a little damp two mornings after they supposedly disappeared. These were the types of clues I sought out. And more than once they had led me to a killer who had covered up all the big stuff quite well.

At that point I would have to bring in the authorities for the "real" science, like DNA checks, blood typing, ballistics reports and fingerprinting. The stuff Knudson was equipped to handle. That's when I usually ended up feeling like a good hunting dog must feel. "Thanks for pointing out that dead bird, boy. I'll just lift it out of the brush now, take it home and eat it. That's a good boy, Jobe."

So I was resolved this time to incontrovertibly prove my case before Knudson got any piece of evidence at all. Fate had finally dealt me a good hand, and I'd be damned if I turned it over to Knudson to bite it.

Elizabeth Greene had unsettled me. On the one hand, it was hard to believe she would kill her husband for financial gain. Her business seemed to be thriving, and the financial statement that Megapolitan had obtained the last time she had applied for coverage on her business verified she was doing very well indeed. On the other hand, of all the suspects, she was holding an insurance policy in the highest face amount: 500,000 smackers. Coupled with that, I have an instinctive mistrust for people whose expressions I can't read accurately. Most of us offer tell-tale clues to our inner churning psyche with the standardized facial contortions our species has evolved in its long climb down from the monkey tree. I had learned to depend on these clues in my career as a salesman, and as good as they were at detecting moments when I should press or back off from a sales technique, they were even better in the field of crime detection. But Ms. Greene stumped me. Her frozen features, numbed by scalpels, sutures and no doubt the latest botulism injections, left me in the cold as to her real intentions. She was going to be a tough nut to crack.

Her file had said her missing husband was an ex-Marine and former first baseman for a Triple A team in Tacoma. He had his own contracting business, which was currently solvent, but just barely. They had two separate corporations set up for their businesses and though the contracting business was struggling, and occasionally in the red, its bills were up to date. Not so his community service. According to the investigation file Officer Greg had slipped me, he had more than once been pulled over while driving under the influence. In fact, he'd had his driver's license revoked. But that hadn't stopped his drinking. According to Elizabeth's deposition on the missing person report, lately he had taken to getting plowed in their recently completed greenhouse. Seems Elizabeth's husband had a little murder problem of his own: Mr. Greene, in the conservatory, with a bottle. Murdering his self-respect.

Chapter 10

I'd reached the freeway by this time and had to negotiate a tricky series of onramp merges that nearly ended up killing me. My number was almost called. And the person calling it seemed to be doing so while viciously cutting me off while she had a cell phone pressed to her ear—her attention fixed on some faraway location where the recipient of her blather was safe and warm and not about to be hit by the fender of her Lincoln Navigator. Which at that moment wasn't navigating very well at all, having left it's presumed pilot four miles back when she speed-dialed her aunt in Southern California to use up her free long-distance minutes.

What possesses people to use cell phones for non-emergencies to hold inane conversations while they're driving on a freeway totally escapes me. Is their life really so full that they have to cram in that chat with Aunt Lillian while they're barreling down the highway at 20 mph over the speed limit and trying to jockey a latte cup to their flapping lips?

If I had a nickel for every traffic violation I've witnessed that's caused by someone dropping his or her attention from the road to deal with a freaking cell phone, I'd be able to quit this P.I. racquet and buy an island in Micronesia. Truth is, only one in ten people is enough of a multitasker to handle the necessities of both driving and phoning at the same time. And even those don't do either task well. But five out of the other nine think they can—and juggle burgers and coffees, and talk to their passenger, and listen to Rush Limbaugh at the same time.

"What's that whining noise Honey, a siren?"

"Nah, I think Rush just found another irregularity from the Clinton administration."

"Hey! Look out for that long red truck with those ladder thingies."

"What's his problem? Where's the fire buddy? Oh, there's the phone again, Hello... Aunt Madge... How's the pilate lessons...?"

It's funny the scenarios that play in your head while you're careening towards a jersey barrier and praying it hasn't been too long since you last had your brakes checked. I finally fetched up in the breakdown lane, unclutched my hand from the steering wheel and unlimbered my middle finger in the direction of the bitch in the Lincoln. I'd like to give her a hot rod. Too bad I didn't carry a gun. It's times like this that I'm in complete sympathy with road rage, especially when it's directed at the right targets. I consider it a form of community service. I think they need to start a new organization called M.A.C.S. Mothers Against Cellphone Stupidity.

I negotiated my way back onto the freeway and took the turnoff to the Westside. I thought I should at least drive by the house of suspect number two on my list, a Mr. Mark Wasen, before hustling home to greet Miranda when she got off the bus. Suffice it to say this guy lived in a pretty posh part of town. Not the kind of place that has lots of big houses with four car garages up front on tiny lots. Those were the homes of the intermediate rich. Too much yard work is not an overwhelming desire for that class of gentry, particularly since social security laws have tightened and illegal immigration has fallen off. No, the Wasens lived in one of those developments where every home has at least a five-acre lot. The houses are set way back from the road, their backyards either running down to the shores of the Puget Sound below or the slopes of the hills above.

Mark lived with his father. Or had lived with his father before ol' Dad turned up missing one day. Mark's father was a self-made man, and like most second-generation wealthy kids, Mark was a leech. 35 years old and still living at home. The wife/mother had died from a combination of lung cancer and cirrhosis a few years back, too much drinking and smoking at the country club Bunco parties I guess. Father and son had been bach-ing it ever since and judging by the hearsay recorded in Officer Greg's file, not too peacefully. They lived at a development known as Hillwood, which, not surprisingly, was nestled in a small valley at the foot of a pristine wooded hill. The elder Wasen was known to go off into said woods for long periods, sometimes days, so Mark had no specific alibi for the time of the old man's disappearance. And sometimes having no alibi is the best alibi of all.

Not that that made him any nicer to be around. I'd actually met Mark before. He was a friend of Knudson, or as much of a friend as that type can be. I'm sure they'd shared some inebriated confidences over a cocktail party tumbler or two; boozing it up together at the country club to the sultry sounds of Nancy Sinatra. Yeah. Those kinds of boots were often made for walking over jerks like me. Or at least so they thought.

Mark liked to brag about him and his dad being the only Jews in the country club, as if the current management cared about anything except the color of his money. Or his dad's. My guess was they put up with him not because he was a Jew or in spite of him being a Jew. They put up with his dad's money in spite of Mark being an asshole. Nonetheless, the scion from Zion, as they referred to him behind his back, cut a wide swath of annoyance through the crusty older club crowd, and Mark's dad often found himself regretting having not worn a condom some 35 years previous.

I drove by their "estate" to get a look at the lay of the land, maybe get a feel for how it may have gone down, if in fact Mark was the mastermind behind removing his father from the country club permanently with a little, shall we say, dis-membership drive. Just as I was slowly cruising past the white-enameled front gate, one of those new BMW convertibles came tearing down the drive. Oops. Busted. It was the scion himself. And he probably wouldn't like my pryin'. As he slowed down I couldn't help but laugh inside as I saw his comb-over settle back onto his mostly bald pate. That's one problem with being too rich. No one has the guts to tell you when you look like an idiot. It's beyond me why a grown man would think he was fooling anyone into thinking he had a full head hair when it was combed up from one ear over his head all the way to his other ear and then hairsprayed down. And why the guy would then drive a convertible, his wedge of shellac flipping up like an air foil on a Formula I racer is a complete mystery. Jeez. Out by the bay, he should avoid even standing there. If he caught a stiff wind, that hair flap would sail him to Hawaii.

"I thought that was you," he sneered.

"Just out taking a little country air, Mark."

"Bullshit, Carson. I know why you're sniffing around. Leave well enough alone. It's bad enough my dad's still missing, I don't need nosy parkers like you stirring things up."

"No offense Mark, even if I could follow your mixed metaphor, but I'd have to have a pretty long nose to stir anything up, much less out here on the road."

"You know what I mean. Stay away from here or I'll get my friend Knudson to come down on you harder than a ton of locomotives."

"I'm guessing it wasn't your SAT language score that got you into college," I said.

"What? What is it with you Carson? Why don't you mind you own beeswax and let sleeping dogs lie?"

"Because I'm hoping one of them will wake up and tell me the truth, old friend." I shifted psychological gears on him. "I only met your father once, Mark, but I liked him. If you ask me, it would be nice to find out what happened to him. I'd think you would feel the same way. Why try to scare me off with nasty Knudson when the official investigations haven't been able to turn anything up? Now that I'm here, I'm kind of wondering why you're trying to run me off. If you've got nothing to hide, why not welcome my help? Heck, you don't even have to pay for it."

He looked down and to his right. Classic tell. He was hiding something. Then he narrowed his eyes and looked left. I could almost hear his brain screeching as he wrenched its rusty machinery into motion. He was making a plan.

"All right, Jobe, you're right," he tried to be nonchalant. "Why don't you come back tomorrow? I'll show you around the place. Maybe there's something the professionals missed. Who knows? Maybe you'll trip over something nobody else even heard of."

"Thanks Mark, I'll keep my ear to the grindstone just in case."

I got in my car and drove away. The look of his mystified face in my rear-view mirror had me chortling all the way home.

CHAPTER 11

When I turned on the road that leads into my development I was right behind my boys. I could hear the stereo blasting in their car from three car lengths back — with my windows closed. I'd have to have another talk with Kiah about road awareness. I suppose it would have been halfway understandable if either one of us had had our windows open, but jeez. I'm not a total curmudgeon here. I blasted Hendrix like a maniac when I was a kid. But my Galaxie 500 didn't have air conditioning, at least not unless you consider cranking down the windows air conditioning. So at least we let some of the sound escape before it totally shattered our eardrums.

Oh well. It was time to get home and start planning the evening's food fest for the kids. I had originally scheduled ham hocks and split pea soup for the meal, but somehow the idea of pig wrist bones floating around in green slime wasn't all that appetizing with our little friend the lump resting in a piece in the garage. Still, I felt pretty good otherwise. I'd managed to check in with the police, talk to the insurance company, collect the files, and actually talk to two of the suspects—all before 3:00 in the afternoon.

I trailed the boys inside and went into the kitchen. I dug out some potatoes, scrubbed them and put them in the oven to bake. I was thinking I'd make twice-stuffed potatoes for the brood tonight. They always liked those. I got some link sausages out of the kitchen freezer and popped them in the microwave to thaw. Or defrost. Whatever. My microwave has a button for every permutation of cooking; popping corn, baking potatoes, heating soup, and, of course, defrosting.

Now let me see. Must be that progress we're always hearing about. When I was a kid defrosting was what you did to the freezer compartment of your Kenmore Refrigidator Deluxe. Thawing was what you did to frozen food. I chuckled as I remembered a previous conversation I'd overheard. Mark Wasen was telling a friend how he had "unthawed" a big steak. "Threw it in the freezer, did you?" I'd inquired casually as I passed by. Funny. He had that mystified look then too.

I have to confess, most of the buttons on my microwave are a total waste of plastic. They could have one big disk with the words "Reheat Coffee" on it and it would completely cover me.

I sat down at the kitchen table and opened the files on the case that Greg and Swinson had given me. The bus's brakes screeched outside. Miranda was home. I heard her run up the walk and slam open the front door. My back tingled. I hate it when they slam it open. Miranda wasn't a teenager yet, but she was already starting to develop the self-involved traits of the boys. Slamming doors, stomping feet, crashing cabinets and toilet lids—it's enough to drive a deaf man dumb. In half a second she was breezing into the room.

"Hi Dad, find the killer yet?" At least Miranda was cheerful.

Jack's ears perked up, "Killer?"

"Dad's working on a case where somebody killed and chopped up someone." She was also not above showing off.

"Somebody cut someone up?" queried Jack.

"Who cut one?" asked Kiah as he pounded into the room. I wondered for the thousandth time if he had to walk like a storm trooper because his shoes were too heavy.

"Nobody cut one," laughed Jack, his voice cracking into the upper register, "Except maybe Dad and his SBD's."

"That's the sausage thawing," I protested, meanwhile giving Miranda a glaring look and running my finger across my throat.

"No really, what this about cutting up?" Kiah was always the persistent one.

"Nothing," I said firmly, "Miranda's got an over-active imagination. I was telling her I was working on a case that may involve murder."

"And somebody cut someone up?"

I looked directly at Miranda and slowly said, "I told her one of the suspects was known as a cut up. You know Miranda, a comedian, right?"

"Oh," she said.

"She must have thought I said he cut someone up. You know little kids, never listening."

Kiah had already left the room, apparently figuring he had extracted all he needed to from this reality. It must be time for his Internet combat game. Jack was also drifting away. He picked up the TV remote from where he'd left it at the start of the conversation and headed for the front room. Another rerun of the Simpson's was calling. I put my finger to my lips and looked at Miranda. She mouthed the words "I'm sorry" and came up and gave me a hug.

"I don't want to tell the boys just yet, Mir," I whispered in her ear. "Sorry to make you look dumb."

"That's okay," she whispered back. "It takes one to know one."

"I know you are but what am I," I said.

"Guess what?" She said.

"Chicken butt," I replied.

Just then the microwave binged. We both busted up laughing.

I started frying the sausage and ruminating about the empty lives my first two suspects must lead. Booze at the country club, ping-ponging between the mirror and the plastic surgeon, all in a constant attempt to occupy the voids in their lives with something approximating fullness. When all they really needed was to have kids.

I never really wanted a kid until I had one. Then I suddenly found out what I was missing: The ability to do so much more than I would ever have conceived possible. I found I was capable of doing more things in a day than I ever would have been able to manage when I actually had the time. Seems the less time you have the more you can get done. Oh sure, you have to get up at three in the morning to comfort a squalling infant, but that doesn't mean you still can't work a nine hour day on four hours of sleep, mow the lawn, do the shopping, do twice as much laundry as you ever did when you were single, and still not have time to enjoy a little Ben and Jerry's ice cream before bed. You just have to swallow quicker.

Of course, you have to stay fit. It's important not to let your tiredness get in the way of exercising. Sometimes it's the working out that makes you able to work it out. I pity the poor people who think that the only way to wind down and relax of an evening is to suck back some liquor or fire up a bong. Call me a prude, but tea totaling is where it's at. I get my high from racing with my kids around the house with a Nerf gun in hand, ready to drill them with three inches of Styrofoam if they so much as make one false move.

I turned the sputtering fingers of sausage one last time, took them out of the cast iron skillet and put them onto some paper towels to drain. The potatoes were getting close to being done so I chopped up some onions, white and green, diced a couple of tomatoes, and minced a clove of garlic. Then I got out the blocks of cheddar and the jack cheeses and started to cut them into quarter inch cubes.

Meanwhile Miranda had attacked her homework. She was studying Cleopatra for the famous person report they require in sixth grade and was drawing out a timeline on construction paper with her Crayola felt pens. Progress again. The new Crayola felt pens come in a scented variety, each color matched up to its most popular smell. Strawberry for red, lime for green and licorice for black. Not a Necco wafer clove in the bunch. In my day the only scent Crayolas had was the sweet smell of stearic acid. Every time I smell one, I still get mentally cast back to the first grade, the quivering cells of my hypothalamus transporting me to a hot sticky classroom at Sun Garden School in Garden Grove, California.

Thinking about stearic acid got me thinking about fat, and thinking about fat got me heading to the refrigerator to dig out some mayonnaise. I like to add about two tablespoons to my stuffed potato mix to help bind the other ingredients. As I opened the jar I groaned.

"What is it Dad," asked Miranda, "thinking of the arm-y again?" She made quote marks with her fingers and winked.

"Nah, Mir. I just realized we're almost out of mayo."

"Oh no! Not the greasy knuckle maker?"

"Yep. The greasy knuckle maker." We buy our mayonnaise in the family size two quart jar, which is great because it's cheaper, but bad because eventually you get to the greasy knuckle phase, where the mayo that's left is too deep in the jar for an ordinary butter knife and you have to get your knuckles and the back of your hand all slathered with greasy gunk every time you dip it in. I dipped the knife in with my right hand and for some reason noticed as I did so that I had virtually no calluses on that hand. Which makes sense, since I usually do my fine work with my left. Though I don't write that much anymore, I still have a callosity on my left middle finger from where I've always clutched a pencil or pen.

"Be back in a second, Miranda," I mumbled, and hurried to the garage. I gently closed the connecting door to the entryway behind me and turned on the garage light. There it was, the lump, still lying by the freezer. I unwrapped it a little and looked at the hand. The fingertips had been cut off. Probably shredded in some garbage disposal somewhere. It was a left hand. I looked at what remained of the middle finger. It had a callus on it.

"He's a southpaw huh, Dad," whispered Miranda from the crack of the door. Her head was just sticking through.

"Yep," I said, blood running back to my head. And now wondering why I hadn't noticed the door being opened. Was my hearing going too? "It looks like he's a lefty, Miranda."

We looked at each other. A loud buzzing shattered the silence. Damn! The smoke detector! I smelled the scorched sausage grease before I made it as far as the living room. Miranda grabbed a towel from the dishrack as I turned off the burner and threw open the window. The boys came spilling out their rooms and started yelling at Miranda to start twirling the towel. We all started fanning the air underneath the smoke detector and jumping up and down like whirling dervishes. The buzzing finally stopped. Except for its audio ghosts in my throbbing ears.

"What's for dinner Dad," yelled Jack, "smoked sausage?"

We all laughed.

CHAPTER 12

It was the alarm jangling. I forced myself into consciousness. I had been dreaming of climbing a mountain. My wife was by my side and we had reached a narrow rocky spine. I told her to go ahead. I reached up, concentrating on one hold at a time and trying to reach the crest. I made it to the top and looked ahead. My wife was gone. I looked down to the left and to the right. Nothing but sharp drop-offs in either direction. I scanned the slope ahead. Nothing there. No wife. Nowhere. I start shouting her name. Again. And again. As the echoes bounced back from the barren cliff ahead, I started to scream.

The alarm.

Saved by the bell. I listened for the sounds of steady breathing coming from the other two bedrooms. Had I screamed out loud? The kids sure didn't need anything else to worry about. The rhythmic noises of their slumber reassured me. I hadn't disturbed them. I crawled out of bed and stumbled to the bathroom.

Morning at the Carson household. Another day, another dream dead. Just a few more years until the kids moved out. A few more years to find ways to let them know I love them. A few more years to climb our mountain of life together, before they went on to climb mountains of their own. And I could finally rest.

For now, I'd settle for a shower. I let the warm needles of water massage my back and burn away the tension of my nightmare. I toweled off, shaved, dried my hair, and got dressed. I headed for the kitchen to make lunches for them all. Kiah and Jack were a little mortified they had to take brown bags to high school. But at least they had some food to eat. No toaster strudels or breakfast bars for us. Just oatmeal and brown sugar. Hot lunch for lunch? The salad bar at the high school cafeteria? Sorry kids. Apples, sandwiches and homemade cookies are the best we can do. I hope the other kids don't tease you too much.

I was ready to drive as soon as Miranda stepped on the bus. I pulled out almost before its doors were completely closed. I decided to complete the rest of my suspect interviews before going any further with Elizabeth Greene and Mark Wasen. The next guy on my list was Fred Costner and since he lived in a development very close to mine, I decided to visit him first. Fred was one half of one of those gay partnerships the religious right is always so non-forgiving about. The ones the fundies think want special rights. "Special" in the fundies' interpretation, being things like medical insurance, rights of survivorship, and community property that any common law couple made up of opposite sexes would enjoy on a non-"special" basis.

I have nothing against gay folks. I figure if they've spent enough time together, and are committed to one another, they're entitled to at least the legal protections of any other common law couple. I can't see any reason to deny them basic protections just because they like a different kind of sex than I do. I sure wouldn't want my wife to be deprived of the right to inherit just because she favored a little oral sex from time to time. Or myself to not get dependents insurance on her medical plan because I have a shoe fetish.

I pulled up to in front of a well-manicured yard. The sign over the porch said, "Fred and Bill's Bungalow." I had a slight feeling of trepidation. I didn't like doing this. For my money—literally—I pretty much have to operate under the assumption that I'm about to uncover some wrongdoing. But I couldn't help but remember the suspicious looks and whispered innuendos I got when I was trying to find my own missing wife. Everybody just naturally assumes, in this atrocity-jaded world of ours, that if someone turns up missing the most likely candidate for being the agent of their undoing is their spouse or partner. I guess that's why absolute strangers that engage in random serial murder are often four states away by the time the official investigation gets passed the loved ones and next of kin.

I rang the doorbell and was entertained by an electronic rendition of Barbara Streisand's "People Who Need People." Yeah, we all need people. Just some of us don't need some people. The door was opened by a slight man who looked to be in his sixties. He was dressed in a black turtleneck sweater that could have been silk and cashmere, a plain fronted pair of charcoal colored wool flannels and deerskin slippers.

"Yes?" he inquired tentatively. You could tell by the dark patches under his eyes he hadn't been sleeping much. And the bright morning sun slanting into his eyes seemed to make him flinch even more. "Can I help you?"

I decided at that moment to be straightforward. "My name's Jobe Carson, Mr. Costner, and I'm looking into the disappearance of your partner Bill."

"Have they found out anything? I haven't heard anything from the police for weeks. Are you? Are they? Are..." he ran down into a fit of stuttering.

"It's okay, Mr. Costner. Nothing new yet, but the insurance company thought it was time to bring in their own investigators," (he didn't need to know why) "and so they hired me to see what I could turn up." The truth... sort of.

"Oh, I'm so glad. I'd about given up. Bill just didn't come home one day. And I don't know why. I must have said something or done something. He was so sensitive sometimes. I never knew when he would just go off on a tangent and blow up on me. He'd storm out and be gone for days at a time. At first I thought that's what it was."

"Was he upset the last time you saw him?" I could really feel this guy's anguish.

"Oh yes, very. He always hated it when I would start a new project."

"Project? Is that what happened this time?"

"Y-Y-Yes. I had decided we were going to get ready for Y2K... whenever it came. And I'd decided to use some of our vacation budget

50

to buy some necessities, I mean, it makes sense doesn't it, you can't take a vacation if the computers all across the world screw up anyhow. Can you?"

"No. I guess you can't."

"Well that's what I thought, so I decided we needed to pack away some really good food. I don't like living on crackers and canned chili you know, so I saw this great program on the food channel about dehydrating and shrink-wrapping meat."

My spine went cold. "So you...?"

"So I bought a dehydrator and a vacu-packer gizmo that we could use to make up some wonderful gourmet cuts. Like steak, or pork..."

"You bought a dehydrator and a shrink-wrapper?"

"Sure, do you want to see them? They really work. I've been using them since Bill's been gone, you know, to just fill up the empty spaces in my life. I was hoping when he came back I could treat him to some homemade turkey teriyaki jerky. He'd be so happy. Oh. Where's my manners? Would you like to try a piece...?"

My mind flashed back to the package in my garage. "Um, no thanks—I gotta run. But I promise I'll be back as soon as I find anything out."

"Oh do. Please help, Mr. Carson. I just know Bill's around somewhere. I'm so worried about him. He probably doesn't even know where he is himself. Sometimes he's so scattered. He'd just fall to pieces without me. I don't know what he'll do. He'd forget his head if it wasn't attached."

"I'll do my best, Mr. Costner. I'll do my best."

I tried to walk normally back to my car, but each step seemed to turn my legs to gelatin. I finally reached the door and got in. I didn't dare look in my rear-view mirror as I drove off. All I could picture was the rental videotape I'd seen on the table by his front door:

Silence of the Lambs.

CHAPTER 13

Fern Frenello and her missing husband lived in an older neighborhood on the east side of what was once greater Olympia. One could say they lived in a former suburb of the main city that got uppity some thirty years back and decided to incorporate itself as its own municipality. Which suffered as a result before they got their economic footing. When your main economic base is located in a city three miles to the west it's hard to construct a viable budget from just the revenues, or should I say residues, derived from taxes on retail sales. Especially when most of that retail took the form of convenience stores and video rental joints. How much city staff can you pay with even eight percent of the price of a Slurpee? It was no surprise that every time Blockbuster ran a two-for-one special the voluntary mayor groaned.

But the developer who fashioned Lacey—and built the now defunct mall that was to be its economic lifeblood—had higher hopes in his heart. Unfortunately, his heart, like his mall, suffered the effects of an infarction a few years back, and while he was still alive, his brainchild indoor shopping center had expired. He tried a remodel towards the end, but it was too little and too late to bring back the shoppers. His efforts amounted to nothing more than rouging the cheeks of the corpse.

Fern and her husband had moved into the bustling and energetic Lacey of the late sixties and had bought a three-bedroom house with all the modern appurtenances; shag carpet, avocado appliances, the works. They lived in what was then considered to be a new-fangled development, with curving streets, cul-de-sacs and two-hundred-year-old fir trees saved from the bulldozer's blade by design.

My immediate problem was that the Frenellos lived at the end of one of those cul-de-sacs, so a casual drive-by was out of the question. I could see from the state of the houses as I drove up that most of the residents had been there a while; at least judging by the carcasses of older cars parked halfway up the front yards. Apparently, there were no neighborhood covenants to hamper the personal freedoms of these homeowners. And it was very apparent indeed.

I pulled into the cracked asphalt driveway behind an actual, honest-to-goodness station wagon, circa 1985. It's formerly bright colors, no doubt inspired by the economic optimism of the Reagan era, had given way to a faded memory of peeling paint and popped-off chrome. As I walked past the gloomy hulk on my way to the front door of the house, I couldn't help but notice its rear cargo area. Broken remains of every gadget from here to Ronco eternity were jumbled together in a not-available-anywhere-on-TV mess. I felt a twinge of exasperation. What a waste. Her aging heap had to get terrible gas mileage already; didn't she see that she could get at least an extra three miles a gallon if she'd only unload all that junk from her hind end?

I weaved my way between splintered Taiwanese wicker porch furniture and chipped ceramic pots to the front door. I almost poked out my eye on a shard of wind chime that still dangled from a cord attached to the sagging eave. The spider webs that were clustered in all the nooks, crannies and corners of the recessed entryway spoke of many years of bug harvesting by the industrious arachnids. Sadly, no other signs of industriousness were visible.

I rang the bell. I should say I pushed the button. There was no bell. Not even that electric grunt that tells you the bell is trying to work. Nothing except the tick of my fingernail against the plastic disc. I pulled open the screen door, taking care to avoid snagging my sportcoat sleeve on the twists of wire protruding from its gaping holes. I knocked. The peephole in the door rattled from the vibration. I knocked again, louder this time, and the peephole shook like a castanet in counter rhythm to my tattoo. I heard some thumping noises and noticed only then that the chaotic sounds that had been constant since

I had emerged from my car were coming from a television set inside her house. The thumping got louder. I saw the peephole lens protrude slightly, as if someone was applying pressure from the inside, then the door was jerked open six inches and a voice barked out.

"We don't want any!!"

"Um, I'm sorry to bother you Mrs. Frenello, but I have a matter of grave importance to discuss with y—"

"I told you I don't want any!"

By this time my shoe was automatically positioned between her soon to be closing door and the jamb. I hoped I wasn't wearing my soft Italian loafers. "Mrs. Frenello, I'm not selling anything," I almost shouted.

"Jehovah Witnesses! Mormons! Get out anyway!" she yelled in one continuous hysterical burst.

"Look at me Mrs. Frenello, do I look nineteen? I'm hardly a Mormon missionary—"

For some reason she still hadn't slammed the door. And something worse was starting to happen. Two little dogs had come up to explore. One was a waddley old basset hound, stereotypically woebegone expression firmly graven on its visage. The other was a frenetic little coarse-haired dog of indeterminate denomination, except I was pretty certain he could be described by the adjective "yappy." Sure enough, he caught sight of me and started to do just that: Yap yap yap. Yap yap yap. His high-pitched syllables were soon joined by the occasional bay of the basset hound. Then the little bastard started to tear at the top of my shoe. Which I noticed in dismay were my Italian loafers. I kicked at him a little and Fern screamed out: "Quick kicking my dog!"

"I'm not—" I started.

"Quit kicking my dog! I'm calling the police!"

"But—"

"Get out of my house! Get out of my house! Call 911! Call 911!" she shouted down the street. The dogs were circling underneath and between her legs, the little one darting in and out of her ponderous blue stretchpant clad limbs like an eel from knobby coral pillars. He kept nipping at the cuffs of my trousers and occasionally my ankles as I tried to hold him off with miniature karate kicks to his yipping muzzle. Fern moved back a few inches, perhaps to position herself to thrust her bulk against the door. She bumped against the slowly wandering basset hound behind her. And went down like a tub of cottage cheese. Tub as in ship. Gelatinous flesh bounced everywhere, her limbs splayed like some catatonic sumo wrestler, her sweatshirted girth flopping like a walrus in heat. Her wild red hair and striped shirt made her look like a hideous Raggedy Andy. Except in her case the appellation "Andes" would have been more appropriate.

Then, suddenly, all the sound stopped. Only the TV kept up its disembodied yammering in the background. The yappy dog was sniffing at her groin. The basset hound had backed off to a safe distance, giving the scene a sidelong look of disgust. A disgust I felt rising in my own throat. A mangy cat wandered up and promptly hopped on the mountain of flesh, ascended to the peak of Fern's midsection and stuck up its tail like a flag. It then descended to her face and started licking the sweat from her nose. Fern didn't stir. She was out like a light.

CHAPTER 14

My Mom always told me if someone gives you a gift horse, ride it, so I mentally saddled up and proceeded to do just that. Since it didn't look like I was going to be able to charm my way past the excitable Mrs. Frenello, I might as well use this opportunity to do a little looking around while I, um, "tried to find her some smelling salts." I quickly grabbed the yappy dog by the scruff of its neck and, finding a small bathroom just off the hall, pitched him in. The basset hound had already wandered off to the living room and started a well-earned nap. The cat was happily rubbing its rear scent glands on Fern's bristly hairdo. I took a quick look around.

My God. Here was a place that could use a little something to help clear out the clutter. Something on the order of a small thermonuclear device. There was crap everywhere. Clothes piled on the sagging couch, other clothes draped over the two wingback chairs, balls of what appeared to be used Kleenex spilling out of a pink plastic trashcan by the Barcalounger. The soap opera guide dog-eared on the table next to the can gave a hint as to the tissue's origin.

And Beanie Babies. There were Beanie Babies everywhere. Every flat and semi-flat surface of the room; end tables, occasional tables, coffee tables, book shelves, knick-knack shelves, bric-a-brac shelves, collectable shelves, all of them filled to bursting with Beanie Babies. She had more Beanie Babies than a third world country.

My dear daughter Miranda had once gone through a brief (thankfully) Beanie Baby phase. At the time I figured, what the hell, we could always rip 'em open and boil the beans if that Y2K thing got out of hand. That was before I found out they don't actually use beans in Beanie Babies. They use Styrofoam pellets. And though I expect when the apocalypse comes times will be dire indeed, I don't think many of us will derive much nourishment from Styrofoam pellet soup. Fortunately, my daughter's fancy passed from Beanie Babies to

Japanese electronic babies and I was spared the necessity of forcibly promoting beanie abstinence and breaking her little heart.

But Fern hadn't been so lucky. They still appeared to be her not so secret obsession. And that's not all, every third nook and corner of her house was crammed with something else. Doodads of every sort that all appeared to be related to the theme of organization. There were plastic bins and trays and hampers and baskets of every description, blue and pink and puce and chartreuse. One group of bin-shelves was almost finished identically in some gray marbled looking stuff. Probably an aborted attempt to achieve some sort of decor uniformity with the aid of that granite spray paint they sold on infomercials a few years back. Come to think of it, her entire front room, and I was soon to find out, house, looked like it had been furnished by the RPK triad: Ronco, Popeil and K-tel. If ever there was a supreme target of infomercial penetration this house was it.

I went into the kitchen and was rewarded with a similar enlightenment. Gadgets everywhere, and failed attempts to find a place to put them all. I opened one of the upper cupboards. Big mistake. I was bombarded by an avalanche of faux Tupperware. Cheesy plastic dishes cascaded from the shelves and pummeled me about the head and shoulders. As my granny used to say, this was really starting to get my dander up. Not one of the dishes was nested in its appropriate slightly larger companion bowl or storage container. Why bother to buy nesting containers if you never nest them? Use your old margarine tubs for Christ's sake. It was woefully apparent that Fern never got the simple fact that organization starts in the brain.

I left the pile of dishes on the floor and retraced my steps to the hallway. The yapping behind the bathroom door had ceased and I went down to the end of the hall and turned right into what must have been the master bedroom. A garish comforter lay heaped at the foot of a queen size bed, tangled with the top sheet in a wrestling match with no clear victor. Make your bed, I always tell my kids. That's three quarters of your room looking clean in one fell swoop.

The bedroom maintained the decorating theme of the kitchen and living room—crap everywhere—and a quick glance at the open closet doors assured me that this room was solely occupied by the stertorously breathing mound of flesh currently matting down the shag in front of the door. I took a quick look a little deeper into the closet just in case, but other than a brief mental note about how a certain type of person seems to like crocheted hanger covers, no great discoveries ensued. I could see why the police had given up on this search early. It would take a search warrant and six to eight months of intensive labor to find anything in this trash heap. Especially if you didn't know what you might be looking for in the first place.

I looked briefly in the room on the other side of the hall and could see quickly that this was the catch-all room of the house. The former "whatever" room—bonus room, third bedroom, study, den, sewing room—that always ends up being a repository for all the things families don't currently have in use. In the Frenello's case, multiplied by a factor of ten. And judging by the smell of old urine, either the cat or some rats had found a nesting place of their own, sans Tupperware, in the recesses of its darker crannies.

I headed back in the direction of the living room and opened the door on the opposite side of the hall of the bathroom. I was immediately greeted by the fresh smell of Old Spice. And something I felt I hadn't seen for a long, long time—the horizontal surfaces of furniture. There was a desk, on whose top was a blotter and a penholder, and, aside from a barometer and a boat shaped clock, nothing else. Books were arranged neatly on a bookshelf. A dresser over by the wall was completely bare except for a small valet tray that held nothing more than a set of keys, each of them with a different colored dot at its top, a small, folding pocket knife, its handle worn from constant use, and a money clip, empty. A small cot was set against one wall, the corners of a green wool blanket tucked neatly under its sparse mattress. A striped pillow, visible though the thin white cotton case, was placed on top of the eight inches of crisply turned down top sheet.

Aside from a thin patina of dust, the room was immaculate. Mr. Frenello, I thought, if you're in heaven, aren't you glad? This was obviously his room, and just as obviously, he had insisted on maintaining this one refuge from the housekeeping hurricane Fern. I crossed over to his closet and slid open the door. A group of mutely colored, banded bottom shirts were hung neatly on hangers, and arranged so that they all faced the same way. On the right side of the closet rod were about a dozen brightly colored shirts, their short sleeves in the contrasting hues that instantly identified them as one thing; bowling shirts. I looked down at the bottom of the closet and, sure enough, a bowling ball case was pushed up against the back wall.

As I bent down to open the case, I heard a moan from the front part of the house. I quickly exited into the hall, closing the bedroom door behind me. I went into the living room. The mountain was stirring. And judging by my reception earlier, I didn't want to be anywhere close when it erupted. With a quick frustrated glance at what must have been the door to the garage I stepped over the brooding behemoth and slipped out the front door. I tried to be nonchalant as I hurried back to my car. No one in the neighborhood appeared to notice. No curtains falling back into place or doors closing. No one even out tending their yards. Good. I drove out of the cul-de-sac quickly and headed back towards Lacey. Next stop Melody Lanes. It had been a long time since I had been to a bowling alley.

CHAPTER 15

I pulled into the parking lot of the aging Melody Lanes bowling alley. A broken raceway of lights wound around the big bowling pin up on the sign. The front of the building was red concrete brick, with what looked to be vertical wood wainscoting circling it from ground level to about four feet up. The concrete sidewalk was broken in places, admitting tufts of browning grass. The long blades of the obligatory and ubiquitous dandelion poked through the deeper cracks. Patches and blotches of questionable provenance stained the concrete in a random array. Only two other cars were in the parking lot at this time of day.

As I walked through the double doors I saw the café to my right. Whatever lunch crowd had been there had since retired to their afternoon bottle or nap. I looked over at its Formica counter and vinyl covered stools as I headed to the main bowling area. A slice of time. The menu board illuminated on the wall listed French dips and hamburgers and homemade macaroni and cheese. A small chalkboard proclaimed "Navy Bean Soup" as the soup of the day. Only $1.99 and all the crackers you could eat.

I spied the man I assumed I must be looking for reading a paperback behind the rental counter. He was an indeterminate age between fifty-five and seventy. The look you only see on old codgers that had spent a lot of their early years in some branch of the military. His hair was buzz cut into what they used to call a flat top; a few quarter inch strands combed up in front and fixed into a flat shelf by the original stylist's gel, butchwax. If the platform he was standing on behind the counter was eight inches tall, that put him at about five foot two. As it was we were eye to eye. His grizzled—or should I say gristled—appearance, spoke of years of hard work, most likely out on the ocean, as his leathery features had that permanent tan you could never get, or keep, in the Pacific Northwest. Small, and wiry was my guess, and tough as nails. I couldn't help but think it wouldn't take too long to dehydrate this guy. He raised his eyes up from his studied concentration of Louis L'Amour to give me a questioning appraisal. His name tag said Bobby. "How can I help you," he drawled, in what must have been some ancient dialect from East Texas.

"Wonder if you could answer some questions, Bobby," I said, noting his eyebrows rise in immediate suspicion. Ya don't ask a man questions out West was his unspoken L'Amourian admonishment. I handed him my business card.

"Private dick, huh?" he said, "Name of Jobie Carson?"

"Not Jobie. Jobe," I said. "As in probe."

"Ha ha. Funny. Probe, I like that. But I ain't done nothin' for you to be probin'..."

"Yah. I know that," I found myself slipping into his accent and verbal cadence, "I'm kinda interested in a guy you probly know. Joe Frenello."

Bobby spit into a ceramic cup. Dark brown tobacco juice squirted out of the pursed corner of his mouth in a tight stream. "Yah. I know Joe. What about him?"

"You know he's disappeared?"

"Yah. Can't say as I blame him."

"How so?"

"That wife o' his. Harpy."

"She did look a little, uh, shrewish." I said.

"Yah. She drove ol' Joe crazy. I don't know what he saw in her... ever. But you know Joe. He was a man of his word, and a man's gotta do what a man's gotta do. So he stuck by her even though..."

"Even though?"

He considered a bit and spit another squirt of juice into his cup. I noticed the cup had the name "Bobby" glazed on it in curlicues that looked like a tiny rope. "Well," he said, "I don't like to tell tales outta school, but she 'bout drove poor ol' Joe to the poorhouse. Just kept spending and spending and spending, one of those, what do they call it, shopaholics. And poor Joe just couldn't keep up on just his seaman's pension and social security. Hell, he wouldn't have even been able to afford to bowl if I hadna cut him a deal on a lane during slow afternoons. They fought all the time. I'm surprised she wasn't the one to disappear, you know what I mean?"

"Joe have a temper, did he?"

"Nah, he was a little lamb. All he'd do is yell. He musta loved her I guess. Or stood by her anyhow. But he'd come in here with his face all puffy and red, and bowl frame after frame, and never say a word, just lay down the ball gentle as a kitten and watch it roll. He always seemed to feel better afterwards. Then him and me'd have a chaw and a little jaw, he'd go over and have a cup of coffee and chat with Lulie at the lunch counter and then he'd head home to his own little stretch of hell. Damn. I'm talking too much. You're pretty good, Mr. Carson."

I waved my hand dismissively, "You and Joe like to chew a little tobacco, eh? That's bad for ya, you know."

"Shucks Mister, we'd much rather have been smoking. But ever since they made all public places like this non-smoking establishments, we gotta get our jolt the old-fashioned way." He squirted again for effect.

"Mighty nice cup you got there." I pointed at his spit receptacle.

"Thanks. Lulie had 'em made up for us. All us regulars. We keep 'em under the counter here."

"Did Joe have a cup?" An idea was starting to bubble up through my brain.

"Yah. Sure he did. It's right here. Ain't even been emptied since I last saw him." He brought a cup from under the counter and took off the lid. The room suddenly filled with the pungent odor of refried vomit. We both squinched up our eyes and shook our heads. Bobby put the cap back on quickly.

"Sorry about that Mister, we usually empty 'em a little more often."

"Hey." The idea bobbed to the top. "Mind if I take that to the lab? It might help find ol' Joe."

"Nah, I couldn't do that Mister. If you lost it I'd kick myself. Me and Joe's had some good times together."

"Well how about I just take the spit then?" I heard myself ask.

"What for?" he asked, in chorus with my subconscious.

"I not sure," I told both of them. "But I think I have an idea."

He went over to the lunch counter and got a little paper coffee cup and plastic lid from what must have been Lulie. She gave me a questioning once over and went back to drying a pie plate. Bobby came back, poured the noxious liquid into the cup, capped it quickly and handed it to me. He then the tucked the ceramic cup named Joe back under the counter. Cup of Joe. We'll see...

"One more question Bobby," I said as another idea occurred to me. "Did Joe bowl right or left handed?"

"Right. Why?"

"Just wondering," I said, as my new great theory was dashed to pieces. "You sure?" I persisted.

"As sure as I am he was a size ten shoe."

"Yeah, of course, thanks for your help Bobby. I'll do what I can to turn him up."

"Yah. Sure thing Mister. But maybe you could do me a favor."

"What?"

"If you find him alive, and he don't want to be found, could you maybe let him get lost again?"

I thought about the lovely Fern. "I'll do what I can," I said, "I'll do what I can."

CHAPTER 16

I looked at my watch and saw that it was already two o'clock. Damn. If I hurried, I just had time to make it to the courthouse and home before Miranda got off the bus. Traffic was no worse than usual on the way back to the West Side and as I circled around to courthouse hill, I had time to notice that the sun, which had been playing hide and seek with the clouds all day long, was finally about to emerge victorious. And doing its best to blind me as I tried to negotiate the parking lot without running down any sheriffs' cars. I took my cup o'sputum out of the cupholder on my console, got out of the car and headed towards the coroner's building.

"Hello-o... Jo-obe!" I heard from another direction. The voice was familiar. I turned around and sure enough, over by the espresso cart that services the three main county buildings, there was my favorite enemy's lab tech, the lovely Kathryn. I felt a tingle run up my spine. And a sudden space open up in my chest. The sun broke through again and sent shafts of luminescence down through the boughs of the fir trees. One shimmering beam played across the top of her shining blond locks, like some heavenly spotlight directed only at her. Our eyes met and locked. I took a short breath and started to rush towards her. Her eyes widened in anticipation.

No.

I checked my stride and shook my head quickly. What was I thinking? Not here, not now. I was still married. And the last thing Kathryn needed was a struggling single dad with a missing wife and an uncertain income. Talk about bringing baggage into a relationship. No. Not ever.

She pursed her lips in a little moue of disappointment as she seemed to read my mind. Or maybe she just didn't like what she saw in my hand.

"You're leaking," she said.

I looked down. Oh my God, Frenello's spittle had soaked through the cheap cup. Brown juice dribbled over my fingers. "Oh jeez!" I said out loud.

"Just a second," she said to me. She turned to the girl with the pierced nostril who was frothing up a cappuccino behind the muffin case. "Could I have a little espresso cup?"

"Sure dude," the barista replied, and handed Kathryn a small dark brown cup.

Kathryn passed the cup to me and I poured the noxious juice into it. I noticed its intense odor had abated somewhat. Thank God for everyone in a ten-foot radius... and my hand.

"Thanks Kathryn. You're a lifesaver."

"My pleasure, all that think-on-my-feet emergency room training's gotta go somewhere. It's sure not being used in my stupid lab work..."

"Good to see you anyhow. I'd forgotten it was break time," I said. "But how come you got the duty? Doesn't Knudson know twenty bucks an hour is a lot to pay for a coffee fetcher?"

"Knudson likes wasting taxpayers' money. Almost as much as he likes bossing people around and having them do ridiculous things."

"What you got there?" I asked, looking at the cardboard beverage tray she had picked up after rescuing my hand.

"Same old, same old. Cappuccino with extra foam for Lee Wu, breve and biscotti for Ann the receptionist, short skinny single for me, double espresso and two wedges of baklava for the big man..."

"And getting bigger every day."

"Yeah. I think baklava is a Turkish word that means big ass," she laughed.

"Good one," I chuckled, "but I understand if you use a different inflection it also means full of crap."

"You are what you eat. Can I get you a latte?"

"No thanks, I'm driving. But I could use a little advice." We started strolling back towards the building that housed the coroner's office.

"What about?" she asked.

"Is it possible to extract DNA from any bodily fluid?"

"Such as?"

"Such as spit."

"Sometimes."

"How much would you need?"

"Depends." She was using her scientist voice. "If it was just sputum, not too much. If it was diluted with something else, hard to say."

We reached her office. Luckily, there was no sign of Knudson. Not that I'd let him push me around anyhow. Kathryn put his espresso and baklava on his desk. She gave the breve to Ann, who for some reason gave me a big wink, and then put the cappuccino at the end of Wu's workbench. Wu was the pathologist, autopsy guy, and forensic wunderkind of the coroner's department. The guy that really should be coroner were it not for a little thing called politics. He gave me a nod and went back to scrutinizing something under his microscope. Kathryn and I went down to the other end of the room and stopped by a lab table. I set down my cup.

"What about if it's been diluted with tobacco juice?" I asked.

"Is that what that is?" she asked, and bent close to take a sniff.

"I wouldn't—" I tried to warn her.

She jerked back her head quickly. "Phew. Lots of aromatic compounds in that, and it smells like a little bacterial contamination as well. Is that sample fresh? Because if it is, that guy needs some major dental work."

"No, it's months old by now."

"That could be a problem." She sure looked beautiful when she got that look of concentration on her face.

"That's what I was afraid of." I put the cup on the counter.

"Still," she brightened, "There's a pretty good chance. You got a nice big sample there—"

"CARSON! I told you to stay the hell out of my office!" The room was suddenly filled with the unmistakable presence of Knudson.

"Whoa, Nellie!" I shouted back.

"Why you—" He sputtered. "I'm gonna pound your ass into the pavement Jobe, I swear to God."

I dropped back into a defensive stance. "Have at it Nellie boy, I've been waiting to wade into your lard since the last time you stole my bacon."

"Ann!" he barked out, "Call a deputy. I'm a sworn officer of the law, Carson, and I said clear out." His face was reddening as he blustered.

"Well, in case you haven't checked the constitution lately, Sir, 'officer' does not mean 'dictator' and my private detective's license, signed by your boss, allows me access to this lab."

He growled. "All right Jobe, but you can't interrupt my staff when I call a meeting." He looked around to Wu, who was sipping his cappuccino. Knudson's expression perked up in sudden remembrance. "Oh yeah, that's what I wanted." He reached out and grabbed the cup I'd put on the counter. "Thanks Kitty, where'd you put my baklava..." Kathryn tried to stop him, but it was too late. He lifted the cup and tossed its noxious contents back into his mouth before either of us could say a word. As the viscous fluid passed over his tongue he grimaced briefly. Then he swallowed with an audible gulp. His eyes opened wide for a moment, welled with tears, and then returned to their former snakelike squint. I gagged.

"Now get out of here!" he shouted at me. "I'm calling a meeting." Kathryn and I looked at each other. She was trying to fight down the same gorge in her throat that I was. We each shivered. Then she shook her head in apology. No sample left now. Not unless we broke out the stomach pump and thrust it down Knudson's flabby gob. I turned and left quickly.

One thing was settled. I always knew he didn't have any taste in clothes. Now I knew he didn't have any taste period.

CHAPTER 17

I sat numb as I drove home. Nothing seemed to be going my way. I put myself on autopilot and coasted down the freeway. A Chevy Nova cut in front of me and as the setting sun reflected off its rearview mirror, I was briefly blinded. Fortunately, a Mitsubishi eclipse chose that moment to wedge itself between me and the Nova. I was able to see in time to catch my exit. I had to wait for the school bus to finish unloading before I drove into my driveway. Miranda was waiting for me as I got out.

"Hi Dad," she chirped automatically. Then her tone shifted, "Bad day?"

"Is it that obvious?" Apparently, I'd never win any poker games with her.

"Oh Dad, you'll find the killer soon."

"Or the four killers," I mumbled.

"Really? There's four of them?" she asked excitedly. Just like her mom. You can't keep Miranda down for long.

"That's one of the problems Mir. There could be four of them. Because there are four people missing. And we don't know who the arm belongs to. Or to whom the arm belongs for that matter."

"Can't you just take it to the laboratory and have them do a whatchamacallit test?"

"DNA?"

"Yeah, like the OJ thing."

"Well, Honey, I could do that... but there are two problems."

"Like what?"

"One, it's not like there's a DNA data bank for everybody in the USA. Even if you have a sample, you have to have another sample to compare it to. We could get all the DNA we want from the arm, but unless we have some known DNA from the supposed victim stashed away somewhere, it wouldn't do us a lick of good."

"I see," she said seriously. Poor Miranda, she really wanted to help her old dad out. "Wait a minute, how about blood? My friend Melinda was telling me her dad was going in for an operation and was saving up some of his own blood. Maybe one of the missing people was doing the same thing."

"Whoa! Good idea, Mir. I'll see if I can check the hospitals tomorrow. You are one smart cookie, Honey. Except..."

"What is it now, Dad?"

"That still leaves the other problem. I can't very well show up at Knudson's lab with our little 'package' to check its DNA. He's certain to confiscate it. Then he'll rush in to get the credit as usual. If he knows about the arm, he'll be tipped off for sure that I'm up to something."

She saw the glint in my eye and got one in her own. "Don't say it Daddy..."

"I can't help it Mir. It would be a classic case of forearmed is forewarned."

She groaned.

We went inside to our respective duties; she to finish her Cleopatra report, me to clean up a little and try to think of a way to cobble some leftovers together and make a meal at least mildly consistent with a nutritional pyramid.

I straightened up a bit and threw in a load of laundry. It was "khaki" night. Khakis on Thursday, whites on Friday, jeans on Saturday. I find that if I do one load an evening I don't have a bunch of huge piles come the weekend. Of course, the kids have to go without some, to them, life-threateningly necessary garment from time to time but, hey, that's the downside of life with a single dad. After a while I went into the kitchen to start dinner. Miranda was in the process of using different colored pieces of electrical tape to fashion a scepter out of an old giant plastic candy cane from last Christmas. This was the 3-D part of her school project. Making the Crook and the Flail, symbols of the Pharaoh's power that Cleopatra flaunted. I had some flailing of my own to do. Oriental style.

I took a chunk of pork roast out of the refrigerator that I had cooked the previous Sunday. My dear wife used to make pork roast that was so incredibly moist. My own attempts in that direction erred on the side of overcooking. No possibility of trichinosis in our family. No possibility of succulent, flavorful pork either. I pulled the shriveled chunk of roast from the recesses of the meat compartment. I almost gagged as its similarity to the lump in the garage struck me. I may have to take up vegetarianism if this squeamishness keeps up much longer.

I sliced and cubed and diced the white flesh into small chunks, then got some olive oil heating up in my big cast iron skillet. No anemia in my family either. Everybody gets plenty of iron from just the pan scrapings. Soon the pork was sizzling in the oil and I added some carrot strips and a little bit of red pepper I had left over from the stuffed potatoes. I threw in a handful of diced onion and some napa cabbage that I'd accidentally bought when I was trying to get romaine for a Caesar salad idea that went awry last week. After stirring in some teriyaki sauce and a little hot pepper brew I put in a couple of cups of cooked rice that had been sitting for I don't know how long on the top shelf of the refrigerator. I covered the whole mess and turned down the heat to let the carrots soften a bit. Then I spread margarine on some tortillas left over from burrito night, sprinkled them with sesame seeds and dusted on a little paprika. I rolled them up, put them in a big ziplock bag and popped the whole shebang into the microwave for about thirty seconds.

"Dinner's ready!" I yelled to the household.

"What's for dinner?" Jack yelled back as he stomped into the kitchen.

"Teriyaki Surprise," I replied.

"Oh no..." he moaned. "Leftovers again,"

71

"Hey, you liked all this food the first time," I said.

Kiah groaned as he came into the room. "Not leftovers! Why do we always have leftovers?"

"When you get your own house, you can live on junk food twenty-four hours a day," I said. "Until then, when you're in my house, you just take your lumps."

Miranda looked up from her homework. Oops. Don't say "lump" around dinner time.

"What was it you slaved over the stove and selflessly cooked up for us tonight, Dad?" she asked sweetly.

The boys growled at her.

"Teriyaki Surprise, Miranda dear," I replied. "Set the table boys."

As you can imagine, they were not pleased.

CHAPTER 18

Miranda and I exchanged a few barbs during dinner while the boys glowered at us. I got to hand to that girl, she's got a good sense of humor. Just like her mom. Every time Miranda makes me smile, I think of my dear, departed bride. Funny. Right before she disappeared I remember saying to her that I was the luckiest man alive.

"Why?" she'd asked.

"Because I've got what every man wants."

"Which is?"

"A pretty wife and a full head of hair."

"Now all you need is Viagra and I'll be the luckiest woman," she'd said. And then laughed like a banshee at my expression.

Now looking at Miranda, with her tongue stuck between her lips in concentration and thinking of the boys in the other room doing their homework, I felt that same sense of gratitude. I was pretty darn lucky. The world started to get a little blurry as my eyes misted over.

The phone rang. Jeez. What timing. What's the interruption tonight? Credit card company? Cellphone or long-distance service? Life insurance? I remembered when I used to pay an extra seventy-five cents a month for an unlisted number. I kept getting calls from companies that wanted me to switch my long-distance service. How the hell did you get my number, I kept asking. Then, lo and behold, my local baby bell wanted to sell me a new "for fee" service called "solicitor blocking". Hmmm. Sounds like a conspiracy to me. I'm never one to accept a reasonable explanation when a conspiracy theory will do just fine, but that stretched even my paranoia to the limit.

I picked up the ringing phone.

"Hello," I said cautiously, ready to tell whoever it was I was on the pot if necessary. That shuts them up real quick.

"Hello... Mr. Carson?" It was a low and steamy voice. My underwear suddenly started to chafe.

"Yes. Who's this?" I knew full well who 'this' was. Visions of dried flowers and spice ropes danced in my head.

"This is Elizabeth Greene, Mr. Carson. How are you tonight?" The way she said the word tonight, dipping the second syllable into an even lower register and breathing it out from the depths of her bosom, made that simple word hold a lifetime worth of promise.

"Um, fine," I said. Or squeaked would be more like it. Does puberty ever end?

"Mr. Carson, you're probably wondering why I'm calling. I can only put it this way. I just don't feel we had a chance to get to know each other yesterday morning. I feel if I'm to perform to the best of my abilities, it's important I develop a rapport with my clients. Do you agree?"

"I don't remember saying I was definitely going to use your, uh, services, Miss, Mrs., Greene..."

"Call me Elizabeth please. Or Liza if you like. My really close friends call me Liza."

"Okay, Elizabeth... uh, Liza. But still I don't remember engaging you exactly."

"Oh I was very engaged indeed, Jobe," she purred. "May I call you Jobe? I could just tell that we'll work very well together..."

"Well, my party's a long way off, uh, Liza."

"All the more time to get to know you better, Jobe. And that's very important. I have an idea. You probably haven't seen that much of my work. Tell you what. I did a local restaurant not far from my office, provided the interior decor touches and arrangements and such. Can I interest you in meeting me there to show off my 'wares'?"

"I suppose that would be okay," I heard myself saying. Somewhere along the way the honey in her voice had changed to strands of silk. And I was being drawn into her web.

"Good. Say 1:30. Most of the lunch crowd will be gone by then and you and I could perhaps share a little nibble while we view the interior design. Date?"

"Well I wouldn't really call it a date, Ms. Greene." I tried to fight loose from the sticky strands. "How about 'appointment'?"

"How about 'rendezvous'?" she said as she hung up.

I listened for a moment to the dead connection. "Uh oh," I said out loud. "French."

Just what I needed. A horny lady with a penchant for interior design. And I had a sneaking hunch what designs she had in mind, and in what interior too. The interior of her boudoir, no doubt. There's that French again. The language of love. By the sound of her voice, she was pulling out all the stops, and all the seductive reinforcements too—the cavalry, the National Guard, and Cher backed by the entire US Navy choir. I felt like Custer at the Little Big Horn, with her on the other side ready to Sioux, blue and tattoo me. This was gonna be an all out war of lust, and if I was any judge of human nature it looked like she wanted to hold my line, storm my hill, and conquer one key objective. I could only hope she didn't want to plant a flag somewhere.

Then again, maybe she just wanted to "talk." Yeah, right. I wouldn't be surprised if she had a different exercise in mind for those collagen-ballooned lips. Ugh. The thought of kissing that lock-jawed doll face sent shivers down my spine. Give me natural flesh any day of the week, and throw in extra wrinkles if you like. If I want tight, artificial skin I can invest in an inflatable party doll. And save myself the price of lunch while I'm at it.

For some reason, I didn't get much sleep that night.

CHAPTER 19

I turned off the alarm before it even rang. I had been looking at it on and off for the last six hours. Every half hour I'd roll my body around and assess the elapsed time since my last restless turnover. I must have slept a little. I remember dreaming I had insomnia. It was one of those nights. All the suspects swirling in my brain. All the possible reasons they may have for getting rid of their loved ones. And the person with the best reason for offing his particular loved one, Joe, wasn't even a suspect. He was one of the presumed victims.

I slid out of my side of the bed and straightened the sheets and covers. Funny how easy it is to make a bed if you do it every day. Maybe I should have a chat with Fern. Funny too, how when the person with whom you've been sharing a bed for so long isn't sleeping there anymore, you still occupy only your "side" of the bed. And the other side stays largely un-mussed.

I shuffled into the bathroom and turned on the shower to heat up while I relieved my morning bladder pressure. Then I looked in the mirror. God, I needed a haircut. The old coif was starting to poof out like a tele-evangelist. Maybe I should take up that for a living. Hell, I've had to con enough people in my life. Maybe I should go for the big kahuna and con a whole church full of them at I time. My hair was almost white. I had a good speaking voice. I could FEEL THE POWER with the best of them. Maybe I could even do like that Power Team for Jesus guy and MC a whole act. Combine the worst excesses of the tele-evangelistic circus with the flamboyance of the World Wrestling Federation. Jimmy Swaggart meets the WWF. Ladies and gentlemen, it's Wrestling with Jesus. Body Slam for the Lord. Turnbuckle Smash for Christ. The shower soon washed away my idle fantasies and I slowly settled into workaday mode.

I executed the household morning routine flawlessly. Lunches made, homework collected, backpacks stuffed, checks filled out for fundraising orders, ("What is it this year Honey, window stickers or Christmas wreaths?") money for gas to the boys, and a peck on the cheek to Miranda before she hopped on the bus. As I shambled back into the morning mess, I couldn't help but feel I'd already put in a full day's work. When I got the last of the breakfast dishes rinsed and put into the dishwasher, I dried my hands and sat down at the kitchen table to look up a phone number. Let's see, Wasen, Archibald. Wasen, Frederick. Wasen, George. Wasen, Tulane (must have been born in the sixties). Here it is, I told myself jubilantly, Wasen, Victor. And underneath it a listing that said, "children's phone," with a separate number. That must be for Mark: The thirty-five-year-old child.

I dialed that number. As I listened to it ring on the other end I reflected on how it was just the other day that Miranda had asked me why we said "dial," when in fact we punched in the numbers on our telephone keypad. I actually had to go to the garage and dig out an old rotary phone so she would believe that there used to be this spinning thing on the face of it that you stuck your finger in to "dial" numbers.

"Hello-oo!" answered a giggly voice that shook me out of my reverie.

"Hello," I said, wondering briefly if I'd got the wrong number or if Mark was into a morning suck of helium.

"Hello," she said again. It was definitely a she, and she definitely had one of those voices that were bubbly sweet, but also a little crusty on the edges. I had a mental image of popped bubble gum drying on the corners of a bright red set of lips.

"Hello," I said. "Is, uh, Mark around by any chance?"

"Markie Markie is sleepy weeping," she cooed.

"Could you, possibly, wake Markie Markie up?"

"Oh no! Markie Markie was a big boy last night and he's very wery tired."

This was starting to get weird. "Um, Miss...?"

"Suzie," she answered. I was surprised she wasn't also 'woozy.'

"Miss Suzie, this is Jobe Carson, and I sort of had an appointment with, um, Markie this morning, I'd really appreciate it if you'd just shake him a little or something."

"Oh no! I couldn't do that—" she started, but just then I heard a low groan in the background. I guessed Markie Markie was coming around, and though I don't claim to be a total expert on hangovers, the textured tone of his non-verbal protest sounded like the harsh sibilance that can only be attributed to an advanced case of cottonmouth. I heard another noise that sounded like the phone changing hands.

"Hello," said a voice. Or maybe it was just grating rocks.

"Hello, Mark?" I said boisterously, "How the heck are you, boy?" I did my best to infect him with the enthusiasm of the morning.

"What? Who's this?"

"It's your old friend and private investigator Jobe Carson. I'm on my way out to have you show me around. Remember? To help you find your dad."

"What? Oh... What... What..." Apparently Mr. Sandman had cold-cocked him the night before. With a sand filled sap

"I'll be out there in a half hour," I said. "Like we discussed the other day Mark, people would be mighty suspicious at the country club if you weren't doing everything you could to find your dear old dad. You're going to have to get your own membership now, remember? Which means the board will have to vote on you. So you want to... help... me... right?" I broke it down real slow for him. "That is, I assume you want to keep your membership in the country club. Don't you?"

"All right Carson, what do you think I am, stupid? It's not like I'm dense. I get your drift." He must have woken up sometime during my exposition. "Give me forty-five minutes."

"I'll be there in forty," I replied.

He was growling like a coyote as he hung up. Or maybe that was Suzie.

Chapter 20

I had to stop when I drove up to the entrance of the Wasen estate. An electronic sentry gate barred the way. I pressed a button on a small metal post and heard a tinny voice squeak from its tiny speaker. Nice to know all that old drive-in movie technology didn't go to waste.

"Whaddaya want!?" the voice inquired. Its tone was not gracious.

"Just here for a little bed check, Markie," I flung back with broad cheerfulness.

In reply there was a brief buzzing noise. Then the gate started its hydraulic assisted swingback that cleared the road for my entry. As I drove closer to the main house I noticed numerous outbuildings scattered through the various paddocks. It was easy to see that this had a been a horse-oriented estate at one time, though now the pastures had been replaced with croquet fields and putting greens—and not a little untamed undergrowth. I rang the bell and the door was opened by a youngish woman who I presumed to be Miss Suzie.

"Morning," she whined. Then, honest to God, she popped her gum. I couldn't help but notice the dried residue in the corner of her bright red lips. Her auburn hair was in the cascading disarray that's popular with a certain set right now. Then again, perhaps her head just had a Cuisinart accident.

"Markie said you should wait here," she simpered as she escorted me to the formal sitting room off the foyer. A fireplace that looked as if the last time it saw ash was when Mount St. Helens erupted stood pristine against one wall. Plush carpet, white of course, massaged my feet as I tracked across it to a Victorian era stuffed chair and matching ottoman by the window. It must have been the real deal, its antique authenticity complete right down to the—"Antimacassar," I said out loud.

"Gesundheit," said Suzie.

"Thanks," I replied, "Gute Besserung."

"I just went a minute ago," she said.

So much for German as a second language. This was getting us nowhere. "Actually," I explained, "I was talking about the doily thing on the top of the chair. It's called an antimacassar."

"Aunt who?"

Vapid was the word that jumped into my brain. "Never mind," I said.

Fortunately, we were relieved of plumbing the philosophies of pomade prophylaxis by the huffing arrival of Markie.

"All right Carson. It's about time you got here," he puffed, "I had to hustle like a pool player to get ready."

My confusion over the one-two punch of his paradoxical accusation and complaint must have been apparent on my face because he followed with a quick verbal jab: "But remember, it's not over till the fat lady comes home."

I took that to signify a threat of some sort, so I felt justified in returning one of my own. It always pays to keep on equal footing with a suspect. "Stick it up your ass Wasen," I said, "and give it a twist for your dear old Dad." I hoped he appreciated my subtlety.

It seemed to shut him up. Meanwhile, I continued to look over the sitting room and appreciate the decorator's touch that brought such a fine collection of furniture and artwork together. If it was Mark's departed mother who was responsible, I had to wonder whether his particular combination of DNA had any strings that could produce such chords of beauty. Looking at him sulk, the hair flattened on one side of his combover by what seemed to be dried whipping cream, I despaired once again about nature's gamble each time it threw the survival of our species to the vicissitudes of sexual reproduction.

"How about we look around the place a little?" I said.

Mark shook his head from whatever bovine ruminations he was engaged in and said simply, "Sure. Where do you want to start?"

"How about that door?" I said, pointing at a connecting arch to what appeared to be the formal dining room. I really didn't expect to find anything; after all, the police had been through all this territory months ago. But I enjoyed going from room to lavishly appointed room, drinking in the opulence of the Wasen's wealth, while plump little Markie and his trollop trailed along behind, wondering if they'd left something incriminating somewhere that could make me finger them for murder. But aside from a few adult toys, which Mark would sheepishly look at and then hand to Suzie, nothing in the entire household aroused my interest. That is, until we circled back around to the kitchen.

"Wow," I said in wonder, "do you have a professional chef come in to do your meals or something?" I was thinking of my own paltry kitchen set-up, with its eight dented pans and one French knife.

"No," Mark said, a touch of embarrassment in his voice. "Dad... cooks." The way he said "cooks," like it was some repulsive act he had once witnessed a slug doing to a cockroach, clued me that Mark wasn't entirely happy with his dad's hobby.

"So, like," I said, "all of this food channel stuff is his?"

"Yes," said Mark, "everything you see here he's either cooked or tried to cook a meal with. Or canned something, or preserved something, or God knows what—"

"He's even got a smokehouse out back!" piped up Suzie. Mark glared at her menacingly. She piped down.

"Smokehouse, huh? Mind if we take a look?"

"Um," he said. "Um..."

"Do you have a problem with me looking at the smokehouse, Mark?" I asked slowly.

"Um, no, of course not," he said. "It's just I..." he gave a sidelong glance at Suzie, who was currently oblivious to us, examining what appeared to be a split end on a red hair pinched between her fingers.

I got his point. "Why don't you and I take a stroll through the muddy fields and leave the little filly here to groom herself?" I offered.

"Good idea," he said. "We'll be right back, Suzie."

She didn't answer. That was one hellacious split end.

Mark and I went out the back door and into a small yard that actually had an herb garden in it. This Victor Wasen guy took his cooking seriously. Mark waddled over to the small out-building at the back of the area. It's funny how some people just can't, or shouldn't, wear sweat pants. The material of the ones he had on stretched across his hind end like the fabric on an over-inflated hot air balloon. Worse, the "stride" of the garment was way too short for his bulbous butt cheeks, so he "strode" along with a melvin of major proportions. Wedgie Wasen. I liked that. No wonder he walked funny. My guess was, when it came to buying his clothes, he hadn't been able to make the mental adjustment from large to extra-large. As a result, he had to endure no end of crotch discomfort. The "martyrdom of pride" we used to call it in the clothing business. Sometimes we'd just say a guy was in "size denial."

Mark stuck a key in a small padlock on the door of the shed. He opened the door and flipped on a switch inside as we walked in. The room was flooded with the light from a bank of fluorescents on the ceiling. A big smoker sat over in one corner. In another corner was one of those giant fryers that were popular a few years back, the ones where you can deep-fry an entire turkey. The only catch was you had to buy about twenty-five gallons of peanut oil to do it in. I actually toyed with the idea of buying one, but figured, even if I could afford the fryer, it'd be about two years before I could save up enough for the peanut oil. Mr. Wasen apparently hadn't been so budget constrained. As I glanced around at the stainless steel wall cladding and worktables and mentally calculated their similarity in size to the tables I had seen on my last visit to the morgue, I noticed Mark try to slip something under his sweatshirt. Unfortunately, fancy as his sweatshirt was, with its chenille finish and intricate embroidery, it didn't leave enough room to conceal anything larger than a Roosevelt dime.

"What's that you got there? Markie boy," I said menacingly.

"N-n-nothing," he said.

"Come on, hand it over Mark. I can tell what it is from the bulge. And most people don't have one that high."

His face reddened as he reached up into his sweatshirt and pulled out an honest to God, I'm not making this up because I saw it in a movie, Swedish penis enlarger. Oh my God. The things money can't, or shouldn't, buy. My professionalism ebbed briefly as I indulged in a small snicker. My joy at seeing him squirm didn't last long. I caught sight of something else over in the corner.

"What's that?" I pointed.

"What does it look like?" Mark was sneering now. "It's a dehydrator, asshole!"

CHAPTER 21

This was getting ridiculous.

"All right, where is it?" I demanded.

"Where is w-what?" Mark replied, worried he'd really pissed me off now.

"The shrinkwrapper thing."

"Shrinkwrapper?" he asked, confusion knitting his brow.

"You know, shrinkwrapper, vacu-packer, whatever it is those infomercials sell to the masses."

"Oh. One of those...?" He stalled. "Let me see... I'm not sure I... I..." He started to rummage around under the prep tables. "Here's something, is this what you mean?"

Sure enough, it was what I meant. And a fancy one too. The label said it was a Dee-Luxe Vacu-Packer 2000. In its original box no less. I pulled it onto the tabletop and opened it up. Inside, the machine was packed very neatly in its original nestling Styrofoam, all the warranty cards laid out meticulously and even the original plastic wrapped around the various components. It seemed like sacrilege to go through it all but I did it anyhow. I felt like I was violating the shrine of some sacred sect of fastidiousness; its acolytes dedicated to the placement of everything in its appropriate location, "A place for everything and everything in its place" their guiding credo. I looked over at Markie and his flopping lactose-enhanced combover and couldn't believe he could possibly have put this machine back in the box in its proper order. But the machine had definitely been used. There was even a little post-it note on the top in slightly smeared penmanship that indicated the need for more bags. It read simply: "More bags."

I put down my own little notebook to place the various items back in the box, wrestled the big unit into its Styrofoam bookends, and closed the top. "Give me a hand," I said gruffly to Mark, and we put it back on the shelf under the table.

"This it?" I asked, glancing around, trying to get some glimmer of inspiration from the surroundings. I walked over to the big meat cleavers hanging on hooks on one wall. Their blades appeared sharp but unsullied.

"What were you expecting?" He was sneering again, "Slaughterhouse five-o?"

It was somehow comforting to have the old Mark back. "Could we look at the garage now?" I inquired politely.

"I suppose," he said. He was acting weary now. "You know Carson, I know you can't make an omelet without counting your eggs, but if we have to go through every frickin building on this overgrown horse farm we'll be here from hell to brunch."

I could tell I'd been here too long already. He was starting to make sense.

"I'll be happy to do it myself Mark, if you want to go in and wash that whipped cream out your hair before it turns to cheese. I'm sure Suzie's about done with that split end by now. Give me the keys. By the way, I left your peter pumper on the main table, in plain sight." With a worried glance he hurried back into smokehouse.

I wandered over to the former carriage barn, now garage, and let myself in. I didn't really need the keys. All the doors were wide open. I gave the vehicle bays a cursory look as I went by: BMW convertible, Rolls, Mercedes Sedan, Bright Green Bug (Suzie's I guessed) and a low red Lamborati or something. I confess, cars aren't my strong suit. I guess I'll never make a good secret agent.

What did interest me though was a door off one side of the garage. I tried three or four keys on the ring before finding the right one, twisted it in the lock and opened the door. I found a light switch, flipped it and was once again rewarded by the results of the terminally neat Victor Wasen's efforts. This appeared to be a storage room for outdoor toys. A couple of bicycles were hung on one wall next to a set of shelves. A sea kayak on a double rack hung on the opposite wall.

Scuba gear was stacked neatly on one shelf next to two croquet sets. There was a deluxe jumbo set of lawn darts; "For Your Next Family Picnic!" emblazoned on its box. Everything in its place. Only one jarring note in the whole anal-retentive symphony—the golf bag.

It was lying on the floor, it clubs spilled out in disconcerting disarray. By its fine leather, lovely burnished metal appointments and the initials VW embossed on the front, I could see it wasn't the sort of bag dear old Dad would carelessly toss around. I noticed one of the clubs looked different from the rest. Its cover was slightly skewed, like a sock pulled on too quickly after a hasty midnight rendezvous. I pulled it off all the way and examined the club head. Dried brown something crusted the surface. Either I was a total idiot, or this was blood. I took out my trusty pocket knife and scraped a little of it into one of the small ziplock bags us PI's always carry around. Maybe I could talk Kathryn into a little midnight rendezvous of our own. For some microscopy. I pulled another one of the clubs out and examined its head. Sparkling clean. It looked weird though. I took it out of the bag and pretended to line up a putt. The head was on backwards. Of course, you'd expect me to think that. I golf right-handed.

I headed out to the back forty and went through a number of outbuildings that contained various yard and farm implements. Nothing seemed to jump out as a useful clue. As far as I knew, the elder Wasen hadn't been raked to death. And I didn't imagine the police had found anything in their search. No yellow tape barred my entry anywhere. Besides, the report I'd read earlier had indicated they had seen no signs of foul play. Then again, the police report hadn't said anything about blood-encrusted golf clubs either.

Maybe I was just too dispirited to put my heart into the search. I was at another dead end. Judging by the state of the house, I just couldn't believe Mark was capable of repacking that shrinkwrapper with such close attention to detail. Hell, the only thing he paid that close attention to was his combover. Still, the smokehouse seemed an ideal place to perpetrate the crime in question. All the tools were handy; everything was laid out for the most efficient transitioning of a human being from an intact corpse to discrete, constituent, preserved parts.

I walked back to the house and rang the bell again. Somehow, I didn't feel entitled to barge in just because I had a key. Or brave enough for that matter. Who knows what new dessert toppings Suzie and Markie might be sampling?

Suzie let me in and then headed towards the kitchen. "Mark's in the shower," she said in a voice not at all unlike a normal person and went back to what must have been her next morning project. The split end seemed to have been dispensed with.

"What's that you're up to Suzie?" I asked.

"This sound system thingy didn't work," she mewed, "So Markie told me to take it back to Stereo City. I'm just putting it back in the box."

"I see," I said, and I did. Slowly, carefully, like a repeat DUI offender trying his utmost to pass a roadside sobriety test, she was reassembling the plastic and twist-ties and Styrofoam packing components of the sound system. When she was done, the finished product looked like it could have come straight from the factory. It only needed one last step.

"Could you help me slide this in?" she asked innocently.

"Sure," I said, as I reached over and grabbed the unit. "I've done this before. The trick is not to force it."

CHAPTER 22

As I got back into town my mind was still tossing around the possibility that Markie and Suzie were in cahoots to repackage Victor into neat little airtight bundles. Maybe there was more to that girl than I first thought. It doesn't pay to assume too much from your first impression. Although my experience has been, hoary aphorisms notwithstanding, that you often can judge a book by its cover, I had a sneaking feeling Suzie may have profounder depths that she let on. Still waters run deep as they say. In her case, "still" may end up meaning comatose, but you never know. I made a mental note to check the shrinkwrappee for signs of bubble gum residue.

My more immediate problem was how to handle Ms. Greene. Liza, to her "really" close friends. I didn't particularly want to be a "really" close friend. But as long as she had taken the initiative to contact me, I felt I might as well try to manipulate the situation to my advantage. As far as I could tell, since the number she had called at my home was my family number, she didn't know I was a private investigator. Good. I didn't feel bound to tell her. Not that I thought she would object to a little private investigation. I just figured if I could play along with this seduction thing for a while, I might get her to slip up a bit and offer me something I wouldn't have gotten with a more straightforward approach.

I pulled off the main street and parked in a hotel garage close to the restaurant d'rendezvous. The restaurant was called "Capitole" with one of those accent marks over the last 'e' that indicated you were supposed to make a Hispanic happy noise — like "Olay!" I had been there once or twice in the past with my loving bride and had been favorably impressed by its menu. The chef/owner was originally from the New Mexico area and had transplanted her culinary sensibilities to the great Pacific Northwest. The result was a peculiar fusion of southwest and northwest cuisine; chili meets salmon, apples meet prickly pears, that sort of thing. Usually the dishes worked, though sometimes they sat in uneasy cohabitation on a plate. Kind of like a desert prospector marrying an old growth logger's daughter.

I went in the front door and was relieved to see no one I recognized, or more importantly, that no one seemed to recognize me. A neatly dressed woman came up and I told her I thought I had a reservation in the name of Greene. "Right this way Mr. Greene," she said, and before I could correct her the day chef called her name and summoned her to the steaming dishes on the counter.

I sat sipping my lemon slice garnished water and surveying the surroundings. Some very nice decorating touches indeed. There were a couple of giant old champagne bottles filled with different colors and shapes of pasta interspersed with a number of dried herbs. There were also some smaller, sealed carafes in which pods of garlic and strands of something, possibly saffron, appeared to be soaking, or at least suspended, in pale green olive oil. Sprays of various types of plant matter were bunched artistically on the chest-high divider that ran down the middle of the room. The divider separated diners from each other enough to make them feel private, but not enough to completely screen out their conversations should one bend an inquisitive ear. Something to remember. Ficus trees stood in some of the corners, decorated with hummingbirds and ribbons and little toy southwestern Indian items: Kachina dolls, backwards swastikas, tiny hand-woven blankets. A cactus terrarium was against one wall under a warmly glowing heat lamp. Barrel and ocotillo and cholla tried to out spine each other, while clusters of aloe vera spread along the bottom in healthy profusion.

The waitress had seated me towards the back of the restaurant, facing the door, so I had a few moments to regroup when Elizabeth burst through the door. As her eyes adjusted to the light, I had a chance to witness her in an unguarded moment. She seemed quite fragile, her brow trying to furrow in worry, as she looked around for some sign of me. Then our eyes met, and her face rearranged itself into what she must have thought was her most seductive look, but in fact reminded me of a badly drawn cartoon chipmunk. The waitress had greeted her by this time and was pointing in my direction. Elizabeth, somehow I couldn't call her Liza even in my internal dialogue, strode, sallied, sauntered — all of them sexily — over to the table. I stood like a gentleman and pulled out the chair for her, getting a big blast of designer perfume in the process as it emanated up from where it had no doubt been liberally applied to her erogenous zones. Yuck.

Why is it people who wear perfume can't smell it? And the worse it is, the more they slather it on? Take patchouli for instance. Patchouli is the only scent I know — barring skunk spray, to which it bears passing, and I do mean 'passing' resemblance — that lingers for hours after a person has left the room. I once had a patchouli-douched customer write out and hand me a check for some merchandise she was buying. I put it in the till. Five hours later, when I was cashing out, it still reeked enough to have marked its territory on every bill in the goddamn cash register.

I hate it most when these olfactory-challenged folks go to restaurants. I was all for non-smoking areas in restaurants. Now I think they ought to have a non-perfume area as well. I suppose I should say fragrance. Men are just as bad. Or worse. Kiah went through a period where he was pouring on what must have been a bottle of stinkwater every morning. My whole fricking house reeked. I had to roll down the window of the car when we drove together, so I didn't sneeze every two seconds and accidentally run into an oncoming semi. As you can imagine, father-son relations were a little strained at that point.

Elizabeth read my frown as disapproval of something else entirely. "Don't you like the restaurant?" she asked.

"What? Oh yeah, it's great. I love what you've done with the place."

"You think so?" she breathed. "Really?"

I flinched. She was laying it on thick. I expected her to make that Roy Orbison growling noise next.

"What is it?" she said, "You seem preoccupied. Do I make you uncomfortable?"

"No, I'm fine. I was just thinking of my boys' band concert tonight."

She grimaced. Obviously, she wasn't here to discuss that kind of domesticity. "Do you like my dress?" she asked, opening her lambskin coat and revealing enough cleavage to tempt a eunuch.

"Is that spandex?" I asked. "I've never seen it embossed like that before." The tight-fitting bodice that was engaged in the act of offering up her bosoms to the admiring public had little peek-a-boo palm trees printed on its surface. In real life I had never seen a palm tree with coconuts that big, but the designer of this particular artistic rendition obviously had Freud in mind. Elizabeth looked like she was decorated with hundreds of tiny, sparkly penises. "What's that shiny stuff? Lurex?"

"Could be," she said. "Maybe we could check the care label later. You seem to know your way around fabrics, Jobe. What I was really wondering was what you thought about the fit?"

"All I can say is, don't shoot your tailor. Cause he's a rare one indeed. I've never seen anyone who could alter to the nanometer before."

She heaved her chest forward a little as she adjusted her chair. I got another blast of perfume.

"What shall we order?" she said.

"You tell me."

"How about the stuffed manicotti?"

"Sounds a little rich."

"Oh it is... And so, so creamy. I love the sauce. I could just drink it." She lifted up a breadstick and started to nibble on its tip.

I changed the subject quickly, pointing to a painting on the wall. "That your doing?" A Navajo Indian child was holding a jar of sunshine while a raven and a coyote offered her stalks of corn.

"Oh yes, from an artist I found at a roadside stand around Kayenta. Not far from Monument Valley. Have you seen Monument Valley, Jobe?" She took in a very deep breath. "It's worth a visit, I promise you."

My tongue appeared to be tied. Where's a snappy rejoinder when you need one?

CHAPTER 23

I held up my hand mutely to the waitress and she came over.

"We're ready to order," I said. "I think we'll split an order of smoked salmon stuffed manicotti. And let's try the poblano chili and feta cheese tamale, and a mixed green salad with the house raspberry vinaigrette. Oh, and bring us some focaccia and bruschetta to start."

"You're so manly when you order," Elizabeth said. "Your voice almost makes me tingle..."

"I can't believe it," I joked, "I almost forgot the focaccia."

She got that blank look in her eyes again. Definitely humor-impaired, I thought. She's the kind of person that needs a laugh track to cue her whether to chortle, chuckle or guffaw at a sitcom. I notice those people at parties. They're always a half beat behind everyone else when the laughter breaks out after a punchline.

"I hope you don't think I'm nosy, uh, Liza, but I couldn't help but notice the tan line on your wedding ring finger. What happened to Mr. Greene?"

Her head jerked. "I don't know," she said flatly.

"You don't know?"

"I don't know. He disappeared one day and never came back"

"He must have been pretty stupid to leave a gal like you voluntarily." I used my most consoling voice.

"Well, he was pretty stupid, that's for sure..." she said bitterly.

I gave her a questioning look and waited.

"...a stupid drunk was more like it. Every time we'd go someplace he'd have too much to drink and end up picking a fight with whatever guy happened to be talking to me at the time. It was so embarrassing. And we were just talking too. You know. Sometimes I just needed a little fresh air or sometimes one of my clients would want to show me his yard or veranda or something. It was all very innocent. That's part of what I do, make the host feel comfortable. Make his guests feel comfortable too. I couldn't even go to the parties I planned, couldn't even experience my own success without my lousy drunk husband busting up and ruining the whole thing. I just couldn't take it anymore, I just—"

The waitress chose that moment to put our plates down in front of us. The ravioli, and the tamales, and the bruschetta, all at once. We never did get our salad.

"Sorry," she mouthed and tiptoed off. Elizabeth was dabbing at the corners of her eyes with a tiny linen handkerchief, the initials EG embroidered on one visible corner. I guessed the outburst was over.

"Sounds like a pretty painful memory," I said. "Focaccia?"

My lame attempt at levity was lost. Elizabeth was looking towards the kitchen. Actually, "kitchen" is sort of an overstatement. The setup of this particular establishment had the cooking area right up front in plain sight, its grills and ovens and cook tops barely concealed behind a couple of sneeze guards and some big jars of garnish.

"He's really good with a knife," she said suggestively.

"How so?" I said, glad the heat of her interest was temporarily turned in a different direction.

"Oooh, look at that," she moaned. "He just flipped that piece of fat from a chicken thigh right into the stock pot with the tip of his blade."

"So you understand the finer points of knifesmanship, huh?"

"Oh yes, in my business you can't know too much about all the ins and outs," she paused and took a drink of her wine, "of food preparation. I can filet a salmon, carve a side a beef or even bone a chicken."

"I'd like to see that someday," I said, surprised at myself.

"I bet you would," she dipped a sliver of focaccia in the manicotti sauce and slid it into her mouth.

94

We finished our meal with more of the same type of conversation, innuendos and double entendres flying faster than a piece of chicken fat into a stock pot.

She insisted on charging the bill to her business. We lingered a little, not quite ready to end our comfortable respite. She had picked up her wine glass, her fourth, and was sipping the last swallow when I looked up. Uh oh. Through the plate glass of the front door I detected the bulbous silhouette of my nasty nemesis Knudson. Oh shit, I thought. He'd be sure to blow whatever cover I had. I looked around quickly for a back exit.

"Come on," I said to Elizabeth, taking her by the hand, "I've always wanted to do this." Grabbing her coat, I hustled her out through the prep kitchen. A couple of wild haired punk types were chopping tomatoes and peeling garlic. They looked up in surprise as we scooted past, probably thinking we were some kind of senior dine-and-dashers. I looked over my shoulder and could barely see around the big Hobart mixer to the front door. Knudson was standing talking to the waitress. Behind him stood Kathryn, huddled in her dripping raincoat, blinking as she tried to adjust her eyes to the dim light of the interior. I burst out the back door with Elizabeth laughingly in tow. She was trying desperately to wriggle into her leather coat on the run.

"My," she panted, "that was fun. Did you see the looks on those prep cooks' faces?"

"I always like a dramatic exit," I said.

"And I like a man who can be spontaneous," she cooed, grabbing my arm and pressing her chest against it.

I felt a hard knob. At first, I thought it was a button on her coat, but when I looked down I could see it was a different protuberance altogether. Her breast dug into my triceps. "Saline," I muttered.

"What?" she said, pulling back hurriedly.

"Sailing," I said. "This kind of day would be fun for sailing. It's so blustery."

As if in cosmic reinforcement, or some divine attempt to bail me out of a horrible faux pas, a big gust of wind nearly blew us into the side of the building.

"Let's run!" I shouted, and we ran down to the hotel garage where I'd parked my car earlier. We got in and the windows instantly steamed up. Elizabeth started peeling off her leather coat.

"Do you have a towel?" she asked.

"How about some Kleenex?" I handed her a box I always keep in the car for emergencies. As I watched her dab away at the coat and get the worst of the water off, I couldn't stop myself from feeling a little sympathy for her. She had a vulnerable look of concentration on her face. It reminded me of our common need to hold our own against the onslaughts of nature. Her spandex obviousness was temporarily obscured by her hunched posture and the folds of her coat. One ringlet of her hair had pulled loose from the severe, pulled-back coiffure she had sported earlier. I could see some of the earnest little girl she must have been, artistic perhaps, a little bit controlling, and bent on making her own way in a world designed for another gender, regardless of the intervening frustrations. Once you got past all that seduction stuff, she was a pretty nice person. One day it might be nice to see her with her hair down and her make-up scrubbed off.

"Where to?" I asked.

"I've don't have to go back to work for an hour," she said quietly, "would you like to see what my own place looks like?"

One day may come sooner than I thought.

"I'd love to," I said.

CHAPTER 24

"But I've got to get home in time to meet my daughter when she gets off the bus," I said.

She grimaced again. It made her voice turn sour. "Well okay... If that's what you want."

"Sometimes life isn't about what you want." I was apologetic. "Sometimes life is about what you have to do. Where can I drop you?"

"Back at the store I suppose." She started to pout. She sunk back into her seat, drew her shoulders in and stuck out her inflated lowered lip. I couldn't help thinking I'd feel real safe if we ever had to fly together. One good thing about Elizabeth and all her add-ons, if we went down in the ocean she'd sure make a great flotation device.

"Thanks for lunch," I said as I pulled up in front of her store.

"The pleasure wasn't mine." She sulked in earnest. I turned up the heater on the dash. The car was getting downright frigid.

"Can I call you sometime?" I asked, trying to make peace.

"I don't know. Do you ever have enough free time in your life to do something other than father?" I never knew the word 'father' could sound so despicable.

"Yes," I said defensively, "I just have to plan it more than most people. You of all people must understand planning."

"Of course. Planning's a life and death thing with me. I'm just not used to being, to being..."

"Temporarily set aside—like a fine wine I'd like to savor later?"

Her expression changed. As much as her expression could change. Her lower lip drew in and her eyes opened a teensy bit wider.

"Like a fine wine. Hmmm. I like that, Jobe. You need to let me breathe first. But watch out, I'll go right to your head." She brightened a little. "All right. Call me when you're ready."

She gave me her hand and I brushed it with my lips. As she got out of the car and walked into her store, I was struck by her cat-like grace. She looked like she would be a wild cup of wine indeed. Let's hope she didn't turn into vinegar.

I drove home once again. At least it was Friday. Tomorrow I could wake up late and catch up on my domestic chores. The bus had already left, and Miranda was waiting at the door when I got there.

"Where's the boys?" I asked worriedly.

"I don't know," Miranda said, "I think they had to go in early to their band thing."

"Where's your key?"

"I forgot it," she said sheepishly.

I didn't have the heart to be mad at her. I was madder at myself for lingering over Elizabeth and neglecting my "fathering."

"Mir," I said, "I really want you to be sure to always have your key. Find a place to keep it inside your backpack or something. There're too many weirdos in this world to be standing out here all alone. Remember the lump in the garage? It took a mighty sick person to do that. And that person may just come after me or you if he thinks I'm going to cause him trouble."

"I know, Dad," she said, almost in tears. "I'm sorry..."

I melted on the spot. Nothing more pitiful than Mir's tears. I gathered her into my arms and gave her a big hug. We went inside and played her Nancy Drew mystery game on the computer for a while. She was pretty good at finding clues. The different levels of the game opened up miraculously as she discovered the right sequence of events. Or should I say "Mir"-aculously?

The boys had indeed left early for their marching band performance. Bits of toast and peanut butter and jelly were strewn artistically across the kitchen counter. Perhaps autistically would be a better word. The boys never seemed to be in complete touch with reality as the rest of us knew it, at least as far as things like common courtesy were concerned. I suppose they thought they should live up to the American TV commercial ideal of male slovenliness. I'm sure they could hardly wait to grow up, so they could crush beer cans on their foreheads or get their own beat-up easy chair to fart in.

Mir and I had some grilled cheese and soup and then dressed warmly for the football game. Sitting in the bleachers on a Friday evening in October can be pretty cold, or sometimes, a lot colder. We stayed at home as long as we could. Truth be told, neither one of us were much into the football thing, and we wanted to arrive as close to the half time performance as possible.

Today's football team/halftime band mating is worse than ever. The crowds in the stands, never very responsive to marching bands in the first place, are now often festooned with small radios and earphones that allow them to keep up on "big" games across the state. The band, knowing that no one in the local audience is paying attention anyhow, have taken to crafting their act to please the musical judges they encounter at special shows and competitions. So the routines, and the music, are beyond the appreciation of the average high school football fan. Heck, they even seem a bit esoteric to the casual, John Philip Sousa nurtured schmoe like myself. A classic case of an artist losing touch with his audience, or an audience not caring to exert the effort necessary to appreciate the artist. Andy Warhol—in Norman Rockwell gallery.

Miranda and I got to the game and walked up to the ticket booth. I paid the exorbitant fee, four bucks for me and three bucks for her. Too bad, I mentally groused, that it all went to the football team and none of it to the band. As I looked up over the corner of the stands I saw a sight that made my blood surge. Kathryn. She seemed to be sitting alone. I looked over at the refreshment stand to see if maybe she was still being shuttled around by Knudson, but other than a couple of baggy-panted teenagers fighting over a corn dog, no one was there.

"Look," Miranda said, "isn't that the Kathryn lady that you talk to sometimes?"

If I ever go completely blind, I'll know who to get as a guide dog.

"It looks like it," I said. "Shall we go up and see?"

"I can see from right here Dad. It's her." Hmm, I thought, atypically anti-social for Miranda.

"I know Mir," I bent down to whisper, "I meant should we go up and say hello?"

"I don't think we have to," she said, "she's waving at us right now."

Sure enough, Kathryn had caught sight of us and was gesturing from the bleachers, standing up and down, trying to get us to see her. A couple of people next to her started doing the same thing. Then the people next to them, and so on. Soon the entire stands were engaged in one continuous wave, pulsing back and forth to the driving rhythm of beating drums. I spied Jack in the distance, pounding away furiously on his.

Kathryn shrugged her shoulders as we went up the stairs.

"Sorry." she said, "I was just trying to get your attention."

"You have such a way with people. Have you ever considered politics?" I said.

"It would be a great field if it weren't for the politicians," she said. "Is this the beautiful daughter I've heard so much about?"

"Yep," I said proudly, "This is Miranda. Come up here, girl." Miranda was acting unexpectedly shy.

"Hi," she said, barely into the range of audibility.

"Miranda, this is Kathryn... or should I say Kitty?"

"Don't you ever call me that, Jobe Carson. You know I hate that nickname."

"Sorry Kathryn, just teasing." The image of them in the restaurant was gnawing at my insides. "But you got to admit, old Nellie treats you pretty nice otherwise."

"Ugh," she shivered, "That fat pig is about to make me want to transfer to the lab in Pierce County. Do you know I actually had to go to lunch with him today?"

"No, I didn't," I lied. "You 'had' to go to lunch with him?"

"Yeah, the slimy bastard wanted to go over some reports on his lunch hour. Like he wouldn't have time to do it during regular work hours if he wasn't trading jokes with his cronies at the water cooler. I had to listen to him bitch about his wife for an hour. Thank God his cellphone finally rang and he got called out to some gay guy's place."

"Gay guy?"

"Yeah, some missing persons case the police think they got a lead on. Apparently someone found some blood at the guy's house or something."

"Why would Knudson be interested at this stage?"

"He's sure this guy is a murderer, I guess. At least that's what he said when he rushed me back to the office. And you know he's trying to get the religious right vote in the next election. This would be a perfect case for him to splash across the headlines and solve. County Coroner catches Gay Murderer. He's probably licking his political chops now. You know Knudson."

I knew Knudson all right. It looked like tomorrow my chores would have to wait.

CHAPTER 25

The boys were great at halftime. Freshman Jack, slight as a willow, was stuck with carrying a giant bass drum. Giant to him anyhow. Compared to the one I'd had to lug around when I was in junior high school it looked like the small half of a set of bongos to me. But it was big enough for his generation. He carried it quite well and played the complex rhythms of the cadence perfectly. Kiah didn't have to carry anything. He was in the pit.

The pit is where all the orchestra type percussion instruments are put, like chimes and bells and the tympani Kiah played. Instruments you can't march around with on the field but which are used by the bands in today's performances to enhance the quality of the music. Not that anyone was listening. The crowd sat bored and impassive. Or engaged in other diversions. Kids throwing skittles at each other, moms grabbing the arms of their squirming toddlers, dads tuned in to the aforementioned state "big" game. And of course, there was the mass of high school kids who were there for nothing more than the social aspect of it all, running around the stands playing grab-ass, dissing one another, and occasionally getting into a pushing match just out of sight of the chaperoning parent security force that was salted through the stadium. I went down to the refreshment booth, bought some popcorn for Miranda and splurged on a short skinny single latte for Miss short skinny single herself, Kathryn.

She was pleasantly surprised when I delivered it. I sure did like her sense of humor. And she seemed to be pretty patient with my situation, unlike a certain bionic woman I had met for lunch. Although I kind of like the human parts of Elizabeth, I had to say the artificial parts were not my cup of tea—or any kind of cup. Now Kathryn, on the other hand...

As kismet would have it, just as that thought passed through my brain she reached out and squeezed my hand. I squeezed back. I turned to look in her eyes and—

Miranda broke through from behind and plopped down between us.

"Hi Dad," she said breathlessly, "Jack and Kiah said to tell you they'll meet us at home after the game." I had sent Miranda to check on the boys when they got back up into the pep band section of the bleachers.

"Thanks Mir," I said ruefully. "Here's your popcorn."

Kathryn put her arm around Miranda's back and gave her a hug. "Your dad is real lucky he has you to help him," she said. "He tells me you're the smartest one of the bunch."

Mir blushed a little. "Um, thanks," she said.

"Did I also tell you she's got an ornery streak?" I said to Kathryn.

"Oh, Dad," said Miranda, and squinched up next to me tightly. I put my arm around her too, and we sat there, the three of us, warm for the first time that evening. Or was it years?

We parted before the game got over. Our team was about four touchdowns ahead and quite frankly, I was tuckered. Mir was asleep as soon as she sat down in the car. It looked like I'd be carrying someone into bed tonight.

"Goodnight Kathryn," I said, "thanks for making my evening special."

"Thank you, Jobe," she said quietly. "You get that little girl home. I'll talk to you next week."

I made sure Kathryn had got in her car and got it started, and then got into my own and drove out of the parking lot. I felt pretty peaceful for the first time in a long time. Maybe I'd sleep a little late tomorrow.

Then next morning I slept in till seven o'clock. Ah, the weekend. I know it sounds funny to say that a self-employed person looks forward to the weekend, but I do. Just like any ordinary person. It's all about giving your life structure. If I slept in any old day of the week, soon I'd sleep in every day and then soon I just might not get out of bed at all — till they drug me to the poorhouse. It is amusing though. A guy who can work at his job any time he likes looking forward to the weekend. Kind of like when retired people say they're going on vacation. What does that mean? They're going back to work for a couple of weeks?

I coasted through my morning routine then whipped up some pancake mix for the kids. I started frying our once a week bacon and broke some eggs for an omelet. Mir was up by this time and I got her to set the table and put out the syrup and jam and peanut butter. Miranda likes her pancakes with peanut butter and maple syrup. I used to really hate it when she was younger, but now I just make her scrub the plate. I feel a lot better. Soon I had her wake up the boys. They came grumbling into the kitchen with that "you woke me up too early" attitude I've come to know and love.

"Jeez Dad, why'd you have to wake us up so early... it's only nine-thirty!" Kiah said.

"Because I care about your health and good habits," I said with saccharin sweetness.

To which they replied with a sour look. Nonetheless, they managed to consume a couple of dozen pancakes each while they were busy grousing. As they neared the end of their feeding frenzy (that late night marching takes a lot out of you) I spoke over the chewing and slurping noises.

"Besides," I said, "I wanted you to have a nice meal before I took off."

"You're working on a Saturday?" moaned Miranda, "I thought we were going to go see my old horse?"

"I'll try to be back by early afternoon Mir, and then we can ride Rusty to your heart's content." Miranda's hard stare indicated my apology was not accepted.

Getting rid of the horse we'd leased for Miranda before her mom disappeared was another bitter pill we'd had to swallow. Fortunately, the guy we'd formerly leased it from let us ride it every other weekend in exchange for stall duties three times a week. Today was both a riding and a crap-shoveling day. Yahoo.

I left the dishes for the boys, got in my car and headed over to Fred's "Bungalow." I had a feeling this was the gay couple Knudson was bent on sensationalizing. Sure enough, crime scene tape surrounded the perimeter of the yard. It seemed so incongruous to see the little porcelain yard chipmunks and blooming purple kale peeking out through the sober strips of flapping yellow plastic.

I arrived just as a second police car drove up. Out stepped Officer Greg.

"Howdy, Officer," I called, "What brings you to this neck of the woods?"

"A little piece of paper we call a warrant for arrest," Greg said.

"No way. On what charge?"

"As a material witness. And then we're going to impound the house."

I gave him my best dead pan look. "What are you gonna do? Put it up on jacks and take it down to the sheriff's office?"

"You know what I mean, Jobe. No one can get in or out until we're done with the place, including Fred Costner."

"Why the sudden change?" I queried. "I thought you'd written him off months ago."

"I can't say anything to that."

"What do you mean you can't say?"

"My boss told me to keep you away from this one."

"Why? His buddy Knudson think I'll mess up his little gay bashing scenario?"

"I have no idea. I'm just paid to follow orders."

"You'da made a great guard at Buchenwald, Greg. How about you let me have one last talk with Fred before you cart him off?"

"Nothing doing, Carson, you should've been here before we put the tape up an hour ago. Now no one but county people are allowed on the premises. No one. Not even smarty pants Carson." That Buchenwald cut must have just sunk in.

"You're beginning to sound like old Nellie himself, Greg, when are you getting jackboots?"

Just then another officer came out of the house, leading poor Fred by a chain, which was attached to his nylon zip cuffs. I couldn't help thinking this case was all about modern packaging. But it still dealt with the same old human weaknesses inside.

"Mr. Carson!" Fred shouted, "You have to help me!"

"I'd like to Fred," I called out.

"Get my lawyer, Steve Henderson; he'll know what to do."

"Why the new interest in you?"

"They found some blood in my well."

"Blood in your well?"

"The collection well of my draining rack."

"Draining ra—?

"On my dehydrator, they found some blood in the—" the rest was cut off as the officer put his hand on Fred's head, pushed it down, and shoved him none too gently into the car. "Shut up, faggot," he sneered.

I looked at Greg. "Nice screening in the hiring office at your department." I said.

"Yep," he said, and shook his head in disgust.

"So what's the big deal?" I thought I'd try to pry at least one small fact loose. "You'd expect a little animal blood in a draining table. That's what it's supposed to be draining, right?"

"They found more than animal blood, Carson. That's why I'm here. The lab says some of it was human."

CHAPTER 26

Great. Just what I needed. Knudson beating me to the punch before I even got to the refreshment table. Why hadn't I asked to see Fred Costner's dehydrator set up? I had been so cocky about my feeling that he wasn't the one behind the dismembering—until I saw that videotape at the last. Why hadn't I taken advantage of his good nature and asked to view the premises? More importantly, why had I slept so damn late this morning? How important is cooking pancakes for your family if sometime soon you won't even be able to afford flour? I wanted to kick myself. Except Knudson had already given me a big mule kick right between the eyes. The jackass. How could he be so lucky? And now I couldn't get into Fred's house. No how.

I needed to call Kathryn. Someone had done a pretty quick blood analysis. Or at least worked into the wee hours to get one done. And I'm sure it wasn't Knudson. He didn't know his way around a microscope, much less a DNA sequencer. And I'm guessing Wu told him to buzz off. He probably called in Kathryn for a late night technical tête-à-tête. The bastard. I could just see him now, leering over her late at night while she tried to determine the blood's origin. Of course, maybe the test didn't have to be that elaborate, Maybe that was pretty stock stuff in a forensic lab; having a quick panel test to determine whether blood was of animal or human origin.

And, come to think of it, even if it was human, that didn't necessarily mean it was of Bill's origin. Though why there would be any other human blood in Fred's draining table would be a question worth answering. I really would have to give Kathryn a call. Knudson certainly thought he had enough to go to an inquest. And rules of evidence being a little less stringent there, he must be pretty sure he could at least return an indictment on poor old Fred. If indeed poor old Fred was poor old Fred, and not some Hannibal Lecter in a black cashmere sweater. The videotape came to mind again.

I headed home to take up my chores after all. But first I put in a call to Fred's lawyer. The line was busy. Maybe Fred was making his one phone call. I put in a call to Kathryn at her office but just got the after hours answering machine. Somehow I didn't feel like leaving a message. I dug around in my wallet till I found the little slip of paper with her home number but got a machine there too. I left a message asking her to call as soon as she got in. She must be out grocery shopping or something. Which I also needed to do. I checked over my checkbook to plot out what we could afford to eat the upcoming week and was pretty disheartened. Our cushion was running out fast. We might have to have split pea soup after all. Maybe I'd make some crockpot beef stew; we could have that for a couple of nights. A cheap cut of beef always went farther when I cooked it that way. Miranda had finished dusting and the boys had made a reasonable attempt to clean their bathroom before I'd got home. I got them folding some laundry and then showed Kiah how to iron a dress shirt. He was just starting a new job in the clothing business at my old place of employment. Part time. At least he'd be able to afford to buy his senior pictures.

The afternoon rolled around and Miranda and I took off to do some horsing around. And a bit of mucking about while we were at it. Nothing like shoveling horse crap to round out a great week. Rusty, or Crusty as I call him, because he's a grouchy old fart like me, was happy to see Mir. They had bonded as only a horse and a pre-teen girl can bond, and she rode him around the outside arena with all the enjoyment and abandon of every natural horseman from here to the Mongolian steppes.

After our horse soiree we headed into town to do our own grocery shopping. We went to the regular supermarket then stopped in at Costco, our local membership discount store, to buy some milk, cheese and hamburger. Unfortunately, my morning frustration at Fred's Bungalow had put back my schedule. Costco was a circus. It was sample time, like every Saturday afternoon at Costco, and all the aisles were jammed with people who'd had enough to eat about six years ago cramming all manner of new and improved prepackaged junk food into their slavering maws. Too bad they don't open the store to the starving homeless once a week instead. It's a shame all the free food they give away goes to people who would do a lot better to eat a little less. Then again, maybe Costco is in the pocket of the heart attack medication companies.

As it was I had to nudge a few lard-asses just to jockey my cart by. It was too bad too. We were kind of hungry. And some of that pseudo food looked mighty tempting; especially the ice cream bon bons. But that kind of food always gives me diarrhea. Too many chemicals for my system, I guess. I have a hard enough time sleeping at night. The last thing I need is bloating. I gave it a pass.

As I passed by the "super sausage microwave pizza in a biscuit" demo I caught sight of a familiar mountain of flesh. The last time I'd seen her she was flat on her back with a kitty licking her nose. Now there she was, snarfing down a fried cheese stick at the end of the aisle. The lady with the hairnet manning the pizza table saw where I was looking and whispered.

"Watch out for that one."

"The one at the cheese table?" I asked.

"Yeah her. She's crazy. One time she came by and swept a whole bunch of my pizza biscuits right into her cart. She had 'em all eaten by the time she made it to the end of the aisle. Another time she nearly knocked a customer into the frozen food cabinet trying to get the last corndog sample."

"Sounds pretty vicious."

"Vicious ain't the half of it. One time she was here and got in a big argument with her poor little husband. She was yelling and screaming at him because he didn't want to buy ten pounds of ice cream sandwiches. And then she actually hit him with a pack of muffins. Blueberry too. There were purple spots all over everything..."

"Yeah, well," I tried to bring the involuntary interview to an end, "I'll be sure to not get between her and any free food."

"That's a good idea," she said knowingly. Then, as if for emphasis, she wiped a blotch of pizza sauce from her upper lip.

I watched Fern from a distance. She was too intent on each upcoming sample booth to notice my scrutiny. Lucky thing too. I'm not sure what she would have done if she saw me again. I sure as hell didn't want her to start flinging muffins at me. And I wouldn't like her to see me with Miranda either. I waited until Fern had turned the corner, picked a baby loaf of cheddar off the shelf, and plowed through the gluttonous hordes to the cash register.

Fate took a hand once again. Or should I say flipped me a digit. The coupon printed out on the back of my receipt was for twenty percent off on my next purchase of Vacu-pack Super Dee-Luxe Automatic Freshness Dating Food Bags.

Oh joy. Thanks for the reminder. And here I was hoping for a fried cheese stick.

CHAPTER 27

I yelled for the boys to help us unload the groceries when we got home. I started putting away the stuff that was already thawing while they carried the rest of the bags in. The message light on the phone was blinking. I'd get to that in a minute. First, I divided up the hamburger into one pound globs and put it in plastic ziplock bags, non-vacuum, thank you very much. I told Miranda to take them out to the freezer in the garage. "And don't forget to close the freezer door. But don't slam it and knock over those Altoid boxes again," I said.

We have this thing around the house. I should say I have this thing. I hate to throw away anything that looks even remotely useful. Like Altoid tins. What a perfect little container they make for small stuff. The problem was, I already had a drawer full of separate tins for tacks and push pins, rubber bands and pencil leads and even segregated (by me) small and large paperclips. I'd about run out of small things to store separately. And I still had a zillion Altoid tins. So I stored them on top of the freezer, and periodically, one of the kids would knock them off. Yogurt containers were another thing. Thankfully, I'd figured out a way to save the foil lids, turn the plastic containers upside down and cut the bottoms off, and use them for molds for homemade popsicles. Which I stored in the freezer. They weren't that fancy, but they sure beat the price of "quiescently" frozen confections from the store.

I finally got around to pressing the message replay button on the phone. Kathryn's voice came on immediately.

"Hi Jobe, I just got home and got your message. I have to be at my mother's this afternoon but I'll try to call you when I get back if it's not too late. You're probably wondering about the Costner guy. It looks like it's him all right. I'm sorry. I found traces of human blood in his draining well thing. A lot of animal blood too, but the human hemocyte panel was definitely positive. Sorry again. Take care…"

"What's for dinner, Dad?" Jack asked brightly as he came into the kitchen.

"Humble pie," I said.

"What's that?"

"It's something poor people eat." I started browning some hamburger to go with my darker mood. "Hand me the Bisquick."

That night I lay in bed wide awake till about ten o'clock. No call from Kathryn. Her mom must be getting pretty bad. Alzheimer's was devastating for families. And Kathryn's siblings lived back east so all the responsibility for her failing mother fell on her shoulders. She had a care person come in during the week and a college girl stay most nights, but weekend days and some weekend nights were up to her. It was like having a baby. Except a baby that didn't grow out of it.

I thought I had it bad. At least all my charges had memories and a little bit of instinct for self-preservation. Kathryn's mom was likely as not to wander into traffic or set her head on fire on the stove top. I'm not sure what was worse, wondering and worrying about the person you think is dead, or worrying about someone that should be. Nature plays strange tricks on us, and having a person die one brain cell at a time is the worst.

I turned out the light and tried to get some rest. My last thought was of Kathryn, then the dark curtain of sleep fell for a while, before opening up to the stage of dreams. I dreamed of Fred Costner, and Mark Wasen, each of them holding sharp, glistening chef's knives. The knives shrunk somehow, and gleamed even more, and Fred and Mark were suddenly wearing green scrub uniforms, with masks across their faces. The scene shifted, and they were bending over a figure on the operating table. The sheet on the patient rose and fell with shallow breaths. A nurse was using a felt pen to draw marks on the patient's face. The patient was Elizabeth. She was barely recognizable with her hair pulled back under a sterile cloth cap. One of the surgeons lifted

Elizabeth's hand and then reached out his own hand to the nurse. She gave him the marker. He drew something on Elizabeth's wrist. Then he traced another mark right above her elbow, completely around her arm at the base of her shapely biceps. The door to the surgery crashed open and Knudson burst into the room, pushing a gurney with a huge mound on it. The mound reared up and it was Fern Frenello, a giant meat cleaver in her hand. She got off and started chasing Fred and Mark, with everyone screaming and Knudson laughing like a maniac and spitting brown juice at everybody. I yelled for them to stop and they all turned towards me, silent now, and started to move in my direction. Elizabeth got up from the table, the sheet dropping away to reveal her sculpted nude figure, her breasts standing unnaturally at attention, her nipples like the eyes of an owl, staring unblinking into my fear. She held up one of her arms. With her other hand. The forearm had been amputated somehow at the mark on her elbow. Everyone else was advancing on me now, all of them brandishing their own severed forearms with their remaining intact hands. They started to close in on me, and then beat me over the head with their gory appendages, blood spurting out of the raw end of each one, all the while Knudson laughing and laughing and laughing. I looked through the chaos of flailing limbs and saw my wife over by the door. I tried to fight through the bloody crowd to get to her, but she backed away from the carnage into the bright light behind her. I called out her name. She didn't respond. She just couldn't see me, that was it, she couldn't see me because I was being buried by the crazy people trying to beat the life out of me with their horrible severed arms, "Help," I called, "Help me. Help me, help me…"

A person reached around from behind her and pulled her away. I kept calling her name, but the door swung shut. I went down to the floor, curling into a fetal position and covering my head with my arms. They started grabbing at me then, and shaking me, and shaking me, and shaking…

"Dad!   Dad!"

"Miranda?"

"Dad! Wake up! Wake up Dad... You were screaming."

"What? What?"

"I'm scared dad... You were calling Mom's name..." she was shivering.

"I'm sorry Mir. I'm really sorry." I was shaking myself. "Bad dream I guess. Thanks for waking me up. I'm sorry, Honey. I'll be all right."

"Are you sure, Dad?"

"I'm sure."

"I really miss Mom," she said, her voice breaking. "Sometimes I really, really miss her." She started to cry.

"I know Mir... I know," I wiped at my own eyes. "I miss her too."

We sat there holding each other for a while, till she drifted back to sleep. I carried her into her bedroom and laid her down in her bed, pulled up her covers and kissed her on the forehead. I sat in her room for a long time, listening to her gentle breaths, and saying a silent prayer of thanks for all the good things still in my life. Like Miranda.

I went back to bed and lay in the dark until the morning sun started to peak over the mountains. Then I slept.

CHAPTER 28

I awoke late Sunday morning. Mir was already up and watching television, holding onto her toy stuffed horse and huddling underneath the old afghan. Or are those hand-crocheted blankets called talibans now? A cup of hot strawberry was sitting on the coffee table next to the couch. Only half drunk. She never could get through a whole cup of hot strawberry. Such a waste. Nestle's strawberry drink mix was one of the few indulgences Miranda was still allowed. Each of the kids got to pick a couple of non-essentials so they didn't feel totally deprived. Strawberry mix was one of Mir's. For making strawberry milk. It was Mir's idea one day to make it hot. Hey, if you use chocolate Nesquik to make hot chocolate, why can't you use strawberry Nesquik to make hot strawberry? Yuck.

But Mir liked it so who am I to complain. I try to be tolerant when it comes to other people's taste in food. Her mom used to like Brussels sprouts. I knew that before I married her... and I married her anyway. Her beautiful face glowing with obvious delight as she consumed those little cabbages flashed through my mind as I thought of her. Followed by the acute emptiness I felt when I lost her again last night.

I went into the kitchen and started frying up some corn meal mush I had put up the previous night. "Poor People's Polenta" I call it. You cook up some corn meal hot cereal style, poor it in a loaf pan, chill it in the refrigerator and slice it up the next day into quarter inch thick rectangular patties. Then you fry them slow in butter or oil and serve them up with honey, syrup or jam. Mmm, mmm good. Like a combination of French toast, pancakes and corn fritters. I cooked up some ground sausage patties while I was at it, scrambled eggs and soon our southern fried breakfast was complete.

We spent the rest of the day like most families, alternating between bonding and bickering. I tried to call Fred's lawyer, but didn't get past the message machine. Henderson. The name sounded familiar. All in all, I got an F in detecting and D-plus in fathering that Sunday. I vegged; soft on the G's. We all watched the last game of the World Series that night. It's the only baseball game I'm interested in the whole year. I guess because there's so damn many of them. Any single game just doesn't seem that important anymore except insofar as it establishes an arcane statistic for one player or another. Like: "most left-handed hits from a semi-crouch with three chews of bubble gum" or; "most spittle from a wad of chaw" or; "most bases stolen against a nose-picking pitcher by a crotch-grabbing pinch runner." I guess I just don't have enough time to keep track.

In any event, we all enjoyed the game. It was nice to see a team with less financial muscle than New York actually win. And Arizona is such a likable team. All lean and dried out from the hot desert sun. You just gotta like 'em. Sometimes a little dehydration can be a good thing. The corpulent over-saturated New Yorkers looked like their big paychecks were going straight to fast living and rich food distended guts. Or maybe I was just looking for things to dislike. Not very charitable of me. New York's sure had it hard the last couple of months. At least their players got a nice trip or two to Arizona out of the deal.

I went to bed Sunday still not having talked to Kathryn. Which was probably for the better. I was likely to take the frustration I felt out on her. And I'd hate to shoot such a pretty messenger with the stinging bullets of my ballistic mood. Miranda went through the day hollow-eyed and exhausted, and we kept at arm's length from one another, lest we trigger an emotional outburst neither one of us needed. My anxiety over Fred's arrest slowly seeped away, and by bedtime I had resolved to trust my instincts and pursue the investigation. I didn't believe Fred was guilty. I don't know why exactly. Call it intuition.

Let's hope it didn't turn out to be hubris. And that I wasn't
tripped up by my pride of being a good enough judge of character that
I could tell when someone was a murderer and dismemberer or not.
Not that I believed that Fred was absolutely incapable of murder, but I
figured it would have to be a murder of passion, not a meticulous,
cold-blooded murder with subsequent dissection, preparation and
vacu-pack portioning. It just seemed like all that cutting and carving
would make him nauseous. Besides, lots of people watched *Silence of
the Lambs*. That doesn't make them all cannibals.

My plan was simple. Assume Fred was innocent. It's not like I
didn't have three other people who were missing their significant
insureds anyhow. Let Knudson waste his time trying to tie up Fred.
That would just leave the field clear for me to drag one of the others to
justice. I hoped. There was still nothing concrete to say my little lump
wasn't totally unrelated to all four of the suspects.

I sat in the chair in my room thinking those things through when
Miranda came in to tell me she was ready to go to bed. I followed her
into her room and tucked her in.

"Sorry about scaring you last night, Mir." I said.

"That's okay Dad, I feel better now. I was mostly worried about
you," she said carefully. "I think it's good to dream of Mom. I do it all
the time."

"You do?" There were parts to this girl that kept surprising me.

"Yeah," she said, "We talk about things in my dreams. I tell her
about my day, and how well you're doing taking care of us. And how
much we miss her."

"Oh Mir... I wish I did a better job for you. And I wish you didn't
have to go through all this. And I really, really wish I could have found
your Mom."

"It's okay, Dad. And I know Mom's okay. Wherever she is. When
I talk to her she never seems unhappy. She never seems upset.
Sometimes we just sit and hold hands and look off into the blue sky.

I'll be all right, Dad. And so will she. She said to tell you she loves you."

I was starting to cry again. "And I love her, Mir—" I choked out the words. My throat was so tight I could barely talk. The tears were flooding down my cheeks.

Miranda put her arms around me and hugged me close. "And Dad," she said quietly, "I love you too."

"I love you Mir... I love you."

CHAPTER 29

The Monday morning routine went down like a runaway broken wagon—without a hitch—and I settled in to some serious detective work. I needed to make a break in this case if we were ever going to eat real meat again. I put the cheap beef and vegetables in the crockpot to make stew and got out my notebook to map out the day's plans. Normally I'm not much of a list maker, I figure the time I spend making a list is time I'm not spending doing whatever it is I'm putting on that list to do, but in this instance, I felt it was necessary to plan a couple of things I wanted to check. I needed to go to the hospital as Miranda had suggested and see if any one of my presumed victims had stored blood. I needed to call my friend Kim at the FBI lab in Seattle to let him know I might be sending him a sample he could DNA sequence on the QT, and I needed to make contact with Fred Costner's lawyer. And what I really needed was to see Fred.

I look at private detecting as a lot like what I used to do in the undersung clothing biz. There's a lot of preparation that goes on behind the scenes. I once had a person at a party, who knew me only through the intellectual discourse I was carrying on with other folks that evening, say when she found out I was a clothing salesman: "What a waste." Perhaps so. At least to the uninitiated. But correctly executing the process of taking a male with limited taste capabilities and dressing him in a specific way to achieve a specific end—such as running for political office or applying for a bank loan—and doing so over his and his wife's prejudices in fit and style and color and his wife's natural tendency to want to make all his clothing decisions for him and in the process overcome her natural suspicion of me as both a slimy salesman and a usurper of her territory, is a diplomatic enterprise fit only for those normally qualified for the highest level of statesmanship. Believe me—it ain't easy. Combine that with these other talents: an ability to maintain a store in a pleasing manner with evocative displays and visually harmonious presentations; a good knowledge of profit and loss and basic business acumen; a keen sense of color as it relates to psychology, both of the wearer and the perceiver; and the necessity to keep up with and promote changing styles while making sure one doesn't dress a guy for a funeral in a lime green Nehru suit. Then, to top it all off, throw in the language skills necessary to communicate with people from all walks of life—from RV vagabonds to Governors—in the process turning them from suspicious strangers into loyal customers, all in the space of fifteen minutes, and you have a person who is more deeply immersed in the milieu of life, and more directly involved in extracting a living from it, than most any other professional.

A people sense I could definitely use now. First step, call Fred's lawyer. As if in response to my thought, the phone rang. This psychic stuff was getting out of hand.

"Hello," I said. "Jobe Carson speaking."

"Jobe, this is Steve Henderson, Fred Costner's attorney. Sorry I didn't get back to you earlier. I was at a Scottish Pipe competition this weekend. What can I do for you?" His voice was calm and deliberate, with a touch of irony. Perhaps an occupational tic.

"Have you been able to contact Fred?" I asked.

"Not exactly, but I acted this morning as soon as I got your message. There were one or two rather frantic ones from him as well. I've set the paperwork in motion to have him out on bail by this afternoon. Stupid material witness arrest. I thought those things went out with thumbscrews and iron maidens."

"Did Fred give you any idea about what he was involved in?" I asked.

"Well I wouldn't be at liberty to say, would I? Client attorney privilege and all that. But as it turns out we haven't directly communicated yet. You probably know more than I do. Fred was very insistent in his messages that I make contact with you."

"I don't know much," I said, "Just that he was arrested, and his house quarantined because they found some blood in his dehydrator."

"Great. Looks like I should book a hotel for him as well. I gathered the police thought he was involved in his partner's disappearance. To which I say: 'Poppycock!' Nothing could be farther from the truth. Fred was devoted to Bill in every way. I drew up their survivorship agreement. There's no way I could have sat at this desk across from that man and not seen the affection he felt for him. Truth be told, I had even recommended a prenuptial agreement to Fred when he first started settling down with Bill, but he wouldn't have any part of it."

"I'm sure you know him a lot better than I do," I said. "And I'm glad you feel that way. Those were my thoughts too. I don't believe he had anything to do with Bill's apparent demise. But the public eats this kind of thing up, and I got a feeling the coroner wants the public involved."

"Feeling huh? I take it you haven't read the morning paper."

"No. Why?"

"Because either you're a little post-psychic or you haven't discovered your feelings are already a reality," he said dryly. "The headline reads: 'Coroner Solves Sordid Scandal.' The sub-heading says: 'Knudson Arrests Gay Partner.'"

"Knudson has a gay partner?"

"My thought exactly. I see your humor is as black as mine, Carson. Newspaper headline writers love to dangle participles, don't they? Or is that misplace modifiers? It's been a long time since the language portion of the LSAT's. In any event, we've got our work cut out for us."

"We?" I asked.

"Oh. Didn't I mention? Fred wants me to hire you to clear him. If you're not too busy that is? Do you fellows take a retainer or anything? He said to do whatever it takes. I'm assuming that means an advance of some sort, say, five thousand dollars?"

I looked over at the crockpot. "What if I end up proving Fred is a murderer?"

"Apparently, that's a chance Fred's willing to take, Carson. The five thousand is yours no matter what. Naturally, I would expect he wouldn't tender you a bonus if you got him convicted. He may be gay but he's not stupid."

"No, he's not stupid. And frankly, I'd love the opportunity to rub Knudson's face in his own prejudice. I'll take your offer. But you should know, I'm also working for Megapolitan to uncover any possible wrongdoing in Fred's missing person claim. If you're comfortable with me playing both ends against the financial middle, then so am I."

"I'm confident the truth will out, Carson. Why don't you come by my office this afternoon about 3:00? I should have Fred out, cleaned up and here by then. We can discuss our strategy. Oh, and by the way. It's nice to talk to you again. That suit you sold me is still helping me win cases. You were right. Navy was the perfect choice. Black would have made me look like an undertaker. I hope your private investigator skills are as well-honed as were your skills as a clothier."

That's why his name sounded familiar. *That* Steve Henderson. "Nice to talk to you again too," I said. "The measure of a man is still his character, Mr. Henderson; regardless of his current profession."

"Well said, Carson. See you at three."

I hung up in disbelief. A five-thousand-dollar advance. I looked again at the virtually meatless beef stew crocking on the counter. A wave of relief washed through me. Only one problem niggled at my mind. Miranda got home about three. I wouldn't be here to meet her. I'd have to leave a note. Maybe I'd attach it to a new stuffed animal. I looked down at my list. I added one line: "Buy new pony."

CHAPTER 30

I left the hospital totally frustrated. I had only been able to confirm one fact during the entire hour I'd spent in the building. Hospitals suck. They suck blood, they suck money, and they suck the spirit out of anybody stupid enough to think they could go in and ask a simple question and get a simple answer. The only thing worse than dealing with a hospital bureaucracy is dealing with a hospital bureaucracy while your kid is bleeding profusely from the wrist he just accidentally stuck through a window. Or waiting with your sister in the emergency room in the middle of the night because she had the misfortune to get in a motorcycle crash on a date with an idiot.

Their form held true. Fill out a lot of forms. Customer service at most of today's medical establishments is motivated only by the appropriate insurance cards. Everybody else can go wait in line with the poor people the government says they have to provide medical care for. Hippocratic Oath my ass, hypocritical oath is more like it. I would like to tend to your health but, uh, first, do you have any money?

I was shunted from department to department, like being on a phone answering message tree, in the flesh. Except the music on hold was even worse. For administration, press one. For paperwork, press two. For runaround, press three. For pointless waiting for no reason, press four... You get the idea. I finally broke through and talked to someone who knew something. And what they knew was they couldn't tell me anything. Without an attending physician's request. The hospital was bound to respect the privacy of all its patients. Unless of course they were naked and gutted on a table in an operating theatre and you happened to sneak in with your med school buddy. I finally rushed out to the open air. And tried coughing as hard as I could to dislodge any potential infecto-cocci that may have snuck into me while I was being shuttled back and forth through the corridors of death.

I emerged into the parking lot and ambled wearily over to my car. I'd had to park it way out by the street. I looked across the street at the building of the cable company and thought I saw someone familiar standing by the entrance. I couldn't be sure of the facial features from that distance, but the posture made it pretty obvious. Elizabeth. I got in my car and drove over. As I pulled up I used the button to open the passenger side window.

"Hello Elizabeth," I said.

"Oh, Jobe," she breathed, "you scared me driving up like that."

"What brings you to this side of town?" I asked.

"Nothing much. I had a meeting with one of the executives about decorating a set for their Thanksgiving show."

"Odd, I just got finished dealing with a bunch of turkeys myself."

Her eyebrows notched a millimeter higher. It looked like the underside of her chin was about to pop loose. "Would you like a ride to your car?" I offered.

"Well, funny you should ask," she climbed into the passenger seat. "I was just thinking of calling a taxi. I took my Acura over to the Honda dealership to have it serviced today and they dropped me off here. I was feeling so helpless without a vehicle."

"Try sharing one with a teenager sometime."

"But you could drop me at my office if you're not too busy." she continued, oblivious to my sarcasm. She reached over and gave my arm a squeeze.

"Sure, I'm going downtown anyhow. Glad to." Her hand shifted to my thigh—

A shot rang out. A slug pierced through my rearview mirror and the backside of my front window. Elizabeth ducked as shards of glass sprayed through the front seat. I looked behind me to my left and saw a gray car squeal out into the street. Jesus! I dropped my own car into gear and took off. I'd catch the bastard this time. He was already past the stop sign that intersected with Harrison Avenue, the main boulevard that heads to the downtown area. I pulled up to the sign myself and had to wait as a big Safeway semi roared past on its way to unload at the store on the corner. I tried to swerve around him, but oncoming traffic on the two-lane road kept whizzing past. One guy actually weaved closer to me and there was a big snap and crunch. Christ, there went my left sideview mirror too. Elizabeth was clutching my thigh with her left hand and the handle over her window with her right. I finally scooted around the semi and stepped on the gas. The light was just turning red as I zipped through the intersection. I caught sight of a gray car five cars ahead. I bumped up over the sidewalk to clear another slowpoke in front of me. He gave me some universal sign language as I went past him on the right. The obligatory mother with a stroller rushed to the side of the Mexican restaurant as I piloted my CRV along the sidewalk. The look of horror on her face as she shielded her child from certain doom made me instantly cut to the left. The driver of the next car I had not quite passed slammed on his brakes and laid on the horn. Elizabeth was white now, but I had settled into the groove. Whip to the left when there's an opening, bump up onto the curb when I had to.

The gray car was only two car lengths ahead now and I could see that it had no license plate. And no dealer plates either. At least none that I could read. Jockeying to get closer, I noticed the flashing yellow light that indicated the stoplight around the upcoming blind curve was about to turn red. That meant that traffic from the north would be cutting into my lane real quick. I goosed the engine again and as it dropped into overdrive I whipped around the Nissan Stanza in front of me. One car to go. The light had turned red. I kept going. Just as I entered the intersection, a big Ford Exposition lumbered into the lane I needed to take. I cut over onto the shoulder and then into the far right lane as it opened up at the bottom of the hill. My quarry had stayed to left and headed down Fourth Avenue. I'd had to cut over to the one lane access to Fifth. Damn. I kept him in sight as we raced across our respective bridges over the southern inlet of the sound. The car he was driving was definitely a Hyundai, and there were definitely dealer plates on it. Or I should say advertisements in the license area. I didn't see any of the official magnetized plates hanging from the trunk lid. I accelerated onto Fifth Avenue proper and then cut through an alley to connect with Fourth. I'd been lucky so far.

My luck ran out. I ran smack dab into a cliche. No, not a fruit stand or haywagon being rolled across a busy street like you see in every movie chase scene from the Keystone Kops to the latest Arnold Swartzenwillis flick. Not another kid in a stroller. Not a flatbed truck that cut off the top of my automobile as we barely ducked down to safety. Nope. A real live, honest to goodness, what else would you expect to run into on a crowded road, automobile. The new and efficient Chrysler Cliche.

As what were certain to be my last moments of life rushed through my head in super slow motion, I found myself reflecting on the absurdity of it all. Car names are getting so out of hand. Novas and Sunbursts and Eclipses were bad enough. Then they started naming autos out of articles of speech. The Nissan Stanza and the Volkswagen Precis. Now they have the Chrysler Cliche. It figures. It's the American way; find a successful formula and copy it. What's everybody else naming their automobiles after? Let's try that. Need an action sequence to punch up a boring cerebral movie script? Add a chase scene. It's all the same. Why doesn't somebody just start naming cars Bob or Frank or something? My personal vote goes to GMC. At least they have the Jimmy.

All the other car names have got too damn weird. As I crunched into the rear quarter panel of the new Cliche one last surreal image kept flashing through my mind; My proctologist, driving his new Ford Probe. The crunching of metal and the breaking of glass brought us to an abrupt halt.

I looked over at Elizabeth. She was breathing hard. Moisture glistened on the platinum hairs at her temples. Her face was flushed. The exposed tops of her breasts were wet with sweat. She shuddered.

"Was it good for you too?" I asked.

CHAPTER 31

The inevitable followed. Apologies to the driver of the other car. Checking for injuries, trading insurance card numbers and waiting for the police. The damage to my CRV was minor. I had crumpled my left front bumper and headlight area. My pavement adversary's vehicle had fared only slightly worse. I had put a fair-sized crease in his right rear quarter panel. And his trunk lid was a little buckled. Fortunately, the CRV is not one of those giant SUVs that routinely total smaller sedans on today's roadways. The Lexus of my unintended victim was mostly intact. But still, at current body shop prices, I was pretty sure it would run close to forty-five hundred dollars to fix both cars. Easy come, easy go.

My dilemma was whether to report it to my insurance company or just fork over the cash. I suppose I'd have to report it, especially since the policeman was even now writing me up a negligent driving citation. And in case my inadvertent chase-ender developed any mysterious whiplash complaints it would be better to let the insurance companies fight it out. I did know one thing for sure. My company was going to nail my financial scrotum to the wall. Any time you have an accident on any of your cars and you also have a teenage driver in your household you might as well just direct deposit your paycheck in your insurance company's bank. Because they are going to stick it to you till you hurt. And they ain't gonna kiss you first either. I thought of Kiah getting florid with anger over the injustice of it all, as only a righteous, hates-all-hypocrisy-in-others teenager can. My premiums were going to double. That's the true life aftermath of a car chase that they never dwell on in the movies: The mundane and painful cornholing you get from the insurance companies.

When it was done, the kind officer had also written me up for having an unsafe equipment issue, what with my busted off sideview mirror, my shattered rearview mirror and my hard to see out of windshield.

"But I'm just going to write you a warning on that one, Mister Carson," he said.

"Thanks Officer, Sir" I groveled, "I appreciate it."

"Quite all right, you got enough problems," he said, looking over at the glowering Elizabeth. "So the whole thing started with a gunshot huh?" Somehow his inquiry didn't sound like he put a whole lot of faith in my explanation.

"Yeah," I said.

"You mean to tell me you were just sitting there in your car, and a bullet just happened to go right between both of you and blow out your rearview mirror and crack your windshield?"

"That's what I said Officer."

"Then you chased this... What was it again?"

"A low gray automobile that looked like used bar of soap," I repeated patiently. "I'm pretty sure it was a Hyundai, it had an insignia on it that kind of looked like an H."

"So it could have been a Honda?"

"It could have been, but I'm pretty sure it was a Hyundai."

"Could have been an Acura, maybe?"

"Maybe," I was getting a little tired of the cross examination at this point. "And it could be my imagination that you're going to end up doing anything about it. Sir."

"Now don't get testy, Mr. Carson, I'm just saying it's not likely we'll be able to check three or four different car agencies in time to see who has been out using one of their cars to take potshots at PI's. You agree with everything Mr. Carson said Ma'am?" he asked Elizabeth.

"No, I don't," she said icily.

"What's that?" he asked.

"I don't agree. That it's his imagination you won't end up doing anything. It's fact."

His face reddened. I interceded quickly. "Tell you what Officer, I'll investigate the Hyundai deal myself. It ought to be pretty easy. There's only that one Hyundai dealership in the tri-city area. Over in Lacey."

"I suppose you mean the one that's closed on Mondays?" he said snidely.

"Closed on Mondays?"

"Yep. I know because I moonlight with a private security firm. That's one of the places we check up on. Nights and Mondays, Can't get no Hyundais... Hey! That's pretty catchy. I think I'll sell it to 'em for a jingle or something."

I was learning more about this particular keeper of the peace than I really wanted. "Yeah," I said, "Great one. Do you think we could go now?"

"Absolutely, Mr. Carson. You be sure to get that stuff fixed. And Ms. Greene?"

"What?" she asked.

"Lighten up. I'm just doing my job," he turned and started to walk away.

"So was Eichmann," she mumbled.

He spun on his heel quickly. "What?" he demanded.

I interjected. "She said, 'she knows what it's like, man,'"

He turned around again and hitched up his belt, heavy because it was loaded with all sorts of arcane paraphernalia, not to mention the big riot club dangling behind. It looked like something out of Batman movie. He walked back over to his squad car and squirmed in, getting poked in various tender places as he arranged himself behind the wheel. He had a surprisingly upbeat attitude considering. Driving around with a stick up your butt can't contribute much to a feeling of inner peace.

I got back in my ravaged CRV and took Elizabeth to her store. She got out without a word and sauntered in. I had a feeling my perfect date status had diminished, while my position on her fecal roster had advanced to number one. Pretty ungrateful for a hitchhiker, if you ask me. Still, she'd taken the bullet blowing by her and the subsequent chase with surprising equanimity.

I checked my watch and saw that it was close to noon. What the hell, I thought, and drove over to Lacey to check out the Hyundai dealership anyway. Sure enough, they were closed, and a big chain was stretched across the front opening of their sales lot. I drove into the parking lot of the adjoining shopping center and noticed a small opening around back that someone could conceivably use to pilot a car in or out. As I went back to the front I saw there were about twenty gray cars identical to the model of the one I had chased. I got out of my car to go over and start feeling their hoods. As luck would have it, when I stepped over the chain, up drove a private security car. A guy with a funny hat leaned out of its window.

"Looking for a new car, buddy?"

"Sort of," I said.

"Well, you may have noticed this dealership is closed," he said.

"Yeah, I just..." I started to say, mentally running through the scenario I had recently lived through and realizing this guy wouldn't care a rat's ass about such an unlikely explanation. I shifted gears. "I just thought I'd take a look without a bunch of salesmen jumping on me, you know?"

"Yeah. I know all right, Mister," he said. "Except that's tough shit. You need to get off the lot. Now. This place is closed."

"Yeah. Whatever you say, Sir. I was just going." I got back in my car and drove away while he remained parked at the chain. I cut through the parking lot of the old shopping center as I headed towards the freeway onramp. Still the same old center I remembered from when I first moved to town: Burger Joint, Goodwill place and charity bingo parlor. The only thing different was a new national drugstore where the old private local supermarket used to be. Wonder if they had any aspirin.

I seemed to have a headache.

CHAPTER 32

I still had an hour or two to kill before heading to the lawyer's so I drove over to the new Target store that had replaced Lacey's former dying mall—"the mall-soleum" we had called it towards the end—to shop for a stuffed animal for Mir. Nothing really grabbed me. I'd have to get something downtown. But, as I was looking at all the different size containers people use for organizing this and that in one of the store's doodad sections, I heard a familiar voice. Or I should say voices.

"Suzie, I told you, I don't like purple towels."

"Oh come on, Markie Markie, you promised we could get new towels and washcloths for the hot tub. Don't you want me to scrubby wubby all the hair on your backy wacky?"

"Stop it Suzie. You know I hate that mushy stuff. You can scrub all you want. I just don't like purple."

"Okay... Blue's just so boring. But, remember, you said I get to pick lunch."

"All right sweetie pie," he was getting a little mushy himself. "Anything on the Capitolé menu is fine with me."

Judging by the sounds of their voices they were walking my way. I hurried down to the other end of the aisle and headed for the exit. I had an idea.

It wasn't long before I was seated next to the center divider in Capitolé, my back to the door, and my face buried in a menu. I'd taken a stocking cap and pea coat my son had left in the car and put them on. I looked like any other downtown denizen now, and I was hoping the reservation card that said Wasen on it on the other side of the divider was a clear indication that Mark and Suzie were shortly on their way. The waitress had been a little curious about my insisting on the particular seat I now occupied, but my explanation that my wife and I always used to sit there seemed to satisfy her. I sat sipping a microbrew and waiting for my salad and focaccia. I figured I could pick over a salad for about an hour if I needed to and the waitress wouldn't annoy me with too many questions. I didn't want my voice to give my presence away to Markie and Suzie. I don't know what I expected to find out, but hell, you have to try to turn every advantage you can in this game. The less they knew about what I knew the better.

I soon heard their gushy voices cooing at each other as they came in the door. I buried my face deeper in the menu. The waitress seated them and handed them menus of their own. They chatted about this and that, and then Suzie ordered their food. It sounded like a bunch of things with goat cheese in it. And one dish with lots of eggplant. She was going to have her purple one way or the other. They sat silent until their meal came, apparently savoring their bottle of Merlot.

"Did you get that box repacked okay?" Mark finally asked. My ears perked up.

"Yes," said Suzie around her eggplant morsels, "Just like you said."

"It looks like it's never been used, right?"

"Yeah. I told you, just like you said."

"Good. I've got another box I took out of the secret trunk in the Rolls. Stupid police..."

"I hate packing boxes, Markie," she pouted. "I hate it."

"Well I'm so sorry. But we need to do it. So they think they're brand new when we take them back to the store. Besides, it's your own damn fault," accused Mark. "If you hadn't pissed off Dad in the first place..."

"I know."

"...When he walked in on us he was madder that a March hatter."

"I'm sorry Markie, I told you, I didn't know it was your mom's nightie. I thought it was something you bought for me."

"If Dad hadn't went off like that I wouldn't have had to..."

"But Markie, you did it because he was going to kill me..."

A booming voice echoed through the restaurant.

"Jobe Carson! How the hell are you, old buddy?"

Oh shit. "Uh, Larry," I said as quietly as I could. "What a surprise. How's the Squire Shop?"

"Hasn't been the same since you left, you old son of a bitch. Nobody has any sense of humor there at all anymore. I don't know why you went to that other men's store. Say... Didn't I see your picture in the paper awhile back? Aren't you a private investigator now or something?" If possible, his voice was getting even louder.

I cowered down close to my salad. "Yeah," I mumbled.

"What's a matter boy? Cat got your tongue?"

"No, I'm just a little tired." I nodded meaningfully in the direction of Suzie and Mark.

"Jeez, bud," he persisted, "Looks like you got a nervous tic too. That private investigation stuff working out? It can't pay too well..."

I gestured in the direction of Suzie and Mark with my thumb, and then put my finger to my pursed lips.

"You're going hitchhiking? You're number one? Hell Jobe, I'm a little teapot. You crack me up," he guffawed. Then he looked at his watch and frowned. "Jesus! I'm late. I better go. Give my best to your wife, old buddy..."

He hurried out. The table on the other side of the divider was silent. I looked through one of Elizabeth's decorations. Mark and Suzie were staring at me. Mark had a little piece of purple dangling from his stunned lips.

"Heh heh," I said. "You know what they say Mark... You can't make an omelet without getting eggplant on your face..."

I paid my check and left the restaurant, head held high. Let them stew in their own juices for a while. Meanwhile I had something to do before I got into some hot soup of my own. I walked down Capitol Way to the corner of Fifth. My destination was the "Wound Up Here" toy store. It was only then I realized I'd have to walk right by Elizabeth's. Oh what the hell, it's not like a guy can't shop in his own hometown. I glanced in her window as I strolled past and noticed her intent with some customer, male, pointing out some fabric swatches mounted on the wall. Her eyes slid in my direction, held mine for a moment, then slid off to sparkle artificially at her current conquest. "Thank you, Lord," I whispered under my breath.

Four more doors brought me to the chaotic cacophony of sound and fury that was Wound Up Here; the best dang toy store in all of Olympia. It wasn't too long before I found the stuffed horse of Mir's soon to be dreams. He was nestled in one corner with his head poking over the top of a plastic corral. He didn't seem too unhappy to be removed from the stuffed company of all the other animals of his series. There were lions and pigs and cows and even hyenas. I briefly considered getting a neat stuffed velociraptor for Jack but decided he'd think it was too "cute" for his adolescent sensibilities. I paid the lady at the counter and wandered out through all the various displays of entertaining toys on my way out. Such profusion. Gone were the simple days of blocks and Lincoln Logs. Wait a minute. I was wrong. There was a display featuring Lincoln Logs right over by the window. This store really was cool. I remembered the first time I'd given a set of Lincoln Logs to Kiah when he was four. Apparently, his crazy uncle had got to him first. When Kiah opened the package, he looked at me seriously and said: "I can't have these yet, Dad."

"Why's that, Kiah?" I'd asked.

"Uncle Tobey says I have to start with Lincoln fiber."

CHAPTER 33

By three o'clock I was back downtown. Mir's new horse, soon to be named, was laying on the couch at home, a note of apology pinned to one of his faux fetlocks. Fred's lawyer, the honorable Steve Henderson, Esq. had an office on the top floor of the Conifer Plaza building. Which at seven stories is the highest building in Olympia. As you can tell, Olympia is not a big town. I had a weird realization one day when I was watching the carnage of the World Trade Center disaster on TV. The newscaster said that the pile of rubble from the collapsed buildings was over seven stories high. Man, I thought, that's as high as the highest building in my home town.

Fortunately, Henderson's office didn't look like a pile of rubble. I was greeted graciously by his receptionist and before I could even pick up a magazine Steve himself came out to escort me to his back office.

"How have you been, Jobe?" he asked as we walked down the quiet corridor. The lushness of the carpet virtually eliminated any sound. His voice had the flat quality you normally only get in a recording booth.

"Pretty good, Steve. It looks like the law business is treating you well."

"Can't complain. Any chance I could call you in for a consult on my next wardrobe renewal? I don't trust that guy they hired after you left. He talks like he came straight from the Menswear House. And pushy. I don't like pushy. Then they hired this kid the other day. He's bright, but that long hair..."

"That would be my son Kiah," I interjected before he said something we'd both regret.

"Great kid," he didn't miss a beat, "I was just about to say I thought he had a lot of potential." Henderson's eyes crinkled at the corners while his best jury-romancing smile stretched across his face.

"Nice cover, Steve. Fred here yet?" We were at the door of his office.

"Yeah, he's using my private bathroom to scrub off the jail scum. Come on in and have a seat."

I planted myself in one of his big green leather chairs. I took the opportunity to look around at Steve's office and felt the awe-inspiring confidence one can only get in the presence of the trappings of the legal profession. None of the high-tech uncertainties of the world of modern medicine. None of the fear invoking reactions to the twirling tools of modern dentistry, only the quiet solemnity imparted by the stolid massiveness of oak and cherry furniture, tasteful wall hangings and dark wood paneling. The only concession to modernity was the computer monitor glowing on one corner of Steve's burnished desk. It was a wonderful impression. You got the feeling that centuries of the best human reasoning would be behind whatever endeavor you hired this man to accomplish for you.

"What do you think?" Steve asked, his arms spreading to indicate everything surrounding us.

"Pretty good," I observed. "This place doesn't look like a slimeball like you works here at all."

His eyes fired briefly. "You're just like a smartass I knew in college," he laughed.

"Who does your decorating? No offense Steve, but based on the first time I sold you clothes, the pig I assume you were in college couldn't have made his frickin bed, much less put together a magnificent impression like this."

"Compliment accepted. My directing credo in life has always been to hire the experts, Jobe. That's why I once let you assemble my wardrobe. I use Elizabeth Greene to do my decor."

"Don't tell me you have shrinkwrapper too." One more coincidence and I was going to buy my own damn dehydrator.

"What?"

"Private joke."

"That Elizabeth woman is amazing," he continued. "She has such connections. I swear, that woman could hire anyone to do anything. And quite the looker too. Talk about hot—"

"Down boy," I said, "Get your tongue off the floor. You'll need it for the courtroom."

At that moment Fred came bursting through the inner door.

"I thought I heard voices!" he said. "Oh Mr. Carson! I'm so glad you're here! I really need your help! They've accused me of killing Bill! And I didn't do anything like that at all. I love that man. But I— But I— I don't know what they think about what they found in that dehydrator thing... I can't even begin to imagine what they thought I was doing. And why are they going after me and why are they trying to make me out to be such a crazy person that would do all this terrible terrible stuff and why can't I just—"

"Hold on Fred!" I yelled.

The room went silent. Fred was holding his mouth closed with obvious effort. His brow started to sprout beads of sweat. He was flush with the exertion of his tirade.

"Fred," I said. "Calm down. I'm here to help. I promise. Now take a deep breath."

Fred took a slow pull on the cool conditioned air. I looked over at Steve. He was looking over the tops of his reading glasses, his gaze aimed directly at Fred. I turned back.

"Now Fred. Tell me what the police found. Slowly."

"Well, Mr. Carson," he started again, "I was sitting at home watching one of my new DVD's — they just re-released 'Funny Girl' you know—and there was a knock at the door. A big officer started waving a search warrant in my face. When I tried to hold him back, another officer came in and pushed me over to the wall. They went all over the house and finally ended up in my basement—well actually, we call it our rumpus room—and they started looking through all my new cooking stuff. You know, the stuff I told you about for Y2K. I've put together a nice little set-up there for drying meats and such. Well, they started to go over my new dehydrator—well, not completely new, I just bought it a while ago at Secondhand City—and they saw this fluid well thing. It had blood in it. You know how it is, you get a big hunk of meat, and it just naturally has stuff in it that has to drain off. My new dehydrator has a little refrigerated table and collecting basin off to the side that you use to drain the meat before you stick it into the dryer proper. That way you can use the blood for gravy or soup stock or something without it spoiling. It's quite a deluxe system. I was lucky to find it. That company went out of business after some infomercial scandal. I could just murder those infomercial people. Why one time I—"

"Fred!" I interrupted him before he got wound up again, "So they saw the blood?"

"Oh yes. It was in plain sight."

"Then what did they do?"

"One of them said 'Ah Hah!' and glared at me like a gruff policeman in a bad B movie. Then he called someone on the phone while his partner zipcuffed me."

"Then what happened."

"We all sat there watching 'Funny Girl' until this big fellow with a snarly attitude comes in and looks at the blood in the drainer well. 'I'll fix you, you damn faggot,' he says, and then waddles out the door with it. The police stay with me all night and then in the morning they hustle me into that cramped car. And take me to that awful jail. That place smells so bad. You'd think they could at least find someone to clean up the urine and the vomit. There's a lot of people out of work. Some of them were even in that jail. Why not hire them to come in every other hour and mop up the other cells. It's not like they couldn't keep busy all day and all night the way some of those people were puking and stuff—"

"It's all right Fred. Calm down." It was Steve this time, trying to hold back the tide of Fred's emotions. "It's all right now. We've got a nice clean hotel suite for you over in Tumwater. Any more questions Jobe?"

"Just a couple," I said. "Fred, you say you just bought this new/used dehydrator a little while ago. After Bill disappeared I'm assuming?"

"Yes…"

"Did you save the receipt? I would think that would pretty much establish your innocence right there."

He looked at me sheepishly. "No," he mumbled.

"Well how about the place you bought it from? Would they remember you?"

"No."

"Why not?"

"I was in disguise."

"You were in disguise? Why were you in disguise?"

"You have to understand Mr. Carson. It's not easy being gay. Some people really hate us. The guy that owns Secondhand City really hates us."

"But he's a businessman, right? Your money's as green as anybody else's."

"Well, I guess," Fred explained. "It was partly Bill's fault."

"How so?"

"He knew the owner of Secondhand City was a gay hater so one time when we were shopping there Bill reaches over and grabs me by the buttocks. Then he plants a big wet kiss on my lips. The owner kicked us out and told us to never come back."

"So let me get this straight. You went in, in disguise, and bought an almost brand-new dehydrator." Things were getting bleaker by the minute. "Now I suppose you're going to tell me you paid cash."

"Yes." Fred said quietly. "I paid cash."

My heart sank. And somewhere in my imagination I could hear Knudson laughing like a stuffed hyena.

CHAPTER 34

Steve asked me if I wanted his secretary to cut me a check on the way out.

"I'm surprised Steve," I replied, "With a posh set-up like this I'd expect you could afford the kind of checks with perforations..."

"That's what I like about you," he laughed. "Always the smartass."

"Just don't get me started on people who call accountants bean counters," I said.

"Don't worry," he replied, glancing in Fred's direction, "I've had enough tirades for one afternoon."

We parted company at his door and I headed home. The stew would be just about perfect by now. All the way home I kept looking over at the check lying on the passenger seat. Tomorrow we'd all have steak. Then I'd sit down and do that task I love the very best of all my household obligations—paying bills. And this time I'd actually have the money in the bank when I wrote the check. Yahoo. Look at me.

Paying bills is always an entertaining experience. I love all the reminders they put on bills to make sure you don't screw up somehow. I wonder how much ink they contribute to the environmental wasteload each month printing things like: "Did you remember to sign your check?" and "Did you remember to put your account number on your check?" and "Did you remember to put a stamp on the envelope?" and etc. I mean I'm sure those envelopes are a great idea for Alzheimer's patients and people suffering from short term memory disorder, but the average Joe already knows how to do that crap. And if the instructions are for those other people, the ones who are either too careless and/or idiotic to pay attention to the instructions anyhow, whose greatest goal in life is to stubbornly persist in stupidity, well hell, they ain't gonna change no matter how much ink you slather on an envelope. Like the people I always used to blow whistles at when I was a lifeguard. They'd just continue to run around the pool on the wet decks, despite the rules. And if they slipped and crunched their skull, they'd just get back up and run some more. Then they'd hop in the pool to wash all the blood off their dundering heads. Which the chlorine disinfected fine.

I never thought I'd relish the opportunity to read those stupid reminders on the envelopes, but I did now. And if I got Fred off, I'd be even richer. The thought of which instantly brought my mood crashing down. Getting Fred off was going to be tough. I was pretty darn somber by the time I walked into the front door. Then a whirlwind came out of the front room and started hugging me furiously.

"Oh Dad! Thankyouthankyouthankyouthankyou...!" she said.

"You're welcome, Mir," I laughed, hugging her back

"Does this mean you solved the case? Are we rich again? Can we get rid of that icky thing in the garage now?"

"Hold you horses girl, one thing at a time."

She looked at me expectantly.

"No, no and no," I said. "I haven't solved the case. We're not rich, and we still have to keep that icky thing in the garage."

"Oh Daaaad..." she whined.

"Sorry, Mir, we still got a long way to go. I just got hired on the side by Fred's lawyer to see if I could get him out of a jam."

"Fred's lawyer is in a jam?"

"Very funny, Mir, don't you start too. Fred's in a jam. Knudson wants to hang him out to dry and my new job is to get enough evidence to prove Fred didn't kill Bill. Which will be difficult since no one knows for sure if Bill is even dead. And the really bad thing is; if that arm in the garage does turn out to be Bill's we're in real trouble. Withholding evidence could make me an accessory after the fact."

"An accessory after the what?"

"After the fact. We didn't commit the crime, but we tried to prevent the police from finding out who did. It's like lying, only a whole lot worse. Especially since we're sitting on a key piece of evidence."

"Would they arrest us?"

"They might."

"You mean we could go to jail, Dad, just cause some stupid trash truck dumped a body part in our driveway?"

"It could happen. I doubt that it would stand up in court. We'd just say we didn't unwrap it. It would be hard to prove otherwise. Still, it might be dicey. Given my profession, it wouldn't be a very convincing fabrication."

"You mean lie," she said seriously.

"Yes, I mean lie." Uh oh. Fathering time. "It's still not right to lie, Miranda. Lying is wrong. But sometimes lying can help someone who might be hurt otherwise. Like Fred. Fred is going to be hurt very badly because Knudson doesn't care anything at all about the truth. He just hates gay people. If I tell a little white lie for a little while so that I can reveal the real truth later then it's..." I started to run down.

"It's still a lie, Dad," she admonished. "But I know what you mean. You can't tell the whole truth all the time. When Melinda asks me if she's fat, I don't just say yes. I say she just has big bones, or maybe we can work out together some time. I don't want to hurt her feelings. She's my friend. Having her as my friend is more important than whether I think she's fat."

"But lying is still wrong." I said, trying to reassert my parental morality training.

"Oh, of course," she agreed. "It's just that sometimes other things are wronger."

"More wrong," I corrected.

"You're the moron," she said.

"I know you are but what am I?"

"Guess what?"

"What?"

"Chicken butt," she laughed.

We went into dinner arm in arm.

The boys joined us at the table and regaled us with stories of their day in school. Senior Kiah and Freshmen Jack. On opposite ends of the tumultuous, hormone infused high school years. I knew they must be going through a lot emotionally, but neither one of them let on most of the time. It's funny. Most everybody I've talked to remembers those four years as some of the most seminal in their lives. Or if not seminal, at least more memorable than any other four year segment. I've talked to guys who spent time over in Vietnam who remember their high school years more vividly than their years overseas. I figure it must have something to do with drugs.

The strongest drugs known to mankind: Estrogen and Testosterone. Every single experience is filtered through one of those monster hormones during that time of a person's life. And every single one is graven deeper in the organic memory banks as a result. Most things in life get temporarily stored on the brain's equivalent of a floppy disk. High school experiences get permanently burned on our hard drives. Kiah and Jack seemed to be taking it well, only an occasional irrational outburst to indicate the cauldron of emotions roiling within. Not that those outbursts are easy to take. Many's the time I've been glad there's no firearms in the household during those emotional flameouts.

On the other hand, there have been times when guns seemed like a good idea. Sometimes, like when people started shooting at me, I longed for something to even the playing field a little. But hell, I had enough to worry about. I was happy I didn't have to be concerned that one of these days Kiah or Jack would accidentally kill each other while "cleaning" a gun. The more opportunities for stupidity I didn't have around the house, the less I had to worry. Guns don't kill people they say, people kill people, to which I agree wholeheartedly. There are lots of incidents where people have killed people even without guns. Guns just make it easier. I could conceivably get mad as hell, assault someone and possibly succeed in pummeling them to death with a cardboard box. But it's also likely that such a sustained effort might give me enough time to calm down before I inflicted permanent damage. A gun's damage arrives too soon. A bullet is a lot quicker than regret.

All of which made me feel my current case was not likely to be a crime of passion or accident. It was certainly possible that Fred's partner, Mark's dad, Fern's husband or Elizabeth's drunken idiot had been killed in a moment of sudden anger. It was just hard to believe they could be cut up, dried and shrinkwrapped in that same episode of violent emotion. It's like my mom used to say when I was in high school. You can't make jerky in a frying pan.

CHAPTER 35

Night passed dreamlessly. All the kids soared through the next morning and took off for school, elated perhaps by the prospect of a steak dinner. Unfortunately, Tuesday morning came with not much in the offing for my private investigative skills. I supposed it was worth my while to check the car dealership in Lacey so I paid my bills, dropped them off at the post office and headed over. A semi-uniformed person who I took to be a salesman was just taking down the front chain as I drove up to the lot.

"Great morning!" he smiled.

Good technique, I thought, the last thing you want to say to a potential customer is "Can I help you?" The answer is almost always: "No, just looking," and that has a horrible way of starting out your interaction on a negative note. Plus, it's difficult at that point to reopen the conversation without seeming pushy. Far better to begin with a safe and neutral observation. The weather is a perfect topic. Everyone has an opinion about the weather. And it's hard to offend anybody when conversing about it. Oh, I've encountered a few professional curmudgeons over the years that would get into a verbal brawl over the quality of sunshine—things like: "Good weather? What's good about it?" or "Nice day? My wife died on a day like this."—but by and large most people were easy to feel out during a weather chat.

"A great day it is," I answered, with a smile of my own.

"Wonder if it's going to be as rainy as last year?" he offered, subtly trying to nail down how local I was.

"I don't know," I replied vaguely, "I hope we get some snow."

"You ski, too?" he asked, getting more personal now. I could tell that soon we would be friends.

"Nah," I replied. "I just snowboard." I kept him at arm's length.

"Really. That must be hard." Nice touch. He was making me feel important now.

"Not really, the learning curve's pretty flat. And the good thing is most of the time when you're learning you don't end up as flat as you do on skis."

He laughed. We were buddies now. "I'll have to try it sometime. Those front wheel drive cars really work good on the mountain roads though, don't they?" Time to get down to business. He was testing my knowledge of autos and gradually bringing me around to a car discussion. Good move.

I shifted off to one side. "How come you guys aren't open on Mondays? I was here yesterday and couldn't get in."

"I'm sorry," he said, on the defensive now, "My boss likes to take that day off. Since we all work Sundays anyway to make it easier for people who need to shop on the weekends."

Excellent turnaround. I accused him of doing something wrong and he turned it into something nice he did for me.

Time for me to pull out some inside knowledge. "So your boss isn't just the closer when it comes to a sale, he's the closer when it comes to the lot too, huh?" I grinned.

"I don't know," he chuckled. "I'll have to run that by my manager."

I laughed.

"I'm John," he said.

"Name's Jobe," I replied, "and unfortunately I'm not looking for a car today."

"Well could you at least use a body shop?" he asked, gesturing towards the crumpled bumper of my CRV.

"Yeah. Know a good one, John?"

"Sure do. My brother has one over in Tumwater. I'll give you the number. What brings you to Lacey Hyundai, Jobe?"

"My CRV."

"Yeah I noticed. Smartass."

"No really, my crumpled CRV. It got crumpled because I was chasing someone in a new Hyundai with your empty license plate ad on it."

"So?"

"So… The reason I was chasing him was because he put a bullet through the backside of my front windshield."

"No shit? Wow. I thought that was one hellacious ding in your glass."

"Anyhow," I continued, "I crashed into some innocent by-driver and by the time I was done with the police and got here, these cars were parked just the way they are now. I don't suppose any of them are missing?"

"No, they're all here and before you ask, no, we do not keep track of the odometers. They all get set back to ten every morning no matter what. Our boss figures what we don't know we can't lie about, if you catch my drift."

"I guess I won't ask him then," I said. "You're sure? All the cars in exactly the same place as when you left on Sunday?"

He gave the lot a thorough once over. "Yep," he said. "Everything looks the same."

"How about keys? How easy are they to get?"

"Pretty easy. If…"

"If what?"

"If you're real good friends with that Doberman over there." He pointed to a chain link enclosure with a sleeping black and brown colored dog in it. "He sleeps in the office when the lot's closed. Right by the board we keep all the keys on."

Dead end there. None of my suspects struck me as dog lovers. And even though Fern was a dog owner, somehow I couldn't see her charming a Doberman. I thought for a minute. "Okay, how about this? A guy test drives a car. While he's out with it he makes a copy of the ignition key. He comes back later when you're closed and 'borrows' the car."

"Pretty good Jobe. Just one problem. Wait here." He walked across the lot and into the sales office building. A few seconds later he came out with a giant blue disk attached to a chain, which in turn was attached to a key. He walked over and handed it to me. The blue disk said 'Lacey Hyundai' across the top and 'Tuesday through Sunday' across the bottom.

"Turn it over," he said.

I turned it over. On the back it instructed in big red letters: "Do Not Duplicate!"

"That's a problem all right." I said.

CHAPTER 36

I shook hands with John, thanked him for his help and said goodbye. I got into my car and pulled it around in front of the old shopping center. I thought I'd check out the new national drugstore, Wall-Aid, which I'd heard so much about. What a change to the old place. They had demolished the tired structure that enclosed the supermarket but left the rest of the ancient strip mall nearly intact, pasting some fascia on it to make it architecturally harmonious with the new drugstore. The extra space created on one side had been used to tack on a drive-through pharmacy lane. Excuse me, "drive-thru."

This was the latest aberration in American shopping. A pharmacy drive-thru. Which I thought was odd. The original expanded drugstore concept grew up from the idea of giving customers something else to shop for while they were waiting for their prescription to be filled. While you waited for the doddering old druggist to measure out your medication, you could pick up some notions and potions and even some—Land-a Goshen!—calamine lotion, should you have a mind. Inventories quickly grew from douche bags and corn pads to all the household paraphernalia of modern society; room fresheners and fancy toilet paper, Lysol and Softscrub, candles and candy, magazines and bosom heaver romance paperbacks. Not to mention film developing. Which gave you something else to wait for. And shop during to kill the time. I guess the idea was too successful. Because now people were coming in just to buy the incidentals alone.

Which created a problem. The drugstore kingpins noticed something. Their stupid pharmacies were slowing up the rest of the store. The aging population meant older and older groups of people were coming in to buy more and more extreme and complex medications for their myriad ailments. The blue hairs were clogging the aisles. The aisles of all the ulterior products the corporation had added to originally supplement their pharmaceutical sales. The stores were suffering from Ulterioro-sclerosis. The old folks, with their walkers and their wheelchairs and their general slowness, were getting in the way of the bustling young shoppers who came in to pay top dollar for the latest designer bubblegum-scented hair mousse. What to do? Drive-thru. Now the old folks could stay in their cars and pick up their Anusol and prescription Maalox from the nice girl at the window. Problem solved. Almost. The first drive-thrus were constructed too narrowly for the bulging Buick Electras and humongous Cadillacs of the oldsters. And worse, you couldn't get an economy size box of depends through the little pick-up window. But corrective tweaks were eventually made and today's super-drugstore is almost as nice in terms of speed, ease of shopping, and limited selection as a 7-11.

I got out of my car to give the new place a closer examination. But as I looked through the front window and saw the same standard, efficiently organized and impersonal set-up of all the rest of the new crop of stores I decided not to go in after all. That old local supermarket was more fun. And I knew the people who worked there. These folks all looked like they came from Seaworld, or the Gap. I turned my collar up against the rising wind and walked down the sidewalk. I checked out the windows of the Goodwill Store. Same old place, same tired old linoleum, brand new front. As I came up to the "charity" bingo parlor (all proceeds go to the daily maintenance trust fund charity of the owners) I started aimlessly reading the postings of last week's big winners on the front window. Something caught my eye.

It read: "Tuesday's Double Bonanza Winner - Fern Frenello. $100 Dollars!!!" Apparently, she won both "$" and "Dollars" and judging by the "!!!" everyone was pretty excited.

I was pretty excited too. I had found out something very interesting. Fern Frenello played bingo on Tuesday nights. And if she was like most bingo players, she played on the same night or nights every week, sat in the same chair, used the same lucky marker and wore the same smoke-saturated, stinky clothes. Hmmm…

Thinking of Fern made me think of Joe. And thinking of Joe made me think of his friend Bobby over at the bowling alley. Maybe I'd go over and have another chat with him. Sometimes if you want to flesh out a missing person it helps to just talk with one of his friends. Fill in the gaps in their life so you might get an inkling of where to look for them. As I climbed back into my car I saw a jogger running out by the street.

My blood went cold. It was my wife. My God! It can't be.

There she was though, same shoulder length blond hair, same five-foot two frame, even the same little hat she was wearing the evening she disappeared. She was running with the same effortless stride that always amazed me. No wasted motion, perfect turnovers, as they call them in the running world, no energy squandered by bobbing up and down as she ran. Just a perfect, even stride. When she ran you could balance a book on her head. I'd recognize that stride anywhere. Tears suddenly welled up in my eyes. A reaction beyond my control. I started to weep. Deep, racking sobs shook me. Paralyzed me.

She was getting away. I tore myself loose, fired up the CRV and raced across the parking lot to the street. I drove past and cut in front of her, hopped out of the car and started rushing towards her. She looked up in alarm and stared wide-eyed at my contorted features. Then she turned on her heel, ran across the street and fled into the adjoining field. I was stunned. I couldn't move. She looked over her shoulder after she had gone about hundred yards. I just shook my head in disbelief. And apology. It wasn't her.

It wasn't her.

CHAPTER 37

I sat in the car for a while. I was drained. Suddenly finding my love again and losing her just as quickly had left me shaken.

I thought about how much I missed her. The times we'd shared running and hiking and camping with the kids. The times we'd climbed mountains together in the Olympics. I chuckled warmly as I remembered the time we'd gone to the top of The Brothers and back to our car in seventeen and a half hours of straight hiking, climbing and mountain goat befriending. When Gus the mountain goat had come up and licked all the salt off my lovely bride's sweaty arms. And then, apparently noticing all the water I was drinking, had followed us patiently down from the summit till I chose to relieve both myself and his suspense. I wonder what Gus thought of my vintage.

We'd had some good times together, but what I missed most was the day to day grind. The little idiosyncrasies and misfires that can sometimes ruin a relationship. Or make it wonderful. The constant daily scouring process of smoothing out the lumps in each other. Till we ended up fitting together like two perfectly joined pieces of wood on a fine work of cabinetry. The highs and the lows that make up a rich relationship. The companionship of facing the woes of the world together. And the joy of sharing everything, from the concern over the most inconsequential zit on your baby's butt to the endorphin saturated elation of a thirty-mile run.

Of course it was the run, or I should say the running, that led to her disappearance. Things had gotten a little frustrating around the house, all the conflicting responsibilities of work and childcare and shuttling kids to school events had cut into our family recreation time. No trips to the woods for an entire summer. And we hadn't run or climbed together, just her and me, for a long, long while. My new job was demanding more and more of my time. And taking more and more of my interest. So she decided to start training for an Ultra.

An Ultra is any run over thirty miles. Which, as you might expect, takes some training. To work up to one you need to run every day for a certain number of miles. They call them base miles. Then you try to get in one long run a week. Or, if possible, two. The idea is to rack up the miles spent on your feet. Running, jogging, power walking, it doesn't matter, you just keep upright and keep going. She had taken to running home from work on Wednesdays. It was about ten miles on the main roads, and if she felt up to it, she would add various back trails and loops on the route to notch it up to twelve or fifteen. All well and good while we were enjoying our Northwest late twilight. But as December approached, and her training intensified in preparation for the "Fat Ass Fifty" she wanted to run at Tiger Mountain that January, there just wasn't enough daylight in a day to hold both work and horse-feeding and kid-getting-off-to-school and running. So, self-sacrificial person that she was, she ran in the dark.

Right out of our life.

We'd had a special trunk show at the men's store that night to feature a new shoe line. I ended up staying later than usual. When I got home from work there was no sign of her. The kids were restless and making noises about who was going to make dinner and when. Mir wondered if maybe her mom had gone straight to the stables to feed Rusty already. We waited. And waited. And waited.

Finally, I got in the car and went looking, trying to retrace her presumed route. Unfortunately, I had only a rough idea of what that route was. She had never been particularly detailed about the way she took when she ran home and, truth be told, she changed it every time anyhow. By the time I had crisscrossed all the different possibilities and cursed the driving rain the kept obscuring the various corners and byways, it was midnight. The kids were pretty anxious by this time. As was I. We called the police. Their attitude was less than energetic. They said to wait twenty-four hours and if we still hadn't heard from her they'd start a search. I remember vividly what the officer told me that night.

"Lotsa times wives need a little 'shelter' Mr. Carson. I don't suppose you've had an argument lately have you? Maybe a heated argument...?"

And that was the course it took for some time after that. I was the main focus of suspicion and no trace of where she might have been snatched from or who may have done the snatching was ever found. I sometimes think if I'd been a little more convincing as a distraught husband they would have worked a little harder at trying to find her. Instead, I'm cursed with the lack of emotional expression I developed as a defensive mechanism in my small and bullied youth. Which led the police to think I knew more about my bride's disappearance than I was telling. The hour I couldn't account for when I closed down the store after the trunk show didn't help. I'd been tired that night. Everybody else had gone home. And it had taken a while to put the store back to normal after the rearranging we had done that day to accommodate the event. Honest, Officer.

I miss her. And I wonder what led me to neglect her enough to not run with her on that night, or suggest some other time when we could train together. At least express my concern that she was endangering herself that way. But I wasn't paying attention. I was caught up in my own life. My thrill over taking on a new position and proving myself in the new challenge of a new store with an entirely new clientele. If I stopped to think about her evening endeavor at all, it was as a "little run." Heck, she ran all the time in our neighborhood. What could possibly go wrong?

If I had it all to do over, I'd say my piece. Tell her I thought she was wrong to put herself at that kind of risk. But she'd probably do it anyhow. She was nothing if not spirited. And if she thought she wanted to do something, or train for something, nothing would stand in her way. Her single-mindedness had led many a person to portray her as stubborn. I just knew one thing: When she set out to accomplish anything, she was going to end up accomplishing it.

And I'd seen the triathlon medals to prove it. My lovely wife couldn't swim worth a darn. She had so much lean body mass she sank like a stone. But every triathlon she'd ever entered forced her to swim at least a quarter of a mile, kicking and sputtering and having her goggles knocked off by the flailing limbs of her aquatically faster adversaries, before she got to the parts of the race that she was really good at, the bike and the run. And she always finished the race. Many times with a ribbon and a hunk of metal.

So I guess I had been kind of happy she was training for an Ultra. At least she wouldn't drown. Who'd have thought she'd disappear off the face of the earth. And lead us to all the doubts and all the wondering and all the uncertainty about where she was and what had happened to her.

There's still only one thing I know for sure.

I miss her.

CHAPTER 38

I was finally able to see clearly enough to drive. I turned my car back onto Lacey Boulevard and headed over to Melody Lanes bowling alley. It was about eleven o'clock. I hoped to run into Bobby again before he got too busy. I walked into the building and nodded at Lulie as I went by the cafe. She set down her cup of coffee and walked over towards me.

"Bobby doesn't come in till noon," she said. "You're that private detective he was talking to the other day aren't ya?"

"Yes I am, Ma'am" I said respectfully, "My name's Jobe Carson."

"Cut the Ma'am crap, stud," she said, "I run through charmers like you quicker than shit through a tin horn."

"Excuse me—Sir," I said.

She barked out a laugh. "Just so's we get off on the right foot." She flashed me a coffee-stained smile. "What's this I hear about you looking for Joe Frenello?"

"That's about the sum of it. The insurance company wants to make sure Fern didn't have anything to do with Joe's disappearance."

"Other than being a raving bitch you mean."

"Yeah, other than being a raving bitch. Something more direct, like maybe taking a cleaver to him and chopping him up."

"I wouldn't put it past her. That woman had a temper. She was a discredit to the whole gender. I mean, don't get me wrong, I can get mad. I've cleared a whole bar full of loggers out in one screaming blow up, but I was a timid little minnow next to that big mouthed bass. Here—" She gestured towards the counter. "Why don't ya sit down and have a piece of pie while we talk."

"Ever talk to her much?" I asked as she slid a big hunk of lemon meringue pie on a plate and set it in front of me.

"Not except the time I told her to peddle her papers someplace else," she said.

"When was that?"

"One day a while back. Joe had been in bowling for a while. Then he and Bobby had a chaw, then he comes over for a little cup of coffee. He loved my coffee. Said Fern's tasted like bilge water. And he should know. He sat there for a while chatting. He had his favorite knife out, that man didn't go anywhere without that knife, and was doing some fine carving, holding a wooden ring in that big gnarly right hand of his—I'm surprised he could fit those fingers in a bowling ball—and whittling on it with the other. Here, let me show you."

She reached under the counter and took out an old shoe box. Inside, nestled in a folded dish towel, were five intricately carved wooden napkin rings. I picked one of them up. The name Lulie was delicately etched through a series of leaves and branches on one side. The foliage curved around on either side of the name to connect with a wonderfully rendered view on the other side. Through the twining branches and set off in a field you could see a little farmhouse with smoke coming out of its chimney.

"Joe and I always talked about how nice it would be to live on a little farm," Lulie said, "with woods around and some fruit trees and a couple head of cattle maybe. He told me he was going to carve me a whole set of these. And when the sixth one was done, he would have something really special to tell me." A little tear started to form at the corner of her eye. Then her features clouded up. She frowned.

"Anyways, in she comes in a tizzy, starts yelling at Joe to give her some money cause when she was at the store they said her credit card had been cancelled. Joe tells her he doesn't have any and she starts screaming at him that he's holding out on her and he can't support her like she deserves and ever since he lost his job at the old supermarket her life has gone to shit and so on and so on. That he would give one of his kidneys to his sister, but he wouldn't even give her a hundred bucks when she needed it. She's getting real loud and I tell her to put a cork in it. She turns on me and asks who the hell do I think I am. I tell her I own this here place and if she doesn't like it she can go piss up a rope. She starts coming for me and when I reach down to get my billy club under the counter, Joe jumps between us and starts trying to calm her down. I tell her to leave and not come back or I'm calling the police. Joe leads her out. I don't see him for about a week. We he comes back in he has a fading bruise on the side of his face. I ask him about it and he says he ran into a door. Right. Ran into an elephant is more like it."

"You're telling me Fern used to beat Joe?" I asked, pushing some meringue around with my fork.

"Does a bear shit in the woods? She beat him all the time. And he never struck back. Said a gentleman doesn't hit women. I told him she wasn't no woman, she was a she-devil, but he just shook his head."

I took another bite of pie. "What do you think happened, Lulie?"

"I don't know. I hope he up and left. I hope he just got the gumption to take off. Maybe sign on as a handy man on some tramp steamer out of Tacoma. He didn't have to stay with that horrid woman. He could do anything. They used to keep him real busy at the old supermarket, fixing shelves and building displays, making keys and tinkering with the cash registers. One time they even had him lay some of that new astro-turf down in their produce department, like it was a garden or something. He built the old-fashioned looking display bins for the fruit and vegetables too. Made 'em look just like the wood crates we used to get stuff in back in the forties. He was pretty sad when they closed the old store down. Asked me if I wanted to buy their cash registers or keymaking machine or refrigeration cabinets or anything. But hell, I told him I got no use for any of that stuff. How many people come into a bowling alley looking to get keys made? And I got enough trouble with this old NCR, what the hell am I gonna do with one of those newfangled scanner beeper things?"

I pushed the last crumbs of crust onto my fork with my finger and put them into my mouth. Perfectly flaky.

"Lard," she said. I flinched as I braced for another tirade against Fern. "I use lard, that's how it gets so flaky. Margarine just doesn't cut it. The old-fashioned way is still best. Joe used to eat my pies all the time and he was fit as a fiddle. He was..." she drifted off and stared at some spot in the past. The room seemed to quiet down. The sounds of the bowling alley faded into the distance.

"Thanks for talking to me Lulie," I said.

She didn't seem to hear me. Her mind was obviously on something else. Like a little wood house on four or five acres. A couple of cows grazing in the field. And smoke billowing out of an old stone chimney.

"You find Joe," she finally said. "Find him, and make sure he's found peace."

CHAPTER 39

I went over to the grocery store to buy a few steaks for that night's feast. I drove all the way to the West Side to go to Top of the Food Chain Market. I liked them best for a couple of reasons. They had the best meat for one thing. And they didn't have any of those stupid grocery store club cards for another. I hate those club cards. They make shopping so dangerous. You think you're picking up a bag of grapes for the prominently displayed price of 39 cents but when you get to the cash register, if you don't have a club card it turns out they're $5.99. You go back to the produce aisle to confirm the gouging and sure enough, on a little teeny-tiny price tag it says, "Non-club card $5.99." I've tried and tried to avoid this trap but finally came to the conclusion there's no safe way to do so. One thing's certain—there's no safe way for me.

What I can't figure is how there can be so much difference in price just because of a stupid club card. They say it's to reward and encourage customer loyalty. Loyalty my ass. Call me old fashioned, but I think customer loyalty should be earned with a little thing called service. So rather than sign up for a stupid card, and in the process get my buying habits analyzed and a bunch of new junk mail sent to my house, I want to stay away completely. They might as well just hang a sign on the front of their store that says: "Welcome club members, outsiders get cornholed."

I drove home with the steaks and a few big baking potatoes, some fresh sour cream and a bunch of broccoli crowns fresh for the steamin'. As I drove into my driveway I caught sight of something hanging from my doorknob. It was big and eye-catching and that fluorescent shade of chartreuse yellow green that you can spot three miles away. Damn. Shut off notice. Frickin water company. That was one of the past due bills I had finally paid yesterday too. Bastards. It's not enough that they have to threaten to cut off your water. They also have to advertise to the entire neighborhood that you're delinquent with your bill. Sor-ry.

I ripped it off the door and deposited my groceries quickly. If I hurried, I just had time to head over to the courthouse and catch Kathryn on her break. I wanted to sound her out on the Fred deal.

I pulled into the courthouse parking lot in time to see her blonde coif bouncing along on the way to the espresso cart. I parked hurriedly and jogged over.

"How ya doing?" I asked, out of breath from my little run.

"Why Jobe," she smiled, "you surprised me."

"I didn't want to give you a chance to start the wave again. These people all look like rabid fans."

"No, just disgruntled county workers, having their twice daily pick-me-up before they go back to their rest-of-the-daily bring me down."

"Poor, poor, pitiful highly paid workers with incredible benefits," I commiserated. "I don't suppose they've priced the private sector job market lately? Or the cost of individually acquired medical insurance."

"You're such a downer Jobe. What a sourpuss."

"Well, hey," I said brightly, "Then hows about I buy you a latte for a change." I crowded in and slid a five-dollar bill on the counter in front of the barista. "Short skinny single for my friend and I'll have a grande with four sugars."

"You really do need sweetening up," laughed Kathryn.

"Um, Sir," interjected the barista, pausing momentarily from hand whipping some cream in a big stainless steel bowl, "that'll be six bucks."

"Wha—? Oh yeah," I covered, numbly turning over another five, "I thought I gave you a ten." I'd been away from the overpriced coffee habit too long.

Kathryn patted me on the arm as I started to turn away. "Thanks, Jobe. That was really nice of you, but I still have to get coffees for the crew."

I stood there feeling my face warm up while she rattled off the litany of her coworkers' stimulant requirements to the gum popping coffee jerk. When she was done she turned back to me and smiled. "What brings you to this part of town, moneybags? And why the sudden largesse?"

"I got a new client," I answered.

"Oh really," she replied, "Who?"

"Fred Costner."

There was a sudden silence. "You mean the Fred—"

"The very same," I finished. "Gay old Fred, looking to clear his recently besmirched reputation. Besmirched by your dear old boss I might add."

"I'm sorry about that, Jobe. It really killed me to make that call on Saturday. But the evidence was incontrovertible. Human blood. In his dehydrator."

"But couldn't it have been any old human blood?"

"It could have belonged to anybody... Or at least anybody who was type 'O' Positive."

"Is that rare?"

"No, on the contrary, that's the most common blood type. I don't suppose you know what Bill's blood type was?"

"No, I don't."

"Well Knudson does. About the first thing he did was run a check to see if there was anything in the county records data base on Bill. There was. A supposedly confidential HIV test. Bill was HIV negative, but 'O' Positive."

"Damn!"

"It gets worse."

"How can it get worse?"

"Knudson also noticed in Bill's records that he must have had a heart problem. There was a notation that he was on Coumadin."

"So? What's Coumadin?"

"Coumadin's a blood thinner they prescribe to heart patients. Knudson asked me to run an analysis for that too. And I found it. I'm sorry Jobe. It looks pretty bad."

"But not impossible," I replied slowly. "'O' is a common blood type. I'm sure Coumadin has been prescribed to more than one patient in the history of medicine..."

"But how many of them are missing, and have their blood type in a dehydrator drain well used by their former partner?"

"Still," I persisted, "It's not completely out of the question. What if he bought that dehydrator second hand?"

"That's a pretty big coincidence. You'd have to believe—" Kathryn looked over my shoulder in alarm.

"Goddamn it Carson!" Oh no. It was Knudson himself, "Not only are you talking with my assistant again, now you're making my coffee get cold. Jesus Jobe, when are you going to get a job?" He guffawed loudly and slapped me on the back. I nearly spewed latte on Kathryn's sweater.

"You're in good mood, Sir," I said.

"Yeah. Busting fags just brings out the best in me," he said. "Nothing like starting off the week on the right foot."

"I'm glad you feel that way," I replied. "It takes a man of your stature to really put the big gut in bigot."

He looked at me confusedly, "Yeah," he said, "Whatever."

"And here's something else that'll make you happy," I continued, "According to a recent survey by PFLAG, Gay people and parents and friends of gay people in our county outnumber Christian fundamentalists by about three to one. And, unlike your lazy 'fundie' folk, they have an obnoxious habit of actually going to the polls and voting. If I were you, Nellie belle, I'd fire my campaign director."

All his joviality suddenly disappeared. He looked like Santa drinking curdled milk. "Why you—" he blustered, "I oughta pound your skinny little ass—"

"I think it's too late to get that vote back Nellie, but much obliged for the offer," I cracked.

"Why you sick son of a—" he spluttered.

"Now calm down, Nellie." A sudden inspiration hit me, "Remember your heart condition. Too bad that Coumadin of yours showed up in the sample you planted in my client's dehydrator."

I've never seen something so big move so fast. He reached out, grabbed me around the neck and started squeezing. As his thumbs dug into my larynx I reflected on the wisdom imparted by that old homily about baiting the bear. Or was that bearding the lion? The world was quickly turning black at the edges. I felt myself spiraling down into oblivion. I tried to get my knee up to sharply plant it in Knudson's groin. But my legs were already completely numb. I dimly heard Kathryn yelling for help. Then I heard a big metallic clang. Saved by the bell, I thought.

Then I blacked out.

CHAPTER 40

When I came to a few seconds later I was greeted by an arresting tableau. Kathryn was anxiously stroking my forehead with a cold bar rag in one hand and clinically feeling my throat for signs of damage with the other. Ever the nurturing scientist. The pierce-nostriled barista was standing over Knudson with the giant stainless steel bowl she had been using to whip cream. There was a big dent in the bottom of it, and gloopy white stuff was splattered in various locations about his head and shoulders.

"Grande with whip," I mumbled. Kathryn shifted her attention to my eyes.

"Are you okay?" she asked worriedly.

"Yeah, fine," I croaked. "I always get a little choked up when I'm around you."

"Oh Jobe," she sighed, "Can't you ever be serious? He nearly killed you." She gently touched my larynx.

"Ouch," I said seriously.

"You're going to have a big bruise there. I'm surprised you can even talk."

"Talking's a big talent in my family. Not to worry, we got voice boxes like armadillos. I'll just tell Mir you gave me a big hickey."

She actually blushed. It was quite attractive next to the prim starkness of her lab coat.

"Jobe, I—" she started.

I sat up quickly, and nearly went right back down as I fought off a wave of blackness, "Hey. Thanks for the forehead wash," I said, changing the subject and turning to look at Knudson. Then I caught the barista's eye. "Does that whipping cream cost extra?" A small crowd was starting to gather around Knudson's roughly breathing body. His legs were twitching like dreaming hippo.

"What happened to the coroner?" One of them asked.

"That was the coroner?" the barista asked in alarm. "Oh shit. And I've only had this job for a week."

"And I bet beaning a wild, murdering coroner wasn't in your job description was it?" I asked. "Don't worry. Let me handle this. Do you have any water?"

She went back to her cart. "Only this," she held up a liter bottle of Calistogie spring water.

"That'll do just fine," I took it from her and screwed off the top. I then proceeded to squeeze it out all over Knudson's face. He jerked up; sputtering and spewing like a whale with an abscessed blowhole.

"What the—?" he spouted. "What happ—?"

"Some skateboarder came by, grabbed this bowl out of the barista's hand and bonked you on the noggin." I said, holding up the dented evidence. "Lucky thing too. You were about to kill me."

His face scrinched up in pain. He gave me a really dirty look. "Carson..." he said menacingly.

"You should have your campaign make a donation to the skateboard park," I continued, "That boy saved your political hide. Think of what the voters would have thought next election about having a murderer as a coroner. Talk about conflict of interest—"

"Stop!" he shouted. "Stop your goddamn yammering. You're going to drive me crazy, Carson."

"I'd think this last episode was proof you'd already arrived, Nellie," I backed away as he heaved himself up, got on his hands and knees and started to look like he was coming towards me. For some reason I was reminded of a nature film I once saw of a walrus in rut. He finally made it to his feet and brushed the remnants of almost crusted cream from his suit coat.

"You're just lucky that skateboarder came along, yourself," he growled.

"Yeah, lucky," I said, winking at the barista.

"And another thing, Carson." He was all business again. "I'm getting sick and tired of you hassling my friend Mark Wasen. Quit it. You and your insurance company vultures need to start pecking at a different dung heap. I'll get a restraining order if I have to. Come on Kitty, it's time to get back to work."

I saluted smartly. "Yes Sir, Big K, Sir!" I'd have to work on that salute. Somehow my middle digit extended further than was entirely appropriate. Kathryn shrugged her shoulders and turned to follow Knudson's already retreating corpulence. Hmm. Mark Wasen couldn't be that close a friend, I reflected. At least I can't remember the last time I referred to any of my friends as a dung heap. Even a metaphorical one.

I shook hands with the barista and put a tip in her jar. Then I shambled wearily back to my car. I was still depressed over the ever-tightening noose around my client's neck. I wished I could drag out the dehydrated forearm right now and turn it over to the lab for analysis. Maybe that would clear Fred. Then again, what if it just confirmed the blood type and Coumadin thing? Fred would be in deeper trouble than ever.

I drove home in time to greet Miranda as she got off the bus.

"How was your day, Dad?" she asked, looking pointedly at the purple thumbprints on my Adam's apple.

"Pretty exciting. It's not every day you get a chance to have the county coroner wring your neck." I told her about the encounter with Knudson and the subsequent protection of the barista's reputation. She laughed when I described Knudson covered with dollops of splattered cream.

"Did you feel like sprinkling nutmeg on him?" she asked. We had gone inside and I'd started washing up the potatoes.

"Waste perfectly could nutmeg?" I said in mock disappointment. "Miranda, I'm ashamed of you."

She dug into her homework and I did some chores around the house. Later on I cooked up a sizzling steak dinner for everyone. It was a success. It had been so long since we'd had a chunk of fresh flesh around the place I could have cooked it in the coffee maker and everyone would have been happy. We sat back after dinner, stroking our distended bellies and feeling satisfied indeed.

"I'm going out again tonight, kids," I said.

"What?" they all cried out.

"But I wanted to go to Trevor's," said Kiah.

"I have basketball practice," said Jack

"I thought we could go see Rusty," said Miranda.

"I've got to catch a murderer and earn money for more steak," I retorted to their assorted groans. "But don't worry; I don't have to leave till later. I have to wait for the late night bingo to start."

"Bingo?" they asked in chorus.

"Yeah, a game invented by the Catholic Church to skirt biblical prohibitions on gambling. B-- I-- N-G-O. And Bingo was its name."

"Oh," they said.

CHAPTER 41

I drove through the parking lot of the old shopping center in Lacey. I was looking for an old station wagon with a messy rear end. There were about fifty. I didn't think there were fifty station wagons left on the planet, much less all of them in one parking lot. It was about nine o'clock, the kids were all back from their various sojourns and were presumably even now crawling into bed. Yeah, right. I only hoped they didn't pull what they did last time I had to go out at night: Roasting marshmallows on the stove top in preparation for making s'mores—and then getting diverted into a "snowball" fight with the marshmallows. Or should I say the flaming marshmallows? Oh well, I'd needed new kitchen curtains anyhow.

It was pretty hard to tell which faux wood-clad station wagon Fern's was, so I parked my car and walked up to the bingo parlor. I stood back far enough from the front window so the glare from inside would prevent anyone from seeing me as I looked in. It looked even rattier inside than I remembered. Used to be it was pretty seedy, but it was also the only place in town to indulge any kind of gambling habit, so folks tolerated the filth. Of course, that was in the days when everybody smoked everywhere anyhow and there wasn't a posh tribal casino on every other block. Seems like there's a new casino opening up about every month now. And some of them at locations that appear to have nothing to do with any former Indian reservation. One has to wonder where all those new reservations came from. I admit my local history's a little rusty, but I can't for the life of me remember the Keno tribe.

It took a moment for my eyes to adjust to the foggy atmosphere within. It was like looking at a computer monitor in safe mode, or trying to discern recognizable shapes on one of those blocked TV channels. But soon the unmistakable form of Fern hove into view. The great white bingo player, acrylic velour sweatsuit adorned with a

172

necklace of marker pens, capacious purse propped against her elbow, smoke streaming out of her nostrils as she stared raptly at her cards and cocked her ears expectantly in the direction of the announcer. It was like watching a totally focused sports superstar. She was intent on one goal and one goal only: Yelling "BINGO!" And she didn't care who she had to figuratively dribble through, skate past, end run around or slide into home plate for, she was going to make that goal. It was almost beautiful; the way she juggled her ten cards and her markers and her ever smoldering cigarette; the way she even took an occasional swig off her "Bingo Forever" Western States Playoff souvenir water bottle. One would have thought she had six hands, the way she kept moving things around.

Having seen her house, I had a hard time believing she could be so organized, or so focused. I reflected that she must be like Officer Greg, what I call a serial organizer. Let things pile up to a certain level—because you're incapable of daily maintenance—then in a burst of energy suddenly get everything put away and ship shape. Except in Fern's case, her energy bursts must always run out a little early, more like an energy spasm really, and the job of doing her house gets further and further from completion as she falls ever shorter every time she tries. No wonder she was here. Clean place to sit. Immediate reward for immediate effort. Perfect.

I waited till someone else yelled "Bingo!" and Fern started a new set of cards, then I went back to my car and drove to my real goal— her house. I parked down the block a ways and nonchalantly walked to the end of the cul-de-sac. My black clothing made me less likely to be seen, but was also ordinary enough to pass off as evening walking attire. Everybody wears black tennis shoes these days. And the fact I had obscured the reflective edges with electrical tape probably wouldn't be noticed. As I approached the door on the side of her garage I heard the yappy dog start barking in what must have been the kitchen. I hugged the side of the building in anticipation of a neighbor's house lights coming on and possibly an alerted someone looking out a window, but no such thing occurred. They had probably all tuned out the little yapper, much like most of us tune out car alarms anymore, their frequent hooting and sirening ignored by the boy-who-cried-wolf filters of our subconscious.

The lock was pretty easy to jimmy, and I opened the door and slid into the darkness of the garage. I slipped a black nylon hose over my face, fumbled on my headlamp, and peered around the inside. The narrow cone of light illuminated various odd shapes as I gave the place a quick once over. There were boxes everywhere. An old lawnmower that hadn't seen the light of day in so long it looked like it could use some Vitamin D lay bone brittle in a corner, one rear wheel askew and a ripped bag tangled in its control cables. Rakes and hoes and shovels lay jumbled together in another nook, and extension cords, cable wire and what looked to be head gaskets draped off one shelf, held in place by a clotted mass of spider web. In the far corner was a big metal monstrosity, with two arms that had little clamps on them. A couple of small wheels protruded out slightly in the direction of the clamps. Looked like Joe had found a place for his old key making machine after all. I spent the next half hour poking around, moving boxes and stepping around indeterminate piles of clothes, trash and animal excrement. I stumbled over a pile of newspapers at one point and had the pleasure of gazing back at my own image on the front page of an old community section; that stupid article they did on me when I first started private investigating. I don't know why those pictures of me keep getting younger looking.

I finally shined my beam up to scan the upper shelves—someone had put in some nice shelves at one time—for empty boxes that might give me a clue that what I was looking for was here somewhere. I needn't have bothered. As my light ray descended back to ground level I caught a gleam of metal. There it was, right by the connecting door to the kitchen, an infomercial perfect, shrinkwrapping, Dee-Luxe Vacu-Packer 2000. I involuntarily shouted a word of victory.

174

You could have knocked me over with a feather. Unfortunately, someone chose to use a hoe handle. A searing pain creased the top of my skull and I almost went down. My headlamp was jarred loose and crashed to the floor, its high impact casing saving it from shattering. I wished my head had a casing like that. I turned in time to see the hoe handle coming down again and put up my arm to shield my face. The handle cracked against my forearm and split, apparently weakened by its earlier encounter with my cranium. The light from my headlamp was pointing upward at a forty-five-degree angle and a giant form stepped through its luminous shaft. The light was dim, and dimmer still through the black nylon mesh of my makeshift mask, but I was pretty sure I saw red velour. Fern! She advanced towards me, arms extended in preparation to administer a hug from hell. I tried to back away but tripped over a pile of dishes on the floor. She advanced closer. I still had time. I dropped into an appropriate stance and snapped up a sidekick to her torso. My foot was buried to the ankle. All I got for my efforts was a sharp "huff" from Fern. As I pulled my foot back and reset to administer a roundhouse to her left temple she started to scream.

"Get out of my house!" she yelled, and in a sudden burst of rage flung herself at me. I torqued my body around to change the roundhouse into a mule kick, slammed my heel against one of her thundering thighs and managed to slow her up enough so I could break towards the door.

I'm not completely clear what happened next. First off I slipped; in what must have been a recently deposited pile from ol' yappy, who I could still hear surreally carrying on in the kitchen. That spun me around as I careened against a big stack of boxes. I struggled to right myself and was suddenly face to face with the now ferocious Fern. Or I should say face to chest. In a split second she had wrapped her arms around me and got me in a huge bear hug. She smashed my face into her heaving breasts, crushing my nose against the smoke permeated velour and squeezing the last breath out of me with her surprisingly strong arms. I guess moving around all that bulk builds a lot of muscle.

All I could think of was when I was four years old and a distant relative had come to visit. A big relative. Aunt Vivian I think it was. Everybody had laughed because she hugged me so tight against her suffocating bosoms I blacked out. Which I was starting do now. That wouldn't do at all; blacking out twice in one day was not on my agenda. I got my feet under me and planted them like I remembered seeing heavy lifters do in the Olympics. Then, in one quick thrust, I heaved with all my might, up and forward. The sudden move threw Fern off balance and toppled her backwards against a stack of recycling bins. Glass and cans and mixed paper shot out in every direction. My last image was of Fern flailing in the middle of the heap of trash, trying to flip over and get to her feet like a three-hundred-pound upside down dung beetle. I spun on my heel, swept up my headlamp and sprinted for the door. I didn't stop running till I got to my car. Then I jumped in, stepped on the gas and sped home. I couldn't believe what had happened. What had gone wrong?

Sometimes I'm not too smart. Maybe next time I find a vacu-packer in the dark garage of a murder suspect I won't yell Bingo.

Chapter 42

I snuck in quietly when I got home. But the floor creak at the end of the hall gave me away. I heard Miranda stir.

"Dad?"

"It's okay, Honey," I whispered as I went into her room.

"Are you all right? I had this dream you were wrestling with a demon."

"More like a hippopotamus," I said wearily.

"What?"

"Nothing. Go back to sleep. I'm home and I'm safe."

"Goodnight Dad. Please don't leave us at night again. I get so afraid."

"Goodnight Honey. I'll try not to. I promise."

"I love you, Dad."

"I love you too, Mir. Goodnight."

I went back into my room, stripped off my clothes and crawled into bed. Being home and safe rounded out the day just fine.

Morning broke with another storm on the horizon. One of those big blustery ones that always come up in late October and early November. We used to sell more umbrellas in the fall than any other time at the men's store. More because of the wind than the rain. The rain just gets you wet, the wind turns your umbrella inside out. Then you do get soaked—for the price of a new one.

I hustled the kids off with hump-day efficiency. This was my favorite day of the week. I was going to get some exercise. Wednesday always used to be my weekday off when I worked in retail and I had got into the habit of starting it with a rousing game of racquetball at the club. Racquetball is far and away my favorite sport. Nothing else combines speed, agility and eye-hand coordination like racquetball. Or makes you work harder to achieve your goal.

Think about it compared to other sports. Take baseball for instance. In non-professional baseball, the average team member spends 99.9% of his time doing absolutely nothing. Even in professional baseball, that time is spent mostly working on a chaw, scratching a crotch or readjusting a cup. Granted, if a ball happens to come a player's way in the one and half to three hours he's in the game, it can require an explosive burst of skill and energy to field it, but it's also possible such eventuality may never occur in a whole nine innings. My son Jack is a good athlete. He runs well, he's agile; he has great eye-hand coordination. Yet we would all have to work really hard not to fall asleep at his baseball games when he was growing up. Because he never got a chance to show any of it. The frickin ball never came his way.

Fortunately, he took up basketball in the fall and winter months. There's a sport with some action. But it's still a team sport, still without the one on one, mano y mano aspect of a good game of racquetball. That's the part I like the best; one on one in a game of skill. Every adversary stands a chance of being overcome by the appropriate strategy. And players of unequal attributes can still play a competitive game. Height is offset by speed, agility balances out power, and accuracy weighs as importantly as brute force.

Being a middle-aged man of average height—what some people would call old and short—I delight in playing young, muscled bucks filled with a sense of their own testo-terrific manliness. That's when I get to trot out the codgerly cageyness they find so frustrating. Because racquetball is also a mental game. Doing a good job of predicting your opponent's behavior as they respond to the shot you make puts you in position to exploit their return shot almost before they make it.

As I left the locker room and emerged into the challenge court gallery, I was greeted by the boisterous voice of my friend and longtime adversary Dave.

"Carson!" he shouted. (Dave always shouts) "How the hell are you?"

"I the hell am fine," I replied in a comparative whisper.

"Ready to get your ass kicked?" he blustered.

"Yeah, but I bet you'll be doing more kissing than kicking."

"Ha ha. Speaking of kissing, what the hell happened to your neck? Run into a double hickey machine?"

"Yeah. My party doll is acting up. I think I need to take her to the shop."

"No seriously, those look pretty mean, Jobe. Someone need to really get their ass kicked? I'll be happy to show 'em not to mess any friend of mine."

And he meant it too. Dave is about six foot two and two-twenty plus. A lot of it muscle. He's faster than he thinks he is, and he's a hard man to beat on the racquetball court. He's got reach and he's got power, and worst of all for me, he's got a lot of accuracy too. But best of all for me, he's the kind of friend that would give you the shirt off his back if you needed it, or beat the stuffing out of anyone that gave you trouble. I could tell he was building up a head of steam to do just that.

"It's okay, Dave, much obliged, but the hickey maker had a bad encounter with a big metal bowl. He's nursing a bigger bruise on his noggin than either of these two little thumb marks."

"Okay, but if he gives you trouble give me a call," he said darkly.

"Thanks Dave, I'll do that."

"Cause if anybody beats up on you," he brightened, "I want it to be me. Get your ass out there and warm up."

We spent the next forty-five minutes beating the crap out of each other. I forgot all about my various bruises and contusions from the twin hippos Nelson and Fern and concentrated on the new ones engendered by the thrashing I was getting from Dave. And the thrashing I was giving him in return. The thing about racquetball that I find most motivating is that every ball seems reachable, if only I can expend just a little extra effort. Which usually means I'm diving after one ball or another, jumping up on the wall and pushing off again, and generally rolling around like a maniac trying to get back to my feet in time to field the next line drive that Dave has blasted ricocheting back from the front wall. Suffice it to say, I generally give myself a pretty good beating up by the time it's over. Hey. You got to get your endorphins somehow. I don't have the patience of runners. I need my pain killers to kick in quicker. So I just accelerate the pain input.

We were in our third game when Kathryn walked by the glass. Dave was ahead thirteen to eight at that point. Racquetball challenge courts have a back wall that is made of super thick glass so spectators can enjoy the game. This means that people watch us from the gallery from time to time, usually when they're tying their shoes or stretching preparatory to getting on a treadmill or one of those bizarre recumbent bikes.

Recumbent bikes are interesting. I'm always a little mystified when I see people on them. I'm usually in the midst of a horrendous game, sweat flowing off my forehead and T-shirt clinging to my body in damp disarray. And there they are in a relaxed position—exercising. Relax while you exercise. What a concept. These must be the same people who drive around and around the parking lot waiting for a parking place close to the club building. Let's see. I'm going to the club to exercise, but I don't want to have to walk an extra hundred feet to get to the front door. O-kay...

Racquetball games end when one of the players gets to fifteen points. So Dave had me down pretty good. A couple of his great serves and I would be out. I waved at Kathryn when she caught my eye. She waved back and went over to the treadmill closest to the court. Dave caught the interaction, made a low whistle laden with meaning and slapped an ace to the left corner while I was thinking about getting embarrassed.

"Fourteen, eight," he laughed menacingly.

"I guess it's time for my dramatic comeback," I replied.

And that's what I did. I fielded his next serve perfectly, drifting a full court dink into the front left corner out of his reach. I then took over service and proceeded to whip off six points with a variety of lobs, kills, and passes that left him huffing like an anemic octogenarian with emphysema. Nothing like a pretty spectator to bring out the showman in me. Or is that show off? You'd think the time I'd cracked my head on the monkey bars in first grade would have taught me a lesson about not showing off. But the only thing it taught me was it sure is nice to have a pretty girl leaning over you when you come to.

"Fourteen, fourteen," I gloated.

"I think she likes you," Dave said.

"You're just trying to throw off my concentration big Dave."

"I surprised you can hit the ball at all with your chest puffed out like that. Isn't your posture normally a little slouchier? When Kathryn's not around I mean..."

I smashed a serve into the front wall that came zipping past his ear.

"Long," he called out and guffawed. "Just like she longs for you."

I quickly served another one. Too hard and too low. It bounced in front of the service line.

"Short," he laughed, "just like you always come up."

As he took over the serve I glanced over at Kathryn. She had slowed to a jog and was obviously concentrating more on our game than on her intervals. I hoped she hadn't heard big-mouth Dave.

He fired a serve to my forehand side that came off the back wall so fast I had to run forward to try to catch it. At the last second I launched from my toes and caught the ball on the tip of my racquet, just as it was about to hit the floor again and give him the final score. My flaccid shot sent the ball drifting up and forward. It came down on the front wall eight inches from the floor, dribbling out with all the force of a lump in a lava lamp. He couldn't reach it in time.

"Oops," I said, picking myself up off the floor. "My serve."

"Lucky shit," he said.

I backhand served a slow looper on the left side of the court. It hugged the wall and crawled perfectly down into the back left corner. Dave had to reach deep to dig it out, his racquet smacking against the wall as he tried to propel the ball forward. I was ready by the time his return shot reached the front wall, in perfect position to dink it over to the front right corner at a steep angle. Dave would have to come across the entire diagonal distance of the court to pick it up in time. He was already moving. He thundered across the floor like an angry buffalo. And met a similar doom. He didn't make it. The ball had bounced twice before he even covered half the distance. I heard a hoot from the direction of the treadmill and saw Kathryn hurriedly putting her hand over her mouth, then suddenly turning forward to check her progress on treadmill's control panel.

"You bastard!" Dave yelled. "You tricky, son of a bitching, shithead bastard."

"Woh. High praise indeed."

"Next time I'm bringing my own rooting section," he groused.

"That's fine with me," I said graciously, "but where will they sit, in the poor sport area or over on the loser benches?"

He slapped me across the back to punctuate his praise and stepped off the court. Then he plopped down on the gallery bench and mopped his forehead with a big rag.

Kathryn just gave me a big smile. High praise indeed.

Chapter 43

We sat there catching our breath for a few minutes. Dave's seemed to be a little more evasive. I occasionally looked over at Kathryn and watched her running along on the treadmill. The five foot mile I call it. Five feet of looping rubber proving the mathematical truth that a circle has no end. Except exhaustion. She finished and got off the machine, wiped down the handrails and came over and sat two tiers above us in the gallery. Dave was back to normal, talking loud enough to wake the dead about his new turkey fryer and what a great deep-fried turkey he was going to make for Thanksgiving.

"But Thanksgiving's on a Thursday," I said.

"What's that got to do with it?" he asked.

"It's not a fry-day."

Dave groaned and slapped me across the back again. I was getting more injuries since the game got over than I got in the whole damn game.

"No really," I said, "Sounds interesting. But can you stuff 'em?"

"I don't see why not," he said.

"I'd just think the little bread chunks would come floating up. Your turkey would be surrounded by a halo of croutons."

"I don't think so. Besides, I use oyster stuffing."

"Oyster stuffing?" I winced. "You're sick."

"I love it," he smacked his lips lewdly. "What do you think, Cutie" he turned to look up at Kathryn.

"I'm on Jobe's side," she said, "I only like my oysters raw."

"Oh ho," leered Dave, "I've heard about what those raw oysters do. I bet you like raw oysters too, huh Jobe?" He elbowed me in the upper arm just to make sure I was catching his innuendo.

"I like 'em okay," I said, "Although I prefer to parboil them just a touch. To make sure that greenish-brownish oyster crap ends up in the pot and not my mouth. You never know what that oyster had for dinner."

Dave grimaced.

"Really Dave," I continued, "the idea of eating something that you stuff up the ass end of a turkey has always been a little unnerving anyhow. I'm not sure I could deal with sticking ocean phlegm balls into the same orifice."

"You always did have a way with words, Jobe. I think I'm gonna be sick."

"That's just the adrenalin from your whuppin wearing off." I was all sympathy.

"Yeah. Screw you too. I gotta go," he said softly. Then he bellowed. "See you lovebirds later..."

Kathryn and I looked at each other sheepishly as Dave's booming laugh echoed down the corridor.

"How are you?" I asked.

"Fine," she said. "You?"

"Fine."

"How's your neck?"

"It's okay."

We sat there in silence for a while.

"Um," she said.

"Yes?"

"I was wondering if..."

"You were wondering if..."

"If... If maybe you would like to go to dinner some time," she finished in a rush.

I was stunned. She took my silence as a no.

"I know you have your kids to think about and I know we haven't really known each other that long and I know your wife is still missing and I know that people may talk about us and I—"

"Whoa! Whoa Kathryn! Hold on."

It was her turn to be silent

"Of course I'd like to have dinner with you," I said. "You just caught me by surprise. I don't think of myself as very date-able."

"Oh, Jobe... Of course you're date-able. I feel so foolish asking you out, but I figured you'd never ask me..."

She was right. I'd probably never ask another woman out again. It was all so scary. What would I do? What should I do? What would the kids think? What would Mir think? I shook my head slowly. I remembered my encounter the previous day with the runner that looked like my wife. How I had felt. How I felt still.

Kathryn had slid down to the step I was on. She reached over and put her hand on top of mine.

"Jobe," she said quietly, "I know you don't want to let go of your wife. I know you feel guilty. Let's just take it easy... and slow. Do some things together... as friends. How about this? I know a nice little place downtown that I used to take my mom to before she got too bad. It's run by a Sicilian. What a character. His name is Eugenio. That's 'Ay-you-gen-ee-oh.' And don't you dare call him 'You-gene-ee-oh.' In Italian you pronounce all the vowels."

"Like in that cheese," I agreed. "It's 'Pro-vo-loan-eh' right? Not the Americanized version 'provo-lone.' Jeez. Sounds like a Mormon mortgage. I'd like a Provo loan please..."

"You got it," she laughed, "You'll like Eugenio, he makes the best pasta in the state. Simple and elegant, all at the same time. And such wonderful, subtle flavor."

"Well... I guess I could use a night out... But I'm buying."

"Not on your life. Last time you bought me something you almost got killed. I asked, I'm paying. How about Friday?"

I mentally checked through my kid calendar. "That ought to be fine," I said. "Friday ought to be fine..."

CHAPTER 44

Kathryn and I said our goodbyes and headed to our respective showers. I took a cold one. I needed to clear my head. The stinging, icy needles did nothing to lessen the pain on my skull though. Fern's hoe handle had raised a pretty good bump. It was no comfort to realize that Knudson and I were probably sporting identical noggin nubs. Oh well, all in day's work. At least I had established that Fern had a vacu-packing machine.

Now my inventory was complete. Murder times four. Everybody on my list did it. Or had the means to. Damn. I blame it on the food channel, and infomercials generally. I'll never get over it. Where else but in the most well-fed country in the world can you find an entire TV channel devoted to nothing but food and its preparation. I guess that makes some sort of twisted sense. It's not like Ethiopia could support a channel devoting twenty-four hours of programming to heating gruel. But really. This is a world where there are countless children going to bed with empty bellies. Hell, that's happening even in this country.

All I can say is it's lucky the food channel is in the upper channel premium package you get from the cable company. Presumably, starving families can't afford to view those channels. I'm guessing it would be mighty tough for a hungry kid from either Appalachia or a rundown urban tenement to watch the Naked Chef prancing around with his broken English accent "whacking food about" and "crammin' in a tin o' peaches" on the underside of a giant loin of pork. Christ. The stuff that ends up on that guy's work table could feed a poor family for a week.

It's a testimony to the surfeit of food in our culture that we're attracted to new and more exotic means to prepare it. Variety is the spice of life and in our case, life is spicy indeed. If spices themselves aren't enough, why, we can afford the means to change our methods of preparation; grill it with a George Foreman grill, dip it in a giant peanut oil fryer, rotisserie it with a free-standing electrical spit that spends most of the year gathering spider crap in the garage. Or dehydrate it and store it in wonderful vacu-packed semi-permanence. And stack it to molder in your basement while half the world scrabbles in the dirt for grubworms to fill out their protein requirements for the month. Ah, America. It's no wonder that its average gut girth has increased twenty percent over the last five decades. The baby boom bulge has transmogrified into the bulging baby boomers. The real tragedy? There aren't enough lipo-suctionists to keep up.

Oh, the humanity.

I toweled off and stumbled back to the locker room. In the shower I got a few inquisitive looks as some of the guys tried to figure out what had happened to me by working out the pattern of scrapes and bruises stippling my body. "Bad night with the dominatrix," I said to one old nosy parker while I was drying off, but I don't think he got it. As I buttoned my shirt I thought about my next move. I supposed it was time to tap into Elizabeth again. It wouldn't hurt to check out her back room and maybe have a look at her dehydrator. So far, I only had her word that it existed. It would be nice to at least confirm that, not to mention pursuing other suspicions I had in her regard.

As I combed my hair gingerly I noticed another shock of gray emerging from behind my well-defined widow's peak. Or maybe it was paint that had chipped off the hoe handle. My eyes looked a little weary, and I had to agree with them. Maybe I'd try to sneak in a nap this afternoon. Nothing like a little nap on the weekday to restore the peace in one's soul. Too bad I'd fought against all those nap periods in my kindergarten days. I sure could use them now. When I left the locker room, Kathryn was nowhere in sight. I noticed her car was gone from the parking lot too. I climbed into my busted up CRV and reflected that I felt as bad as it looked.

I drove over to Elizabeth's Environments. The front door was locked and a sign on the door indicated whomever would be back in fifteen minutes. Kind of a cheesy sign really. One of those where you can move the hands of the clock to show when you expect to return. More the kind of sign I'd expect to see on the door of an old 'five and dime' than gracing the leaded glass of Elizabeth's Environments. Speaking of cheesy. That gave me an idea. I walked down the street to the corner and hoofed it over a couple of blocks to Secondhand City.

Secondhand City had one of those shabby store fronts that pockmark downtown like so many acne scars on the faces of its great old buildings. The windows are dirty, and you can see the backsides of all the jumble that is crammed into their cramped interiors. It was one of those places that wanted to be an antique store at one time but somewhere along the way gave up and settled into being just a plain old junk shop. Or pile.

I went through the front door and a big annoying buzzer sounded in the back. It was loud enough to sound in the front too, one of those penetrating noises, like a cross between a pneumatic drill at a tire store and an air horn on a semi. You know, a welcoming sound. Not the same in timbre, somehow, as the delicate tinkle at the entry of Elizabeth's Environments. As I glanced around the interior and mentally compared it to the elegance of Elizabeth's, I wondered what it was that was so valuable it needed the equivalent of an air raid siren to warn of intruders. A grizzled old fellow in a ratty Pendleton shirt ambled out of the back room.

"Yeah?" he said. Coldly.

"Good morning." I smiled.

"Yeah—?"

I decided to keep up the politeness offensive. "Is the owner around by any chance?"

"What for?" He had gone from cold to suspicious.

I lowered my voice. "I'd rather tell him if you don't mind."

He thought about it for a minute. "He's not here."

"When do you expect him back?"

"A while." Talk about terse. This guy was starting to get on my nerves. Either he was the owner and thought I was here to collect a past due bill on that pile of pellets fueling the woodstove in the corner, or he was just one of those terminally taciturn people you occasionally run into in the world of retail that make you wonder what the hell whoever it was that hired them was thinking when they did so. Like calling one of those computer tech support lines and ending up with someone with a thick foreign accent. I'm all for people getting jobs in this great big country of ours, but why hire someone who can't be understood to staff a helpline where understanding is the key to success? And why hire what was obviously a non-people person to work with the frickin public?

"A while, huh?" I said. "Any chance you could narrow that 'while' down to a certain block of time? Like when I should come back?"

"Two weeks," he muttered.

"Vacation?"

"Buying trip."

"Where's he buy things?"

"Vegas."

"Really, I'd figure he'd buy things local."

"Yep."

"Like from appliance stores, with broken packaging maybe..."

"Yep."

"...or the Goodwill, or garage sales."

"Yep, that too."

Wow. Three words at once. I had him warmed up now. "Anything else?"

"People bring crap in."

"Do tell."

Instead he just nodded. If silence was golden, this was one rich sumbitch.

"And what's your name?" I finally asked.

"Curt."

"Figures."

He stared at me.

"Most appropriate name in the English language," I explained.

He stared me right out the door.

CHAPTER 45

As I walked slowly back to Elizabeth's place I noticed that the air was starting to get a little nippy. I could almost smell snow. Great. That meant the kids would need new coats again. It always times out so well, a month before Christmas having to buy the most expensive thing in their wardrobes. Unfortunately, they were all at the ages where hand me downs were out of the question. Unless, of course, Kiah wanted to rummage through my collection of sixties and seventies clothing styles. For some reason, I hadn't thrown any of that stuff away, or at least all of it. I kept a representative sample of the worst fashion excesses of the decades; three-piece brushed cotton suit with twenty-three-inch bell bottom pants, multi-colored disco shoes with two and a half inch heels, love beads, fringed jackets, and body fitting nylon shirts. It was fun to see Kiah mesh together the fashion from all three decades; the sixties, the seventies and the oughts. Super tight shirt and super baggy pants. It looked great.

Too bad I'd thrown away that red nose and grease paint.

My musing brought me to the steps of Elizabeth's. I saw that the sign was down and went through the door. Its tinkling caused Elizabeth to look up from her inventory of holly boughs.

"eX-mas is just around the corner," I said brightly, "Got lots of halls of divorcees to deck?"

"What brings you here?" she asked sourly.

"Why, you of course," I said. "I got a hankering for autumn leaves and dried dogwood stems."

"Private detective business a little slow lately?" she said. Uh oh. Sarcasm.

"Um..." I stalled. It looked like she'd blown my cover. "Well, yeah, but I was in the neighborhood and I—"

"Cut the crap, Jobe. I talked to Henderson yesterday about his annual Christmas party. He said he'd just hired you."

"And how did that come up? If you don't mind telling."

"He said I sounded a little less calm than usual. I told him I'd just been in my first car chase. And with whom. He told me he knew you too. Had just hired you for a job in fact."

"Just like a lawyer. If it's not a privileged communication he's flapping his lips like an English washwoman."

"You lied to me Jobe."

"Well I wouldn't call it a lie actually. If you remember, you're the one that asked me to Capitolé."

"Well misled then. I thought you were interested in me."

"Not that it matters Elizabeth, but the only misleading I did was when I came in here looking to 'decorate for a party'. You're the one that started the seduction treatment."

She looked at me angrily. Her eyes started to bulge a little.

"Seduction treatment?" She spit. "You flatter yourself. I was just trying to get your business. That was salesmanship. I wasted my valuable time, when I could have been working on other clients, and you, and you—"

"Had a fine lunch with a nice companion and a little run through the rain. Not to mention an exciting car ride. Excuse me. You're the one who was misleading. At least it sure looked to me like you were enjoying yourself."

She stuck out her lower lip again and bit the inside of her cheek. I could tell she was going to go stubborn if I didn't try something quick. And I still needed her cooperation. Time to try a different tack. I needed to appeal to her innate sense of fairness. I put on my most pitiful supplicant look.

"Hey Elizabeth. It's not like we didn't enjoy each other's company anyhow, right? I'd say it's pretty darn obvious your 'salesmanship' was having an effect. I confess. When I first walked in here I was trying to fool you. But all that changed after I got to know you." This tack was turning real tacky. "Can we just start over? I admit it, okay? I'm a private investigator. And you're an interior design specialist. Let's go on from here."

I stuck out my hand. She gave me her own and I slowly brought it up to my lips. She flinched briefly as I tickled her knuckles with my mustache but held still as I lightly touched her smooth skin with my lips. She was staring hard at me as I looked up over her hand and into her eyes. She was trying to gauge if I was serious, or if this was just one more part of my act. I poured all the sincerity I had into my return gaze.

"All right, Jobe," she said tentatively, "I'd like that."

She'd bought it. I grabbed her other hand and swept her into a light embrace. I wasn't sure whether I could keep my face from looking too jubilant. I caught my reflection in the wall mirror behind her. I didn't like what I saw.

"And you know," I said softly, "I could really use your help."

She stepped back. "Anything," she breathed. Uh oh. She was turning on the 'salesmanship' again.

"Just a small something at this point." I said.

"Oh darn," she said, "I was hoping it would be something big."

"You said you had a dehydrator in the back room. Can I see it?"

"No. You can't," she said sharply, our mystical moment suddenly shattered.

"Why not?"

"It's, uh, at the repair shop."

"The repair shop? What could go wrong with a dehydrator?"

"I don't know, it just stopped working one day." She seemed to think that wasn't convincing enough. "Maybe the heating element wore out or something. I've been using it a lot lately."

"Have you?"

"Yes. Nothing better on a cool autumn evening than coming down here and firing up the dehydrator. It's actually pretty nice. I've got a little apartment in the back..."

"Do you come here often at night?"

"Is that question professional... or personal...?" She said coyly.

I felt better. She was using that syrupy voice again. I guess sometimes it's hard to keep a good salesperson down.

CHAPTER 46

"What say we check your backroom anyhow?" I said.

"Fine with me, Jobe," she cooed. "I've got nothing to hide from you."

"I'm glad," I said.

We headed through some honest to goodness beaded curtains into a small hallway. A bathroom door opened off one side and a small stairway led up from the other. A couple of steps forward brought us to a large room. There was a big work table in the center of it, covered with seasonal paraphernalia. Large metal shelves lined the surrounding walls. The shelves contained various white boxes, clearly labeled, some of whose contents were discernable through their semi-opaque plastic. Very organized. A triumph, in fact, of organization. I'd like to turn her loose in my garage.

"Pretty impressive, Elizabeth. I'm amazed that you can keep everything so perfectly arranged."

"It's really not that hard, Jobe. You just need to set up a system, and then, more importantly, follow it. I used to get so frustrated when I worked for other people. The management would always set up these time-saving and labor-saving systems, and no one would ever follow them. This one boss I had kept making all these forms for us to fill out. Then he'd complain to high heaven every time something would go wrong, often because he himself hadn't filled out the form completely. A form, or any system for that matter, is only as good as the people willing to pay attention to it and stick with it. Now that I'm on my own, it's simple. Once the system is set up, it's only a matter of maintenance. Which I do in little bits all the time. Clean while you work, as my first boss used to say, and you won't have a big mess at the end."

"Yeah, but lots of people can do maintenance." I said. "The hard part's starting the big job in the first place."

"Not if you use my other trick. Break it up into manageable increments. Don't look at a job as a three hour ordeal. Just tell yourself you're going to go out for five minutes. For example: Say you're cleaning your garage and it's a big rummage heap..."

"Wait a minute. When did you go to my garage?"

"I don't need to. Most men seem to need a least one slovenly hole in their life. I don't care how organized they appear, how neatly they dress, or how immaculate their car is. Somewhere, somehow, they've got a pile of crap where they can root around like pigs in a wallow..."

"I'm glad you have such a high opinion of the masculine gender. I never thought of it that way before. So my garage is actually an atavistic return to my genetic roots as a boar in a mud hole. Thanks. And here I was carrying around all this anal-retentive guilt. I feel much better."

"So your garage *is* messy?" She probed.

"Yeah. It is."

"Well here's what you do. Go out tonight, for just five minutes. Maybe when you take out the trash. And sort through one pile or another. It doesn't matter where you start, just start."

"But there's so much crap..."

"Quit whining. I hate men that whine. So start somewhere, and just work for five minutes. It's kind of like the first few minutes of a run. I, and most people, always dread those the most. But soon, if you stick with it, it gets easier, and then most of the time, it gets downright pleasurable. You look pretty fit, Jobe. Would you like to go for a run Saturday morning? I bet you haven't jogged around the lake in a few years. What do you say?"

"Maybe," I stalled, "But let's get back to my garage."

"That's about all there is to it. Just start somewhere. Then keep going, a little at a time, till things start to sort themselves out. My guess is it won't take as long as you originally thought. And you'll end up working longer each time without realizing it till one day you find you're done."

"Sounds possible..." I said cautiously.

"It works. Look around you. Do you think I could plan all the events I plan without having a system that worked. Remember, a job is only as big as its smallest increment. I once butchered an entire cow in less than three hours. And it was my first time. I cut and sawed and trimmed and even packaged. The butcher who was teaching me was amazed."

"If you don't mind my asking, what the hell were you doing butchering a cow?"

"My wild youth," she laughed. "There was a time I wanted to prove I could do any job any man could do, and better. Being a butcher just struck my feminist fancy."

"I see," I said, reappraising my earlier estimation of her abilities. Sometimes you can't judge a book by its cover. Something caught my eye over in the corner. A vaguely familiar machine was setting on a smaller work table.

"What's that?" I asked.

"That?" she said. "That is a Super Dee-Luxe Vacu-Packer 2000."

"No kidding," I said, my blood running both colder and quicker. "And why would you need that?"

"For the same reason I need a dehydrator, Jobe. Who knows? Maybe I want to package up some exotic snacks for a boat cruise, or preserve some special herbs... All kinds of things."

"It's just that I've seen a lot of these lately," I said, "Yet I've never had the occasion to use one myself. What's so special about the Dee-Luxe Vacu-Packer 2000?"

"Well, it holds more different sizes of bags for one thing," Elizabeth said. "The older models could only pack smaller items. If you wanted to vacu-pack a leg of lamb or something you were out of luck. Plus… See that bulge on the left side? The new vacu-packer has an automatic bar-coding and freshness dating attachment."

"Yahoo," I said, "I got a coupon for you I got at Costco. Just one more question: Who the hell would need an automatic freshness bar-coding whatever?"

"Mostly nobody, except someone like me," she said. "I find it particularly helpful for managing my inventory. But I think it's really just one more thing a manufacturer throws in to make their product look more impressive. Like all the software options you have on your computer that you never even look at or the million cycles you'll probably never use in your dishwasher. All the bells and whistles. People have to have them, even if they never, ever use them."

"Yeah," I agreed, "People sure are funny." She sure had a good handle on human frailties. And she was a lot deeper thinker than I'd imagined. I gazed around the room in awe, comparing it to the dishevelment or Fern's place. What a broad and wonderful range of behaviors in this species of ours. It's a wonder we manage to get along at all. Like mismatched roommates in the great college dorm or our world, some of us tidy, some of us pigs. The beauty is we all seem to make it to the commons to enjoy dinner.

Elizabeth had eased closer as she'd pointed out the features of the vacu-packer and was now slipping her arm gently around my waist as we stood together. I unconsciously put my arm over her shoulder and gave her a little squeeze. We stood there for a minute or two, each of us caught up in our own reveries. She turned in front of me and put her hands behind my neck.

"I'm sorry I was so angry earlier," she said, and stood up on her tiptoes as she pulled my head forward. I felt her warm breath on my face. Then she closed her eyes and kissed me on the mouth. The moist fullness of her lips pressing urgently against mine gave promise of an unrestrained hungry passion. Her tongue played briefly against my teeth and then thrust deep into my mouth, wrestling with my own in a surrogate struggle for both dominance and submission. I pulled away, gasping for breath. I was filled with a sudden sense of overwhelming guilt—the memory of my dear bride soiled by an unexpectedly pleasurable retreat into carnal squalor.

The pig had found a waller.

CHAPTER 47

The bell tinkled in the front of the store.

"Damn," Elizabeth spit out, "Customer." She gave me a searching look and headed for the front room.

I felt like spitting too. I roiled the taste of her around in my mouth and looked vainly for a place to discharge it. Not a toilet in sight. I went over to the vacu-packer and examined it more closely. Sure enough, it looked like the one I'd seen before. Except that one was packed neatly away in a box at the wonderful Wasen residence. Now there was a wallow. Come to think of it, I still had unanswered questions about Markie and Suzie and their proclivity for repackaging. It was high time I paid them a little return visit. Maybe I'd get really lucky and Mark would be playing pinochle with Knudson or something. I could catch both hogs in the same place. And have it out once and for all.

I looked around for a back exit. Somehow I didn't feel like trying to sidle past Elizabeth and her customer. I didn't think I could keep the guilty look off my face. Hidden behind a roll-away tailor's jenny in the back of the room I found a door. It had a button lock in the knob and an old-fashioned throw bolt across the upper panel. No alarm appeared to be in evidence so I took a chance, threw the bolt, and opened it. I braced for the blast of a siren. Nothing. Outside of the door was a little vestibule area. Other doors door led off either side to what I presumed were extra store rooms. Another door was directly ahead of me. A big two by four was across it, wedged behind iron brackets mounted to the door jamb. I removed the board, opened the door and stepped out into a dark alley. The looming backs of three-story buildings cast shadows along its length. I went right. After about fifty yards I came out on Capitol Way, opposite the Batdorf and Bronson Coffee house. Thinking I could use a cup of coffee about then, I jaywalked across the four lanes of traffic and headed into the warm, wonderfully scented atmosphere of B&B.

There's nothing like the smell of fresh ground coffee. Or finely roasted beans. One of the nicest things about the last decade is the emergence of small specialty coffee roasters who have learned that the many and myriad tastes of the versatile coffee bean have been a treasure only waiting to be discovered. The infinitesimal and almost undetectable difference we consumers once faced between Maxwell House and Folgers has been expanded to reveal the dark and wondrous joys of Sulawesi, Arabica and Sumatra Mandheling. I ordered a steaming cup of my favorite; Dancing Goats blend. I like it mostly because of the name. The barista gave me a quizzical look for some reason, perhaps because I didn't look enough like a hippie to appreciate the full-bodied taste of Dancing Goats, and I went over and sat down next to the window to collect my thoughts.

All kinds of folk peopled this little espresso bar, and it was always entertaining to see the vast variety of adornment everyone thought appropriate to their particular lifestyle. And accepted in others. Suit and tie clad lawyers mixed freely with dress-casual state workers—though dress-slovenly would be a more accurate description—and multiply pierced young folks and tattooed women with pink mohawks interfaced comfortably with blue-haired oldsters whose own fashion favorites—puffy teddy bears on the moms' sweatshirts and Dockers slung under the dads' sagging bellies—betrayed their middle American origins. Just some parents out to visit their college kids. The great thing was they all found common appreciation and sustenance in the humble pit of the coffee cherry. And the warm atmosphere and supplementary pastries made for a wonderful bond. Today's espresso bar must echo the hometown tavern ambience of a bygone era. Or perhaps the sense of community and togetherness once inspired by folks gathering around the woodstove in old time general stores.

I was staring out at the sidewalk, mentally sympathizing with the poor folk on the benches outside suffering under the curse of their cigarette addition, when I spied a familiar form; Kathryn, walking briskly in the direction of the men's store where I used to work. She saw me. My heart took a leap in my chest and I smiled broadly. She smiled in return and angled into the doorway. I got up as she hurried over to my table. As she took a closer look at my face her smile suddenly turned to a frown.

"Don't tell me," she said, "you just got out of disguise." For some reason the word 'disguise' trailed off into a snarl.

"What?" I asked dumbly.

"Your face. I didn't know you wore lipstick. At least not bright red..."

I wiped at my mouth with the back of my hand and was shocked to see red grease all over my knuckles.

"I—"

"I'm sure you have a very good explanation, Jobe Carson. And I have a very good reason to get the hell out of here."

She spun around and walked quickly to the exit. She was out on the sidewalk before I could utter another word. The people at the table next to me were talking in lowered voices. I looked around the espresso bar. Everyone seemed to be looking in my direction, or was turning back from recently having looked in my direction. One old lady with crocheted lollipops on her sweater stared at me while absently rubbing the corners of her own mouth. I sat back down and sipped at my coffee. Every now and then I wiped my mouth with the little napkin they'd given me to put under my cup. It came away with red streaks four times before a couple of faded pink smudges indicated I was probably fit to go out in public. I got up and deposited my now empty cup in the trash, grabbed a weekly newspaper on my way out the door and headed for my car two blocks away. It seemed like everyone was staring at me as I walked along the sidewalk. When I reached my car, I tried to look at my reflection in the rearview mirror.

Nothing. I still didn't have a rearview mirror. I used the mirror in the visor instead. The aptly named make-up mirror, I thought ruefully, and saw that I had indeed got rid of all the traces of lipstick. But not all the traces of regret.

I stared at my reflection for some time. Trying to figure what it was about me that led to these ridiculous lapses in judgment. I'd better get my act together soon. People were depending on me. I should stick to the important tasks at hand and quit getting diverted by my own selfish lust. My client Fred had a murder charge hanging over his head. And somebody had died. And most of all, my family expected me to provide for them. Fair enough. My kids hadn't asked to come into this world. I had brought them of my own free will. It certainly wasn't their fault that their mother had disappeared. I needed to focus on getting this problem solved and bringing home something for them to live on. Which I sure wasn't accomplishing by getting lipstick smeared all over my face by a rutting interior decorator. Or being chastised by an angry lab tech for that matter.

It was time to bring home the bacon. And I knew just the pig I planned to start with. I put my car into gear and slipped into westbound traffic. Wasen Wallow, here I come.

CHAPTER 48

I pulled up to the front gate of the Wasen estate and pressed the call buzzer. The wind was blustering pretty hard and I couldn't quite make out what the little speaker was squawking, so I got out and stood right next to it. With the gusts blowing all around and having to bend down to talk to the little disembodied box, I felt like a penitent at a drive-thru for sinners. "I'm sorry father for I have sinned, I'm on a diet and I super-sized my last meal." Would that my problems were so simple.

Mark's voice crackled over the radio. "You're supposed to be staying away from here, Carson."

"But Markie!" I shouted. "I need to talk to you!"

"I thought Knudson told you to leave me alone. Why the hell are you here?" he squawked back.

"A little thing called the constitution, Mark. I haven't committed any crimes. I certainly haven't harassed you. You ask me out here last time, remember?"

His response was garbled by a particularly strong gust of wind that set the trees shuddering and shrieking overhead. It looked as if a big old fir bough was about to crack down and crush my car.

"I didn't get that," I shouted into the box. "What do you say you open up the gate and we discuss this inside? I've got some information about your dad I think you want to hear."

"What?" his voice rasped.

"Nothing doing. Let me in first."

I waited for a few moments. The wind was really blowing up a storm. Black clouds in the distance were racing along the treetops. The long grass in the fields was being pushed down in various random patterns. You could follow the eddies and thrusts of the wind as it played across the open areas. The alternating ripples, traces, billows and depressions looked like the impressions of ghost horses rolling and frolicking in the empty pastures.

Then the rain started to come down in sheets. Although down is a misnomer. The spray was mostly horizontal, the droplets the size of dimes, and they pelted my eyes and face as I struggled back into the car, my coat flapping all around and tangling me up as I tried to shut the door and settle into the seat. A buzzer sounded, and the gate began to swing back. A blast of wind caught the large sheet metal warning sign bolted to the light tubular frame of the gate. The sudden force against the impromptu metal sail made the whole mechanism swing violently backward, to the edge of the road and beyond. I heard a squeal as the metal wrenched beyond its intended terminus. The wind kept beating at it and the gate twisted some more, finally tilting downward and planting itself into the field at a distinctly non-functional angle. Victor, should he ever return, would not be pleased.

I navigated through the opening carefully, hoping the wind wouldn't reverse direction and send the disabled gate flinging back into my vehicle. I had enough dents for one job as it was. I drove up to the house and parked as close to the front entryway as I could. I hurried up to the door and beat on the giant knocker as the wind buffeted me from behind. The door was opened a crack by someone within and then a big gust caught me from the rear and literally propelled me inside. I slammed into Suzie, who went sliding across the polished tile entryway. The door slammed back against the wall, its resounding oaken boom echoing all the way to the darkened opening of the den, where I could hear the big screen TV blasting out its own grunts and crunches from what could only have been a football game.

I grabbed the door and forced it shut, went over to Suzie and helped her off the floor.

"First down, Chargers," I said, and pulled her to her feet. "We've got to quit meeting this way,"

"Thanks," she said, "I told Mark this floor was too slippery."

"Venetian tile is such a pesky surface," I commiserated. "If I were you I'd get some of that indoor-outdoor carpet stuff. You can get it wet and vacuum it and everything."

"I know," she said seriously, "We had it in my Mom's mobile home before my stepdad burned it down."

"That's why trailers make such terrible meth labs," I joked.

"I know," she said even more earnestly, "That's what I told him. But he didn't listen."

I decided to change the subject. "So, been packing any boxes lately?"

Before she could answer, Mark schlepped into the room. His sweatsuit was even more disheveled looking than usual, the drawstring of the pants loosened so they sagged low enough to reveal his paunch, which protruded pinkly from the top of his not so tightie not so whities. The zippered jacket hung loosely on his shoulders and a sleeveless undershirt let tufts of hair poke out from various portions of his chest, shoulders and armpits. His trademark combover lay lank on his head like a week old, roadkilled possum, scalp pimples and tanning bed burns showing through like swollen blowflies. Pretty.

"Sorry to catch you before your shower, Mark," I said. "Really, really, sorry."

"Not as sorry as I am," he said. "What's this important news about Dad?"

"I heard he's been sighted out on the Georgia Straits," I lied. "Or at least someone matching his description. In a large sea kayak. What color was that one that's missing from the garage?"

"Red," he said. "You're sure?"

"No one's sure about anything, Mark. Maybe it was just a red herring."

"But herrings are a lot smaller than kayaks," Suzie said.

"Shut up!" Mark barked at her. She looked quickly down at the floor.

I was studying his reaction. Was he worried that his dad was alive, or worried that I thought the dad story was a red herring? Or relieved that people would at least think his dad was still alive? Since I had made up the whole story anyhow, it was hard to say. Maybe I should try to flesh it out it to trip him up somehow.

"What was the old fellow wearing when he disappeared?" I asked.

"I don't know," Mark said.

"But Mark," Suzie offered, "Didn't he have on his raingear when he di—"

"I said shut up!" Mark yelled. "And I mean shut up NOW!"

"There's a clue, Mark," I said calmly, "If he had on his raingear when he 'di—'maybe he was intending to go on a journey."

Mark looked at me cautiously; I think he was trying to figure out if by journey I meant a brief trip, or something more permanent.

"I don't know. I don't know anything. And it won't do you any good to keep asking. You can't squeeze blood from a sow's ear."

"But if you keep digging random holes, who knows what you may turn up?" I said. I decided to switch targets. "Say Suzie, didn't I see you at Secondhand City Saturday?"

"No," she said doubtfully, "I haven't been there in a couple of weeks."

Mark started to shout at her again, but the cat was already out of its skin.

"So what's the big deal with you guys taking back appliances?" I asked.

"None of your business," Mark said.

"I'm guessing it's very much my business, Mark. It seems a little odd, a rich person like you going to all the trouble to take a used appliance into a place like that. Why not just give it to the Goodwill? Charitable soul that you are and all."

Suzie jumped in again. "Because the Goodwill doesn't—OW!" Mark had slapped her face.

"I said shut up and I mean SHUT UP!" he screamed. Then he turned on me, "Now get the hell out of here before I call the police. Suzie will back me up that you're trespassing. I saw what happened to my front gate, I'll tell the police you crashed into it. I'll tell them you broke in here and started slapping Suzie around—"

"Why you son of a bitch," I said. "I'm gonna kick your fat lying ass."

I started to advance on him, but he had grabbed a cell phone from the sagging pocket of his sweatpants. He had already dialed a 'nine' and a 'one' by the time I got two feet. His finger was poised over the other 'one,' ready for an instant emergency call, not to mention an automatic trace back should I decide to ignore the threat and pummel the holy hell out of him. Another reason I hate cell phones. They're too damn handy. I stopped short and gave him a mock salute instead. Then I turned around and headed for the door. Suzie was rubbing the side of her face and looking at me with haunted eyes. She had traded a meth lab for this?

It looked like neither one of us thought it was a very good trade.

CHAPTER 49

I drove back home feeling frustrated indeed. I had blown my cool. As a result, I didn't get a chance to probe Mark very deeply. Worse, I had stood witness to a domestic violence episode and done nothing about it. My nerves still jangled from the adrenalin seeping out of them. I pulled into my driveway in time to see Jack and Kiah heading out to Jack's basketball practice.

"How late's practice tonight, Jack?" I called.

"Seven thirty!" he shouted back.

"Got your shoes?"

"Yeah."

"Got your shorts?"

"Yeah!"

"Got your..."

"I got *everything,* Dad," he said.

I watched them drive off and waited patiently. I had noticed something, but Jack's sarcasm had silenced me. Soon Kiah's brake lights came on. He turned into the neighbor's driveway, backed out and headed in my direction. As he pulled up next to me, Jack got out the other side. He walked over and retrieved his gym bag from where he'd left it on the porch.

"Mind taking your skateboard off the sidewalk while you're at it?" I asked pleasantly.

He did so, but not without a glare at me full of that barely contained rage only teenagers can harbor.

"Have a good practice," I called as he got sullenly back in the car. That's my Jack. A lot of parents get pretty upset at that sort of behavior. But I figure, you gotta ride that stuff like a wave; stay on top of it, go with the flow, and keep looking ahead for the real rocks poking out of the swell.

I went inside to find Miranda curled up on the couch with the latest Harry Potter book. She had absolutely devoured the first three inside of two weeks. The fourth was about to be engulfed as well.

"How was your day, Daddy?" she asked over the top of the book.

"Fine," I answered, "Sorry I'm late, Honey, a big worm came out of a cave and swallowed this child I was holding."

"That's nice," she mumbled.

I shrugged to myself and went into the kitchen to inventory the supplies for dinner. Tonight's menu called for basic red spaghetti. Something all the kids liked. I took out the hamburger, onions and spices and set to work Although I can put a batch of spag on the table in half an hour, since I had some time tonight I decided to do it "slow simmer" style. I started frying up a pound and a half of hamburger then mixed in half a chub of pork sausage. It was the ten-ounce chub, in case you're wondering. I peeled an onion, cut it in half across its north/south axis and then placed a series of longitudinal quarter inch cuts almost all the way to what would have been the hemisphere's Arctic Circle. I then flipped it sideways and cut along latitudinal lines so the onion's own natural segmentation allowed it to fall apart in perfectly diced pieces. I brought the frying pan over to my cutting board and scraped the onions off into the steaming hamburger. I added garlic and onion powder, ground about a teaspoon of whole oregano between my fingertips and dusted it through the mix. I did the same with a couple of pinches of anise seed, then ground in some black pepper and threw in a teaspoon of salt. A splash or two of wine and soon the whole mess was simmering fragrantly. I sliced up four large white mushrooms and stirred them in.

While I waited for the hamburger to brown I filled up a big pot with water, added some olive oil and salt and put it on another burner, ready to boil when the time came. I cleaned up my cutting board and work area, Elizabeth's admonitions about incremental work habits briefly wafting through my mind, and put some dishes in the dishwasher. Funny how the kids had learned to pick up, rinse and load their dinner dishes, but every other meal or snack left the counter by the sink littered with milk-clouded glassware and scummy plates.

I opened a couple of cans of cut stewed tomatoes and poured them in the hamburger mix. I then added two small cans of tomato paste and the same amount of water. I repeated the spice additions, omitting the salt this time and adding a teaspoon of concentrated lemon juice and a tablespoon of sugar. I stirred it all up and turned down the heat to let it slow simmer for the next hour and a half.

Cooking always helped me collect my thoughts. Puttering around with the known combinations of ingredients that made up my recipes seemed to help my subconscious get in the mood to categorize the seemingly disparate items in the cases I was working on. I was thinking it was time to call a family meeting. I was pretty sure I had gathered all the information I needed to crack this case. I even had a prime suspect in mind. But I wanted to run all the info by the kids and see if they had any insights. Or any spins on the clues that I had overlooked. I always liked getting feedback from the family at this phase of a case. If nothing else, sometimes just presenting all the facts in a coherent manner helped to lead me to a conclusion.

Let's hope it worked this time. I hadn't heard from Henderson, but I knew he was anxious for something that would make him feel better about taking Fred's case. Lawyers, despite all the jokes to the contrary, are far from stupid. Especially business wise. They understand full well how a high-profile case can bring in more clients, or turn them disgustedly away. Taking on the county coroner was bound to be risky business. I didn't want to let him down.

I threw in some laundry and watched the early news. Surprise, surprise, the world was still going to hell in a hand basket. Afghanistan was still being bombed and the Taliban was still shouting defiance. Oh well. What did the government expect? Trying to reason with a fundamentalist is like trying to put toothpaste back in a tube. It's bound to be both a messy and a frustrating experience.

By the time the boys got home dinner was ready. The sauce had matured perfectly. And the fresh garlic cloves I had minced and heated in the microwave with butter, then spread generously over French bread, were a sweet and succulent counterpoint to the robustness of the spaghetti. We all ate our fill.

As I wiped the last dribs of sauce off my plate with a final crust of bread I announced to them all: "Family meeting tonight."

"Oh boy," shouted Miranda. "We get to solve the case!"

Kiah put his most serious and introspective look on his face.

Jack was ever the practical one. He asked simply, "What's for dessert?"

CHAPTER 50

We sat around the dining room table. The dishes had been cleared and cleaned and the tablecloth removed. The kids each had a notepad and pencil in front of them. I had pinned a big piece of butcher paper to the wall, listed the various suspects and the clues amassed against each of them so far. While I was writing I'd given the children a synopsis of the case to date.

Miranda was the first to speak:

"You mean Knudson actually drank that guys spit? Eeyew. That is really gross..."

"No grosser than the way Jack smacks his mouth when he eats," said Kiah.

"Or you look when you're talking to your girlfriend," teased Jack.

"Shut up!"

"You shut up!"

"You shut up!"

"Both of you shut up," I shouted. "We're trying to solve a case here. Jack. You first. What do you think?"

"I think that Mark guy did it," he said.

"Pretty quick judgment," I said. "I'd like to think that too. He's certainly the perfect asshole. But why else?"

"Look at what he stood to gain. He's got free run of the place that his dad used to live in, all that money, and all those cool cars. And now he doesn't have his dad looking over his shoulder and hassling him every time he wants to do something."

"Very good Jack, and very passionate. Sounds like I better watch my backside. But that's just motive, what about means?"

"Look at the list. He's got all the right tools. He coulda chopped up Pop in that shed thing, dried him and wrapped him and no one would have seen him."

"By the way," interjected Kiah. "Why are you so sure all these people were shrink-wrapped or vacu-packed or whatever?"

"Let's just say that piece of information fell out of a truck one day," I said, slipping a glance at Miranda. "Accept it as a given. What do you think, Kiah?"

"I think it was that Elizabeth chick."

"And—?"

"She wanted to off her husband so she could screw around with other guys and not worry about him barging in drunk."

"But what about the income from his business?"

"Nice try Dad, but you said yourself it was in the red. The guy was a drag, dude. If I was her I'd want to off him too."

"Okay, say she did. What about this? When I was shot at, she was in the car."

"Maybe she hired someone to shoot at you."

"Maybe..." I mulled it over. He had a point.

"How did she react after the chase?" he persisted. "Was she at all surprised?"

"Not very," I replied, remembering. "You're right. She seemed to take it pretty calmly, considering. Of course, it's always hard to read her expressions. How about means?"

"She covers that pretty well too. You said she's got a dehydrator and a vacu-packer. And it sounds like she's got a pretty private area in the back there."

"I don't know," I said doubtfully, "Somehow I can't picture her using the area where she usually dries flowers in quite that way."

"Come on Dad, like you always tell me; start thinking with the organ in the upper part of your body. Someone who can butcher a thousand-pound cow in under three hours could make short work of a two-hundred-pound biped."

I shivered. The image of Elizabeth laboring over the bloody dismembered corpse of her husband, a quasi-frown of concentration on her brow and that focused look she got when planning a project was somehow tough to stomach.

"Besides," Kiah said, "doesn't she stand to rake in the most dough of all these people? That's a pretty pointy finger right there. And speaking of fingers, why do you list whether the victims are left or right-handed?"

"Another thing I'm pretty sure has relevance," I explained. "Let's just accept that too."

He looked at the butcher paper chart. "Why do you list Elizabeth's husband as 'left handed' with a question mark?"

"Something I haven't confirmed yet," I said. "I always seem to forget to ask for some reason. I presume he is because he once played first base on a minor league team. And most decent first basemen are left-handed."

"But Dad, what about—?" I cut him off with a sharp look. Jack, our resident baseball aficionado, was starting to contradict me with what I was sure was a bevy of right-handed first baseman statistics.

"So I don't see anything that definitely lets her off the hook," Kiah finished triumphantly.

"And I don't see anything that definitely snags her either," I said.

"Or rules out that Mark guy," said Jack. "Just because she coulda done it, doesn't mean he didn't"

"Don't be stupid, Jack," Kiah said. "Why would he want to kill his own dad? You get mad at Dad sometimes—me too—but do we really want to kill him?"

Jack looked at me seriously. Gym bags notwithstanding, it did seem a little farfetched. "Maybe his dad didn't like Suzie," he offered. "Or maybe his dad threatened to cut him off. Or maybe his dad died accidentally but it looked like Mark killed him, like in those mystery stories, so he panicked and thought of this weird way to get rid of him."

"Good thinking, Jack," I agreed, "That's a wrinkle I hadn't thought of. Let's see; the old man had an accident and it looked like Mark had a motive so he did all the butchering to cover it up anyhow. Post-meditated manslaughter. I like it. It fits his psychology."

"Yeah, and that Suzie chick helped him clean everything up. Even though he's a slob, she puts everything back in boxes perfectly, right? Maybe that's why they keep trying to take things back to stores and stuff."

"That's too obvious, and weird Jack," interrupted Kiah. "Why doesn't he just take 'em to the Goodwill, or the dump for that matter? Who'd ever know?"

"Good point, Kiah," I agreed. "Why the elaborate return effort? Unless..."

"Unless what?" Jack said.

"Never mind, we'll come back to it later. Miranda, I haven't heard a peep out of you. What do you think?"

"I think Fred did it," she said flatly.

"Why would you think that, Miranda? Fred's my client."

"He just seems too nice. In the books I read, the people that are too nice are always the ones you have to be suspicious of. And remember that icky video you saw on his table? About that cannibal guy? I think he has a deep, dark secret."

"Come on Miranda," I said lightly, "You've been reading too much mumbo jumbo. I doubt that Fred ate Bill."

The boys exchanged glances.

"A video rental is hardly evidence that will stand up in court, Mir," Kiah said.

"Yeah, lighten up, sorcerer girl," Jack sneered. "What did you do? Read his mind? Or feel his aura?"

"Dad," Mir persisted. "You said yourself he had all the equipment in his rumpus room. And so far, he's the only one attached to a definite piece of scientific evidence: The blood. It sounds to me like the coroner picked the right guy."

"But what about the shooting at my car? How do you explain that?"

"I don't know," she said. "Maybe somebody else doesn't like you. Remember the first time you were shot at, on the street? You hadn't even talked to any of the suspects yet. So who knows?"

"Certainly not me. Except that it would be a pretty unusual coincidence. Even so, I still don't get a strong motive vibe from Fred."

"Maybe Fred thought he had a good reason to murder Bill. Maybe he has a new lover, or Bill did. Maybe he was tired of Bill going out on him all the time. Maybe he was sick of Bill's temper and stuff."

"A lot of maybes, Mir. And some good ideas. I'll think about it. But my gut feeling says it's not him. If you talked to him I think you'd feel the same. His anguish is genuine. He really does miss Bill."

"But Dad," she protested. "That doesn't mean he didn't kill him. It just means he's sorry he did."

She had a point. We all sat there staring at the butcher paper for a while. I was briefly struck with the irony of my choice of material for a chart. Then I set about considering all the kids' arguments as objectively as I could. They were certainly persuasive. Means, motive and opportunity were about evenly distributed amongst all the suspects. I came to a conclusion.

"I think—" I began.

That's when the doorbell rang.

CHAPTER 51

Dammit. Who the hell was that? If it was another fourth grader trying to sell me a Christmas wreath I was going to burn down the school tomorrow. I went irritably to the front door. As I opened it I caught the glint of light on brass. Then a big guy in uniform thrust a sheaf of papers in my face.

"We have a warrant to search this house. Are you Jobe Carson?"

"Yes, I am," I said, adrenalin surging through my arteries. "Why would you have a warrant?"

"Evidence in a murder case. Mind opening up the garage, Mr. Carson?"

Uh oh. They knew right where to look. What was going on?

"Sure Officer, just let me find my shoes," I said. Stalling wasn't really going to help me any at this point, but I couldn't help trying to think of a way out. "I didn't know there was a murder case going on." I heard myself say lamely. Quick thinking, Sherlock.

I led them through the side door that went to the garage. When I flipped on the light the first thing I noticed was a pool of water next to the freezer door. Which was hanging open. Damn Miranda, I thought, I've told you a million times to make sure the freezer is closed when you get out a Popsicle. The next thing I noticed was that the policemen, there were two, had pushed past me and were heading straight for the green plastic bag. The lump. And it was sitting in the puddle of water. The bigger policeman grabbed the package and lifted it gingerly. By now we had all crowded through the confined space that opened into the garage proper. He slowly unwrapped the dripping plastic.

"Oh shit!" Kiah and Jack said simultaneously.

"Ah hah!" said the policeman.

"Oh Jesus." I said. Not because the arm was now revealed and I was suddenly in the position of defending myself against a withholding

218

evidence charge in a murder case. But because the arm had changed. It was no longer a dried, dehydrated, shrivelly, not very human looking piece of meat. Now it was a full, plump, saturated human forearm, livid in its realism, looking suddenly like it had just been forcibly removed from someone who may still be in the vicinity. I checked an impulse to grab it and go running into the street to ask if anyone had accidentally left it behind.

"You're under arrest, Mr. Carson. You have the right to remain silent. You have the right to an attorney. If you cannot afford an..." His words droned off into my subconscious. What I was focusing on was the looks on the kids' faces. They were stunned. Their Dad was being arrested. Jack and Kiah were looking in horror at the arm. Miranda had a look of guilt on her face...and fear. Fear that I would be taken away forever. Kiah was the first to move. He rushed at the policeman that was holding me and started pushing him away.

"Leave my Dad alone!" he yelled, and started beating at the guy's chest. The other policeman came up behind and pinned Kiah's arms to his side with a big bear hug.

"Cool it boy," he said. "I don't want to have to arrest you too. Tell your kid to settle down, Carson."

"He's right Kiah. Ease up. It's all a big mistake. I'll get this taken care of and be out on bail by morning. Call the lawyer—Steve Henderson."

The policeman told me to put my hands behind my back and proceeded to zipcuff me. It was another first for me. My first experience with zipcuffs that is.

I'm not sure why zipcuffs are so popular these days. Because they're sure a lot less comfortable than the old metal handcuffs. Maybe it's easier for the poor policeman because he doesn't have to lug around a key. Not that keys ever mattered anyhow. There have always been a lot of amateur Houdinis out there. But what I don't think officialdom realizes is that us criminal types that aren't magicians don't need bolt cutters any more. Just one snip from a strong pair of pinking shears and we're free. Who says progress isn't good?

"Do you have a relative you could call to watch the kids Carson? Or should we call CPS?" the bigger policeman asked.

"Kiah, call your aunt. Have her come over till I get bailed out."

The cops led me to their squad car and I had the pleasure of seeing my neighbors peek through their windows at my unceremonious deposit into its plastic back seat. That'll be a great tale at the next homeowners' potluck. The smaller policeman was carrying the arm now and rewrapping it as he walked. It's funny how during times of crises I have a great awareness for detail. As he walked through the spotlight on the side of his patrol car I could see what looked to be a tattoo on the arm's wrist. I hadn't noticed that before. Somehow the swelling caused by the rehydration must have stretched that area out more. The shriveled shrunken skin had previously obscured it, or perhaps it had been hidden by the folds of the vacu-wrap.

That's when another car pulled into the driveway. I should have guessed. The lettering on the door saved me the trouble. It read: "County Coroner." Knudson extracted himself from the driver's seat.

"I'll take that Officer," he said, and let out a low whistle as he partially unwrapped the green plastic. Then he leered at me. "I got you by the short hairs now, Carson. I hope you brought some pain medication, because withholding evidence in a murder case is a major offense—with major punishment. I'm gonna enjoy sticking it to you and watching you squirm." He thrust the arm at me in an Italian salute. My own return hand gesture was obscured behind my back. So I tried to spit at him instead. All I got was a pitiful little noise. For some reason my mouth was too dry.

I wiggled around in the back seat as we drove off. I tried to catch Miranda's eyes and the eyes of the boys. And at least give them a nod of reassurance. This was not the setback I needed. It didn't take a private detective to figure out what must have happened to the arm.

When Miranda had left the freezer door open, its defrosted ice seeped out onto the garage floor. For some reason the plastic wrapped arm had fallen off the heap and into the puddle. Sparky must have penetrated the vacu-pack when he was gnawing on it that first day. The water from the puddle had slowly rehydrated the arm. Just in time for the police to find it. Some people have all the luck.

As we drove away I kept trying to put together why the police had shown up at my door. Who could have tipped them that I had a severed arm laying in my garage? Who might have told someone, who then told someone, who told someone who cared? There was really only one possibility. It was as plain as the name of the ruling that forced the cops to read me my rights.

Miranda.

CHAPTER 52

The ride to the police station looked strange through a heavy metal screen. And the general ambience was different than my own vehicle. The rear of the police car reeked of what seemed to be two competing smells—bleach and vomit.

"You guys need to put one of those little cardboard evergreen trees back here," I joked nervously. "Or how about a 'stick up'?"

"You're gonna be getting a stick up somewhere if you don't pipe down, Carson. Now shut up. We're trying to listen to the radio."

I shut up. Police sticks have their place, but I didn't want inside of me to be one of them. The buzzes and squawks coming over the radio left me mostly mystified. I always have a hard time sorting out what the various people are saying. I once had a friend with a police band radio receiver who'd listen to it all night long. "D'ya hear that?" he'd say, "A three-forty-two on a one-adam-twelve. That must be serious." All I ever heard was static.

A voice I knew cut through my reverie.

"Yeah, we got that queer bastard nailed to the cross now," it said. "I'm gonna see that faggot roast on the fire yet. I got the evidence laying right here on the seat. And I'm going to do the analysis myself. Just to make sure. This chain of evidence is staying with me all the way. Not only that, but we got Carson on his way to jail too."

"Congratulations Nels," another familiar voice said. "I'll tell Suzie to bring one of her friends over to the house tonight. Ditch Betty and stop out for a jolt. I can't wait to hear how you plan to...." the words faded off into static again and another voice, presumably the dispatcher, started calling for a drunk to be picked up at the mall.

I hunched in the back seat angry and depressed. Why is it dipshits always prevail? As if to underline my upset, the evidence of dipshittery was suddenly surrounding me everywhere. Christmas lights. Christ. It wasn't even Thanksgiving yet.

What is it with people? Earlier and earlier every year. They'd already started stringing those stupid curtain lights from their eaves. I growled. One of the policemen looked around and growled back. That type of light has got to be the worst aberration in Christmas decorations in a long, long time. Icicle lights I guess they call 'em. Boring. The bright glow of a fourteen inch by thirty-foot sheet of white lights may cheer some souls but to my variety loving sensibilities it looks like the equivalent of landscaping with astro-turf. I've never been one for easy uniformity. So when seventy-five percent of my neighbors started festooning their roofs with "stalag-lites" I chalked another one up to the Gap-ification of our culture. Of course who was I to talk? Here I was, the refined cultural connoisseur, zipcuffed in the plastic back seat of a squad car that smelled of puke, old donuts, and copfarts. Good taste certainly pays off in this great world of ours.

We pulled into the station and the polite policeman yanked me out of the car and flung me into the processing area. I held up a number for him and did a couple of glamour photos, got my pinkies smudged and emptied my pockets into a manila envelope. Processing done, and relieved they had skipped the orifice search, I was herded down a hall and pushed into a fine scented cell which, much to my delight, already housed what looked to be an interesting and stimulating bunkmate. He smiled. Uh oh. The specter of the Gap again. Except this time it was the gaps in his teeth. I hoped they wouldn't make him whistle too much in his sleep.

"Now get yourself a good nights' rest, Carson," the attentive officer said. "Here's a blanket." He handed me a rip proof blanket, but not, I noticed, soil proof, and closed the door with a clang. It's so nice basking in the gentle ministrations of our public servants. "I'll bring some toilet paper in the morning," he finished.

"Thank you, Sir. How do I call room service?"

"Funny, Carson. Why don't you try pulling that bell rope on the wall over there?" I looked where he indicated and saw a nice rendition of exactly that. In two dimensions. Some artistic drunk had managed to smuggle in some kind of crayon and had done a credible representation of an old-fashioned butler's pull rope.

"Ha ha," I replied. "No seriously, how do I get in touch with you when I need something?"

"You yell, idiot," he growled. "What do you think this is, The Bellagio?"

"What about when I need to use the bathroom?" I asked.

"You're in the bathroom," he grinned, and pointed towards a stainless-steel pedestal. It was standing about eighteen inches out from the middle of the back wall. And about two feet from the bunks on either side. I had originally taken it to be some kind of heating or air conditioning unit. Apparently it conditioned the air all right. In the olfactory sense.

"You go to be kidding," I said, "You don't expect me to drop my drawers in front of God and Joe-Bob over there do you?"

"Maybe you should have thought about that before you broke the law," he said righteously.

"Somehow the dynamics of crapping in a cell just didn't enter my mind," I said. "And besides. No one's proven that I've broken any laws yet. Maybe that arm was sent to me as a gag gift. Maybe someone planted it in my garage. Maybe—"

"Don't get all lawyer-y Carson," he interrupted. "Around here you're guilty till proven innocent. Until your attorney can spring you you're just an ordinary everyday criminal to us. Let's just hope you haven't eaten anything lately that disagrees with you."

No sooner had he said that than my gut began to roil. As he walked away the cramps started. Visions of hamburger left out thawing too long rushed through my brain. And straight to my bowel. Sweat started to bead my forehead and I shivered as the chills washed over me. I looked over at the lidless, stainless steel throne and then at the gap-toothed, grinning hick sitting expectantly on the bunk.

"How-do?" he whistled. "My name's Clevus."

It was going to be a long night.

CHAPTER 53

It's no surprise to anyone who has spent any time in jail that some of the most profound treatises on human nature, from Seneca to De Sade, were cultivated by such surroundings. The dehumanizing experience of exile and incarceration seems to distill the essence of the human spirit. Having someone else in complete control of your most basic freedoms, like where you go and what you do, makes their absence more poignant and their hoped for return more precious.

Henderson finally sprung me the next morning after he'd got a judge friend to schedule an early arraignment. It helps having a lawyer who's president of the regional bar association. Even judges face the prospect of disbarment. The judge was appropriately stern and menacing and set my bail at twenty-five thousand dollars. Henderson put it up with a personal check to save us the cost of a bondsman. We left the courthouse complex much the worse for wear.

"You look like you've been through hell," Henderson said.

"It was either that or hog heaven," I said, "At least heaven for one hog I know, name of Clevus. I didn't get much sleep last night."

"I'll say. You look it. And you seem to be looking a little green around the edges too."

"Something I ate," I explained. "Mind driving me home real quick? The chauffeurs that brought me here seem to have left."

"Sure thing Jobe, I don't mind being your taxi driver. Just don't forget to tip. I've been stiffed by you criminal types before."

"Yeah, okay," I said distractedly. My attention was suddenly elsewhere. Walking across the campus was a figure I had last seen an eternity ago, or was it yesterday morning? Kathryn saw me too and started to angle in our direction. Then she hesitated. And veered away instead. I tried to catch her eye, but she kept her head forward and her mental blinders firmly in place. I suppose she had a right. Another woman's lipstick and jail time were not your best harbingers for a good relationship.

"Friend of yours?" The ever observant Henderson intoned meaningfully.

"More of an ex-friend, I think," I replied.

"She work around here?"

"Yeah. For Knudson in fact."

"Ouch," he grimaced. "How long as she been an ex-friend?"

"Since yesterday," I said sadly.

"That's too bad. That might have been a good angle to help Fred. Nothing like an inside track to the coroner's office when the coroner happens to be crucifying your client." I could hear the faint tone of disapproval in his voice. Under the deafening blast of sarcasm.

"Sorry," I said, and I was.

"I don't mean to pry Jobe, but I've seen that look on a woman's face before. I'm guessing she was more than just a friend. What'd you do, kiss another girl or something?"

"Yeah." Sad gave way to morose.

"I don't suppose you thought about the fact that pissing off your friend might affect the outcome of your work in some way?" This time it was his harshest courtroom voice.

"Look Henderson. I'm sorry. Okay? Ease up. Cross examining won't help. Or nailing me to one for that matter. I'm tired, and I'm sore, and I feel like Elvis just before he died. Let's just get me home to a hot shower and a few moments of peace and quiet."

"Whatever you say, Don Juan. I suppose I can always send my secretary to hit on Dr. Wu."

"You'd have more luck playing her on Knudson himself. "He's dipped his wick in more candles than you'd find at a pope's funeral."

"You have such a way with words, Jobe. Too bad you can't control your lips in other ways."

"It wasn't my fault," I lied.

"It takes two to tangle."

"That's 'tango'," I corrected.

"Not in your case. Cause you got this sucker all knotted up now."

He had a point. We got into his car, one of those Plymouth limited edition roadsters, and headed back to my place. When I got home I found a note from the kids' aunt and another one from the kids saying they had gone off to school. The aunt's note was disapproving as well. Miranda asked me to call the school office when I got in. I did so and they paged her. When she came on the line I told her I was okay and would see her later that afternoon. Henderson had driven off, telling me to meet him at his office around one o'clock. I unloaded all my tension and took a hot shower. For about twenty minutes. Hell with the power bill. Ever since that "three minute shower" campaign to curtail energy and water usage, I've always felt a little scummy anyhow; like I never get completely cleaned off. I rinsed till my skin was puckery.

I stepped out of the shower with a big question ringing in my head. Or should I say pounding. Pounding like a primitive drumbeat. That tattoo on the arm's wrist. What could it signify? I mentally ran through the dossiers of the people on my list. Bill's vitals had said he had a number of piercings. Could be, lots of pierced folk have tattoos too. Fern's husband Joe was an ex-merchant marine. Good chance of a tattoo there. Mark's dad was pretty straight laced, but Elizabeth's husband was an old navy flyboy. Again, certainly a possibility.

I found myself calling her first.

"Elizabeth, quick question: Does your husband have a tattoo on his wrist?"

"Yes," she said disgustedly.

I was cautious now.

"Which wrist was it on?"

"His left. Why? I hated it. It was a stupid thing. It was the date he and his girlfriend first met when he was in the navy. Before she dumped him for a better man. Like I should have done. We were going to have it removed but never got to it. I made him wear an I.D. bracelet over it in public. Why do you ask?"

"Just trying to nail down a couple of loose ends," I said. "I'm putting out search parameters to some of my colleagues in other cities. You never know. I'll let you go."

"Jobe," she said hesitantly.

"What?"

"Nothing. Stay in touch. Let me know how it's going."

"I will," I said, and hung up.

That's one, I thought, and looked up the number of Fred's hotel.

CHAPTER 54

The hotel receptionist answered on the second ring.

"Artesian Suites," she said cheerfully.

"Yeah," I replied, "I'd like to speak to Fred Costner please. I'm not sure of the room."

"One second," she said. "I'll pull him up on my screen."

"That's okay. I'll just speak to him in his room."

"What?"

"Nothing."

"I'll ring you," she said.

"Ouch," I said.

"What?"

"Nothing," I explained, "I've just never been rung before."

"Listen Mister, it's been a tough day. If you got something to say just say it."

"Never mind," I said sheepishly. "I'll just wait while you connect me with Fred."

But it was not to be. The receptionist got back on the line quickly.

"I'm sorry sir. That party doesn't answer."

I forewent my opportunity to ask how she could tell Fred was having a party and thanked her politely instead. I grabbed the phone book and looked up the number to Melody Lanes Cafe. Lulie answered on the first ring.

"Melody Lanes Café. What's your poison?" she said.

"Lulie. It's Jobe Carson. I'm running down a lead. Do you know if Joe had any tattoos?"

"He sure did. A big one on his arm. Why do you ask?"

I felt a tingle of anticipation. "Which arm?"

"His left one."

"Where on his left arm?"

"Where do you expect? Where every sailor from here to Shanghai has one. Right down from his shoulder. And his was a classic too, a big boobed girl sitting on an anchor with all sorts of snakes and curlicues spreading out around his arm. It was quite the work of art. He must have sat through many a painful session. He used to brag how he had parts of it done in different cities all over the Pacific Rim. Well, he didn't really brag, that wasn't like Joe, but you could tell he was proud in an odd sort of way that each part of it came from a different port of call. Kind of a living souvenir. Like those hats RV folks wear with the pins all stuck in 'em. Except in this case the pins were stuck in him."

I wasn't listening. I was too disappointed. This definitely took Joe out of the equation. Tattoo all right, but in the wrong place. Tattoo bad. I really didn't like Fern at all. Especially after she'd almost suffocated me in her garage. I was hoping I could pin something on her. But I guess not. I broke in on Lulie.

"I appreciate your help Lulie. I better go now. I need to check on some other things."

"Okay Jobe. Having any luck tracking down Joe?"

"Not much I'm sorry to say."

"That's too bad. When I saw you in the police reports in the paper this morning I thought you were up to something good. Withholding evidence huh? I was hoping it was evidence that would nail Fern to the wall."

"Me too," I said. "Me too. But a little needle just took her off the hook. I'll be in touch."

I hung up the phone and sat there for a moment. Damn. I tried Fred's hotel again. The receptionist was curt and efficient. It wasn't long before a voice I knew came on the line.

"Yes?" Fred was tentative.

"Fred. Jobe Carson. I got a quick question for you. Does Bill have any tattoos?"

"Why yes, Mr. Carson, lots of them. Tattoos, piercings, even a little scarification. He was really into what they call body art. Although I sure didn't see the art in it. Looked like he had a bad date with Rosie the Riveter if you ask me. I never saw the point of all that piercing and needle stuff. But what do you do? It was just another of those prickly subjects between us. If I had a dime for every argument we had over where he was going to stick his next piece of jewelry, I'd be—"

"Specifically Fred," I interjected, "Did he have a tattoo on his left wrist?"

"Oh yes. A weird design. He said it was a Mayan codex thing. Looked more like a bar code to me. I used to joke that he could use it in the grocery store to get an automatic twenty percent off any item. Just run it across the scanner while the checker wasn't looking. We never tried it though; it could have added an extra hundred dollars to our bill for all we knew..."

I listened to him ramble for a while as my memory brought up a picture of the tattoo I had seen on the severed arm. Mayan codex pretty well summed it up. I was going to have to call this case the winter solstice caper. Things were getting darker every day. I just hoped Henderson didn't want his advance back. Not to mention the bail money. I shook out of my depressing reverie and tuned back into Fred, who was still going full tilt.

"...and the time I went with him to the piercing convention at the Space Needle you'd have thought they didn't make so many surgical steel hoops in the whole country. And there were more studs than a builders supply store. When we went to—"

"Fred!" I shouted.

"What?"

"I gotta go. I need to get back to work on the case. You hang in there, okay?"

"Okay," he said. "Mr. Carson?"

"What?"

"You don't think Bill's alive, do you?"

"Hard to say, Fred."

"Well I think you're wrong," he said. "The other day as I was lying in bed here, I just realized that through all my worry I never paid attention to one thing. My real feelings. I don't feel like Bill is dead. I can't explain it, but I'm sure he's alive. Deep down in the core of my being I just know his life force is still going. It's there, pulsing away like a beating heart. Do you understand Mr. Carson? I know that he's still alive."

He was good. He had me going there for a bit. And who knows? Maybe he was telling the truth. Maybe Bill was alive somewhere. Maybe a certain someone had just relieved him of one of his tattooed limbs to test out a new dehydrator. Maybe someone like Fred.

"I gotta go," I said curtly.

"I feel like I'm being cut off," he said.

"Join the crowd," I said, and hung up.

One more call and my roundup would be complete. I checked my notebook for the number and punched it into the phone. The line buzzed eight times before a sleepy voice answered.

"Yes?"

"Suzie, Jobe Carson. That man of yours around?"

"No," she said slowly, "He had an early round of golf with Knudson. You'll have to call back at a better time."

I jumped in before she could hang up

"Suzie! Wait a minute. Maybe you can help me."

"I don't know..."

"Just a quick question: Did Mark's dad have a tattoo?"

"Um," she hesitated, "Not exactly."

"What do you mean 'not exactly?'"

"He had some numbers on his wrist."

"Numbers? How so?"

"Mark's grandfather was in a concentration camp in Germany during the war. Mark's dad tried to duplicate the numbers on his own wrist when he was a kid. With a pin and some ink. Mark's grandfather beat the hell out of him for it. Victor showed it to me one time. It was pretty crude. Kinda all mushed up and blurry. I asked him why he didn't have it taken off with laser surgery or something. He said he kept it as a reminder. Of how the road to hell is paved with good intentions. And something else..."

"What's that?"

"Of how hot tempers run in his family."

"Do they?"

"Do what?"

I was remembering that slap she had taken across the face. "Do hot tempers still run in the family?"

"Not really," she said quietly. "Mark just gets under a lot of pressure sometimes. And I don't help. I'm trying to do better."

"You'd do better to help yourself to someone without a 'pressure' problem Suzie. Really. Hitting someone like he hit you is not normal."

"What would you know about normal?" she asked sharply. "He hits me a lot less than my stepdad did. And he's getting better. Really." Before I could contradict her, she hung up.

Somehow she didn't sound convincing. But at least she'd answered my question about Victor. That brought the total to three. Elizabeth's husband, Victor, and Bill. All of them with tattoos. All of them lefties. All of them still missing. And all my instincts coming up blank.

The phone rang under my hand and scared the hell out of me. I picked it up with a strange sense of impending doom.

"Jobe, it's Kathryn. I thought you'd like to know. Knudson just had me call the media. He's having a coroner's inquest, and he got the Sheriff to arrest Fred again. He's claiming Fred is a public menace."

Chapter 55

I hung up the phone, went into the living room and collapsed on the couch. Everything was falling apart. And worse, Knudson was winning again. That fat, pompous bastard. He was trying to gather all the publicity he could by having a coroner's inquest. He had enough evidence already to turn the case over to the regular prosecutor. But no. That would make him just a bit player in the legal process. He didn't want that. He wanted to champion his role for all to see. And get as much press for his next election bid as possible.

But that wasn't what was really bothering me. What was really bothering me was everything that was happening was flying in the face of my instincts. Fred just couldn't be the murderer. It just didn't feel right. It rubbed as painfully against my intuition as a finger on a cheese grater.

Intuition is a funny thing. I believe in it with all my heart—and brain. Not in any mumbo-jumbo sense either. I'm not about to start my own psychic hotline. Intuition is much more pedestrian. It's like an unknown processor clicking away on our brain's hidden hard drive that occasionally spits up important knowledge. Look at the facts. The great moments of inspiration in science have come at odd moments, like Newton's apple and Gell-Mann's quarks, but not until and only after the inspirees have crammed their heads full of the relevant data. Then, bingo, while they're not paying conscious attention, out comes the big nut.

I'd learned to trust my intuition over the years for that reason. Never to force it mind you, but trust it nonetheless. And in this instance my intuition was screaming that Fred was not the culprit. And that someone else was. A new inspiration hit me at that moment. Maybe I could use this inquest thing to my benefit. The information I could get in Fred's defense may not be substantive enough for a court of law. But it may be persuasive enough to convince a citizen's panel. After all, the main purpose of an inquest was to gather evidence from the public and interested parties, and from that determine whether an indictment should be issued against a certain individual. If I could derail Knudson's plan there, I might save all the trouble of proving beyond a reasonable doubt that Fred was innocent.

Because I've never really believed that it was up to the authorities to prove perpetrators were "guilty" beyond a reasonable doubt. The average jury member's mentality could be summed up in the infamous words of my former boss. "If he wasn't guilty, the police wouldn't have arrested him." Given the popularity of that stance, and the generally intolerant nature of jury pool peers, I didn't have much hope for the annoying and gay Fred once the wheels of justice rolled over him. Call me cynical.

But first off I needed some preparation. I got up from the couch and went back to the phone. It was time to gamble a little. I had my own suspicions about who the murderer might be. In fact, I was pretty damn certain. But that meant another thing too. I was pretty sure who the murderer was not. Besides, it was more than intuition this time, it was force of habit. I had gone through my whole life without kissing a killer. And I wasn't about to start now. I dialed Elizabeth's number one more time.

"Hello, Elizabeth's Environments."

"Elizabeth. Jobe again. I wonder if I could ask you a favor. Are you going to be at your store for a while?"

"Sure Jobe. Anything for you... I'll be here all day."

"Would you be able to break away for a little bit to run an errand for me?"

"I think so. My appointment book looks pretty sparse today. What did you have in mind?"

"A little intrigue."

"Oh boy. I love intrigue."

236

"Think you could do a little acting?"

"Really Jobe, I work with the public every day, don't I?"

"Good, I'll be there about 1:30."

"I'll be waiting with 'bated breath," she said.

"Then you better lay off the caviar, that's not the kind of fish eggs us po' folk use for bait."

She just laughed.

I called Henderson and told him I'd see him at 1:00. He was pretty pissed about the Fred situation but I got him calmed down by telling him that at least Kathryn and I were back on speaking terms. Though he got upset all over again when I said I was going to meet Elizabeth at 1:30. I couldn't blame him. Here he was shelling out all this dough and I was getting all the girls. I reminded him that the apparently positive nature of my romantic entanglements was more than offset by the amorous attention of Clevus the previous evening. He conceded that I had a point.

I then called my friend at the FBI lab in Seattle.

"Kim, how long to run a DNA analysis?"

"Less than 24 hours, usually. The new machines make it easier than a load of laundry."

"I may be sending something up to you next week. Could you squeeze me in?"

"I don't know, Jobe. Things are pretty booked up right now."

"What about if it meant smearing Knudson's face in a pile of his own crap?"

"Why didn't you say so? In that case, I could have it done yesterday."

"Great I'll send it out UPS Previous Day, and we'll have him suffering by last Tuesday."

"I'll be standing by," he said through his laughter.

One more call. My fingers nervously tapped out the number.

"Coroner's office."

"May I speak to Kathryn Olson please?"

"One moment."

My heart fluttered like an epileptic telegrapher.

"This is Kathryn."

"Kathryn, Jobe."

Silence.

I bulled ahead. "I'm sorry about the other day. There really is an explanation. Really. Could I make it up to you over dinner? Maybe we could go to that favorite place of yours. Please?"

"I don't know, Jobe."

"Kathryn," I said slowly. "I don't know either. I don't know anything. I'd just like to have a nice dinner with a very nice person. Let's just say it's my way of thanking you for all your help. How about it?"

I held my breath. Time stretched to infinity.

"Okay Jobe Carson. Just this once. But you'd better pick a nicer shade of lipstick this time. Bright scarlet's all wrong for your complexion."

"But what else would go with my red face? Let's say tomorrow night at 7:30."

"Awfully short notice Mr. Carson. I have a pretty full social calendar you know."

"Tell your cockapoo to get his own dinner."

"Ouch. You really know how to sweet talk a girl, don't you?" She laughed.

"Hey. I'm the one who should be hurt. If you remember, we already had a date for this Friday. I'll pick you up at 7:00."

"All right. See you then Jobe."

"Thanks Kathryn. Thanks."

I hung up feeling pretty good. It always helps to make a plan. Not to mention a date with a pretty girl. I made some lunch and lay down for a couple of winks. Maybe while I was napping my intuition would come up with another brilliant stroke.

CHAPTER 56

I awoke with a start. Warm blood flushed through my body as the fog cleared from my head. The phone was ringing. I looked at my watch. It was 1:02. I went into the kitchen and picked up the receiver.

"Where the hell are you?" Henderson snapped in my ear.

"Uh... Sorry," I stammered. "I must have fallen asleep."

"I'm not accustomed to people sleeping on my nickel, Carson."

"Sorry. It's been a trying couple of days. What's up?"

"Obviously not you," he was calming down. "I thought we were supposed to be meeting here at my office... Now."

"Sorry Steve. Maybe we should skip it. Is there anything we really need to accomplish? Fred's not there, right?"

"Right. No thanks to you and your formerly secret appendage. Fred's locked up so tight I can't even get any of my judge friends to spring him loose. Knudson's screaming in their collective ear, and to the media, that this guy is the worst thing to come down the pike since Hannibal Lecter. They're all worried the next time they stand for election the public will accuse them of turning loose a psychopath and Willie Horton them into early retirement."

"Then I have to act quickly. I don't want Fred to suffer any more than he has to. When's the inquest scheduled?"

"Knudson's got everybody stirred up for early next week. Apparently he doesn't have a big witness roster, and he's already called the jury administrators to come up with a citizens' panel. Looks like Tuesday at the latest. Maybe even Monday if he gets the citizens seated."

"He can't present his own evidence and conduct the inquest, can he?" I asked. "I heard him say he was going to do the analysis himself."

"My guess is he'll let the assistant coroner conduct the actual proceedings, but that he'll schedule himself as the star witness."

"Can you petition the inquest for special testimony?"

"I might be able to get you on as a character witness. And Knudson will probably let me speak just to make everything look fair."

"Good. That fits in with my hoped-for scenario just fine."

"What do you have in mind?"

"You'll have to see for yourself. I hope to get Fred off the hot seat by getting someone else on. You might need to be ready for some of that thinking on your feet that you're so famous for."

"You sure Jobe? I could move for a delay. Give you some time to nail things down."

"Not necessary," I said, more confident than I felt, "I want to bring Knudson down when he's puffed up the most. I owe that bastard the worst night of my life."

"All right then. Keep me informed."

"I will Steve. Thanks for your help, and your support."

"Let's just hope I'm not propping up an idiot. Fred is in a real tight spot. I know, and you know, that Knudson's out to get him; even if he has to bend the evidence to do it. I hope you have some mighty powerful stuff."

"Thanks for the vote of confidence, Steve. Jeez. As if I needed the extra expectations. I'm already under more pressure than Christ's Mohel."

"All I can say is, moil schmoil, you just better produce, Carson."

I hung up and looked at my watch again; just enough time to get to Elizabeth's store. Phase one was beginning. This plan better work.

I rushed downtown, parked and went into Elizabeth's place. True to her word, there was no one around.

"What can I do for you, Jobe?" she asked breathlessly.

"A little bit of drama," I replied. "What I'd like you to do is find out something from the guy over at Secondhand City. Apparently he thinks I'm some kind of snooper out to get him on tax charges or something. He won't tell me a thing. He won't even admit he owns the place."

"What do you need to find out?"

"First, if he's the owner. Secondly, if he ever purchased a piece of equipment; specifically, a food dehydrator from a private party. Like a couple that came in maybe, or a garage sale or something. Lastly, and most important, who he remembers selling that particular dehydrator to."

"A dehydrator?" she asked. "Like the one I had in back?"

"The very same."

"Can I ask why?"

"I'd rather you didn't, but I'll tell you this: Henderson will be really happy if you help."

"I'll go right now. What's the guy look like."

"You'll know him. Name's Curt. A man of very few words."

"But a man nonetheless."

"Exactly. Use your 'acting' skills, if you know what I mean."

"What makes you think I have 'acting' skills?"

"Elizabeth Honey, you could 'act' the robes off the pope himself. Now get on it. I got a client simmering in county hell."

She took a few moments to freshen her makeup and then headed over to Secondhand City. Forty-five minutes later she was back. I guess some guys need a little more acting than others.

"I think I got just about everything you need, Jobe," she boasted, flush with the thrill of victory.

"Do tell," I said.

"First, he does remember buying a dehydrator recently. He's only bought one in the last six months. Some lady came in with it all boxed up and looking new. I asked for a description, but he got real canny at that point. I'm pretty sure he knows though. Second, he also remembers exactly who he sold it to. He was rather graphic on that subject. Said he fobbed it off on a flamer for only twenty bucks lower than list price for a new one. Told the guy that it was brand new, never been used and so on, got it at a warehouse scratch and dent sale. He was quite proud of himself. Especially since he only bought it for about thirty bucks from the mysterious lady in the first place. Said he really screwed the faggot good, wasn't fooled by his disguise for a minute, recognized him from when he was in with another one before but decided the best way to get back at them both was to take their money."

"I knew he was an entrepreneur."

"And quite the Lothario as well," Elizabeth laughed. "He asked if I was doing anything this Friday. He wouldn't let me out of the store till he showed me his special treasures in the back room. That man has some antiques you wouldn't believe. And I'm glad I went. Because here's the really good part—I found something there I think you could use. In case Curt needs some 'help' with his memory sometime."

"What's that?"

"Not so fast Buster. You owe me a lot already. There's a price for this one."

"And that price is?"

"Dinner at the finest restaurant in Seattle. With me. On you."

My first thought was of Kathryn. The last thing I wanted was to upset her again. Then I thought of Fred sitting in jail, wondering if he'd ever get out. Then I thought of Knudson, laughing wickedly as he drove away from my house with the arm. Then I thought of the arm, and who I was sure it belonged to. And to whom it needed to be returned. It was only one dinner. And Elizabeth was not a completely objectionable companion. I'd just have to try to explain it to Kathryn. I hoped she'd understand.

"All right," I said. "Deal. What's the big secret?"

"Mayan artifacts."

"What?"

"Mayan artifacts. He has a whole display case full of illegally acquired Mayan antiquities. Tomb robber stuff. The feds could burn him for having them big time."

"Beautiful, Elizabeth!" I swept her into my arms and gave her a big hug in congratulation.

She hugged me back and laughed. But as she turned up her face to mine I remembered the last time we'd found ourselves in such an embrace. I touched her lips briefly with my fingertip, put my hands on her shoulders and pushed her gently back.

"I gotta run," I said to her bewildered look. "Thanks a lot Elizabeth. You've earned a dinner for sure." I hurried out of the store and headed home. I felt like I hadn't seen my kids for a week. And for some reason I suddenly felt dirty. Maybe if I started now, I'd be able to take enough showers by tomorrow night's dinner.

CHAPTER 57

The kids and I caught up on old times that evening over delivered pizza. Jack and Kiah were particularly interested in the gruesome details of the jail's toilet facilities. "You mean you have to crap out in front of God and everybody?" Jack asked with blasphemous incredulity.

"If you stop to think about it Jack, you're always crapping out in front of an omniscient God."

Kiah, recently from the theological debates of his 12th grade humanities course, laughed knowingly.

"Still," I continued. "It weren't pretty. Especially without pillow soft, two-ply tissue."

That dispensed with, conversation turned to my having kept the arm in the garage a secret. Neither Kiah nor Jack could believe it had been there under their noses for so long. Jack, always the one to pull wings off flies and similarly engage in acts of hands-on scientific experimentation, was particularly peeved that he had missed the opportunity to explore the experience of independent limb manipulation. It wasn't long before the inevitable question came up. Kiah was the first to broach the subject.

"What I don't get is... Why did the cops suddenly come busting down our door... and then go straight for the arm? They didn't search the rest of the house at all. Who else knew about the arm besides you, Dad?"

I looked at Miranda.

Miranda looked down at the floor.

"You told her?" Jack protested. His incredulity was working overtime.

"She and I discovered it together." I said.

"And you didn't tell us?" They both said to her, with older brother vanity fully punctured and hissing.

"No," she muttered.

"But you did tell someone, didn't you?" Kiah said. I think he has a future in the prosecutor's office.

Miranda's silence spoke volumes.

"Who did you tell, Honey?" I asked gently. "It's okay, I understand."

"I told my friend Christen."

"Christen, huh?" I probed. "That wouldn't by any chance be the same Christen that's on a basketball team with Knudson's niece?"

"I guess..." She was pouting now.

The boys and I looked at each other and shook our heads.

"Oh well," I said. "All's well that ends well."

"And that's swell," said Kiah.

"And I knew she'd tell," said Jack.

"And you can go to hell," said Miranda.

We busted up laughing.

Next morning dawned foggy and cold. Winter was upon us, and the days for the next three months would alternate between gray, cold and dry and gray, windy and wet. Only one thing was certain, they'd all be gray. Time to break out the Seasonal Affective Disorder light banks.

Kids off to school, I puttered around the house for a bit and decided on my next move. It didn't seem safe to put all my eggs in the Secondhand City basket. I needed something more impressive than the testimony of a Mayan artifact smuggler. I called up Kim at the FBI lab.

"Could you requisition a specific piece of tissue from the coroner's office without alerting the coroner?" I asked.

"Probably," he said after some thought. "Because we sometimes are called in to verify results, we have the power to perform quality control inspections on short notice. What did you have in mind, Jobe?"

"I need a DNA analysis. The specimen is a severed arm that the coroner has in his possession. I have reason to believe he is may tamper with the results."

"How could he do that? If he does a DNA analysis of the tissue it can only give one result."

"I don't know if he's going to do a DNA analysis. I'm not sure if has another specimen to compare it to. I think he's just going to type blood and do a gross examination for identifying marks and such. I'm just worried he'll do his best to obscure any evidence that doesn't lead to his conclusion. And since he's the coroner, he's calling the shots. I'd just like to have a DNA read-out on record. Just in case."

"Sounds reasonable. Hold on..."

There were rustling sounds and muted voices on the other end.

"Wait a minute," Kim said. "Speak of the devil. I just got a FedEx shipment from Knudson's office. Let me open it up."

There were more scratchy noises, and the sound of paper being cut, then a rip.

"Yo ho. There's a couple of samples...and a request for a DNA analysis. Seems their machine is on the fritz. Of course I don't know if this is your severed friend. Do you have a chain of evidence code number?"

"No, but I could probably get one. I'll call you right back."

A quick call to Kathryn and I had the code number. I called back Kim. It matched.

"All right," he said excitedly. "We won't have to go through a mock inspection after all. Old Knudson may have just handed us the keys to the candy store."

"Good. Maybe we can send him an all day sucker."

"Or some dum dums," he said. He was laughing as he hung up.

I put the phone back on the hook. Then I nearly jumped out of my chair when it rang under my hand.

"Jobe. This is Lulie. Can you come down here to the café?" There was urgency in her voice.

246

"Sure thing, Lulie. I'll be right there."

I drove quickly out to Lacey. As I pulled into the parking lot, I saw one of the new Volkswagen beetles parked across two slots. Jeez. When will people learn to park their frickin cars? You'd think every third person fails the "straight in parking" portion of their driving examination the way vehicles are skewed helter-skelter everywhere.

I walked into the café and was greeted with a disturbing scene: Lulie, sitting on the customer side of the counter, her arm around the shoulders of a sobbing young woman. A woman I knew too well. Suzie.

"You know each other?" I blurted out.

Lulie shot me a dirty look.

"Of course we know each other. Suzie used to work for me."

Suzie was still crying. She looked at me and started a wave of sobbing as well. Her face was a mess. There were scratches on her forehead and she had an angry looking welt on the side of her cheek. A big purple bruise was starting to form around the edges of her right eye. Her hair was tangled and clotted with blood that had oozed from her forehead. Lulie had a wet bar rag and was dabbing at the edges of Suzie's lips, which looked like they'd almost been bitten through. Probably when she got the red mark on her chin. Which was no doubt caused by a sharp uppercut to her jaw.

"Mark?" I asked quietly.

She nodded her head and started to moan.

"Did you call the police?" I asked Lulie.

"She won't let me," she answered. "Said she'll just say she ran into a door. I don't know what to do."

I shrugged my shoulders. What can you do?

"Suzie. Why don't you tell me what happened?"

"It's not easy..." she looked up at me through smeared mascara. "It's all your fault you know."

"My fault?" I asked.

"Yeah," she said, a quaver in her voice. "Everything was fine till I told him this morning that you called yesterday."

"What did he say to that?"

She burst into another spasm of tears. I waited. Lulie gave her another hug.

"He asked me if I said anything or if you asked anything and I told him what I had said about his dad's tattoo and temper. Then he blew up. He said I had no right to go blabbing family secrets. He started slapping me around. After a while I fought back. I scratched him and hit him. That just made it worse..."

Another wave of sobs overtook her. Lulie and I exchanged glances while we waited it out. Suzie sucked in a ragged breath and continued.

"Pretty soon he knocked me down and jumped on me when I was on my back. He had my shoulders pinned under his legs and was starting to choke me. Calling me a dumb bitch and squeezing my neck so I couldn't breathe. I got one arm loose and reached up and dug my fingernails into his cheek. He screamed and rolled off and I got up and ran out the door. I drove here..."

She started crying again; long racking sobs that shook her whole body. Lulie held her close and waited for it to subside. I reached over and took her hand. That's when the full magnitude of the event hit me. I looked down at Suzie's fingertips. I could see clotted blood crusted around her nails. I waited for a while longer while she settled down. But I didn't let go of her hand.

"Lulie," I finally said, "Could I have a little plastic to-go cup? With a lid. And do you have a toothpick? Preferably an individually wrapped one."

She looked at me questioningly but got what I asked. Suzie was quieter now. The worst seemed to have passed.

"Suzie," I said, "I need to do something that could help you, and may end up helping everyone in the long run. Is this the hand you scratched Mark's face with?"

I held up the hand I was holding.

"Yes," she said.

"Lulie," I said, "remember this. You may have to testify to it someday."

I unwrapped the toothpick and ran the tip of it under Suzie's fingernails, sliding loose little gobbets of flesh. Flesh that I hoped would render the DNA signature of Mark Wasen; a signature significantly close to a man with a homemade tattoo. Who golfed left-handed. Lulie watched me use another freshly unwrapped toothpick to scrape the specimen into the cup.

"It's funny," she said.

"What's that, Lulie?" I asked.

"How different men are."

"How so?"

"Well, you take a good man like Joe. Struggled all his life. But he'd give you the shirt off his back. Hell, he once donated a kidney to his dying sister. One day, when it was really busy here and my dog got hit by a car out in the parking lot, Joe took him to the vet because I couldn't get away to do it myself. One of the nicest men you ever want to meet, and he's stuck with that horrid wife. And here he is missing. Then you take a bastard like Mark, never had to do a day's work in his life and he treats everyone like shit. I don't know what you're planning to do with that stuff, but count me in. I'll testify to whatever you want. Or do whatever you want. We don't even have to go to court. We can go over and commit a little justice right now. When I was a girl back on my parents' sheep ranch, I harvested my share of prairie oysters."

I looked at her. She had picked up a wicked looking paring knife while she spoke. She was serious. I couldn't help crossing my legs.

"Maybe soon," I said. "First I got to make some calls. Thanks for calling me here. I think you've finally given me the last thing I've been looking for."

I grabbed the cup and gave Suzie a gentle pat on the back.

249

"Stay with Lulie for a while," I said, though I didn't have much hope it would do any good. "Try to get some perspective. There are lots of men who aren't assholes. Why don't you ask Lulie to tell you more about Joe?"

I went back home and made some calls. One of them was to FedEx.

CHAPTER 58

When the kids got home I announced another night of delivered pizza.

"Oh no..." moaned Miranda, ever-conscious of eating healthy.

"Can we get buffalo wings too?" inquired Jack. He should have lived in New Orleans. Somewhere in the genetic shuffle he had acquired the Lagniappe gene; always lobbying for something extra. If I offered him a new car, completely decked out with A/C, surround sound, automatic windows, locks, and the full rally sports package, the first thing out of his mouth would be: "...and leather seats?"

Kiah blew out a sarcastic snort.

"What?" Jack asked, cueing in to something other than barbequed chicken appendages.

"Dad's got a date," Kiah sneered.

"It's business," I said.

"Business with who?" asked Miranda.

"Kathryn," I mumbled.

"Oh." She turned abruptly and headed for her room.

"Hey," I said to the boys, "Beats leftovers, right?"

They went silently into the front room and turned on the TV.

I picked up Kathryn about 7:00. I'd fought the urge to put on an extra sweater before I left home. I was pretty sure it was only locally chilly. I rang the doorbell of her little house. She opened the door and greeted me warmly. She was dressed in a lovely cinnamon colored silk and cotton top and a short black skirt. Her black leather jacket set off their simplicity and elegance. She spoke a few words to her mom's caretaker and then we got into my battered vehicle and headed for Trinacria.

We parked a block away and walked to the small restaurant. As we opened the door my mind was flooded with what must have been some Jungian collective unconscious impression of neighborhood bistros in Sicily, where soft Mediterranean breezes caused gentle waves to lap at the rocky shores of a stunning island. Olfactory gusts of garlic and peppers blew through the warm air of the cafe to the sound of keening operatic voices, whose echoing tones extolled the vicissitudes of love in a language I could not understand but could somehow comprehend.

A waitress came up to where we stood.

"Yeah," she said, "Reservations?"

"Yes we have, Heather," said Kathryn, "It's under Carson I believe."

"Table number one," she said and led the way back to a small table by an old piano. Funny. She had only spoken a total of five words but had somehow managed to pack in enough sarcasm to fill a volume. I pulled out a chair for Kathryn and looked around. There were only about nine tables in the whole room, seating no more than fourteen people at that point, but everyone seemed to be in a pleasant mood. Not a sour impatient look on the whole lot, which in my experience of the human herd was downright unheard of. There's always at least one person in ten who can't be satisfied. I heard the sounds of a man in the back, presumably in the kitchen, hollering something to someone in a Sicilian accent. His tone was both brusque and artistic, like Michelangelo bellowing for an acolyte to bring him a bucket of paint. Quickly. Can't he see the ceiling is starting to dry?

"Heather!" shouted the voice from the back. Our waitress shrugged knowingly and headed for the rear. Kathryn laughed.

"What do you think?" she asked.

"Fantastic!" I was in awe. "So many different people here and all of them so apparently happy."

"That's why this is my favorite restaurant. It's like a blast from another century—or another culture. I've only heard a cell phone once

252

in this place. And I've never seen that person here again. Eugenio cooks everything fresh and simple. One time he brought me a salad with the freshest, sweetest romaine I've ever tasted. He had just bought it at the farmer's market that morning and it was wonderful. That's all the salad here is really, romaine, with just a little basil and red wine vinegar and oil. I'm sure you'll love it. The salad here is served after the meal by the way. It freshens your breath and adds a piquant counterpoint to the pasta."

A new waitress appeared at our table.

"Hi Laura," said Kathryn, "How's Sheila's baby?"

"Little Eugenio is doing fine," Laura said, "He sits on the kitchen table and tells his dad when the pasta's done. Have you decided what you're going to have?"

"I think so," Kathryn said, looking at me. "Would you like to choose the pizza ingredients?"

"Sure," I said, quickly glancing at the list on the back of the menu.

Kathryn ordered the Broccoli Penne, burnt and hot. I didn't know what the heck she was talking about. I was also noticing with dismay that there was no pepperoni or Canadian bacon or salami listed on the menu.

"What's this 'Coppa'?" I asked desperately, trying not to seem too much the country buffoon.

"It's an interesting spiced ham," Laura said. Another waitress was walking by.

"I think it tastes like a cross between prosciutto and salami," she said. "Hi Kathryn."

"Hi Jody."

"We'll have that then," I said, "and how about spinach on it as well."

Kathryn looked at me questioningly as the waitresses left.

"It just seemed like the right thing," I said.

Heather was soon back with a couple of glasses of the house red wine. A finer vintage never crossed my lips. Like everything else in the place, it was warm, it was robust and it was authentic. Moments later Laura put a small plate of peperonata on the table with a little basket of fresh baked bread. The peperonata was a sautéed concoction of red and green peppers, onions, garlic and, of all things, potatoes. The bread was in the shape of little bow ties, and sopped up the rich sauce of the peperonata with perfect permeability. Andrea Bocelli was belting out a couple of arias in the distance and the room noise was starting to increase. Kathryn and I made some small talk while I absorbed the ambience. I was feeling a little flushed by the time our meal arrived.

Laura placed a steaming bowl of tubular pasta and sauce on our table. The broccoli penne was incredible. Having it burnt and hot, as it turned out, meant that the chef had fried the pasta a bit after boiling it, giving it a chewier texture and nuttier flavor than just cooking it in water could have done. The tomato-based sauce was caramelized a bit and perked up with hot peppers as well. The broccoli bits and garlic cloves scattered through the dish added wonderful alternating bursts of flavor and texture.

I heard another bellowing: "Heather" and soon our first waitress approached our table with a sizzling pizza on a plate. The best mozzarella cheese I was ever to taste was oozing off the edges of the freshly cut pieces and the coppa and spinach were artistically strewn across the pie in delicate distribution. Flavor was obviously important to this mysterious and vocal chef. But more importantly, though I could see he wasn't afraid of quantity, he still understood that proportion was paramount to gustatory enjoyment.

When I bit into the pizza I was instantly transported to tastebud nirvana.

"My God," I said.

Kathryn smiled widely in agreement. "I told you this was a fantastic place."

"Mmmph," I agreed. "And I bet it remains fantastic—because it won't ever be a chain."

"That's true. Which is good. The Red Lobster folk and the Olive Garden folk will keep packing away their endless breadsticks and salad bars, and the folk like us will still be able to get in here and enjoy real food."

"Here's to discriminating taste... and not too many people having it." I lifted my empty glass in toast. The ever-attentive Laura brought a bottle over to fill it. As she walked away I lifted my glass to Kathryn again.

"And here's to a beautiful dinner companion," I said seriously.

"Oh Jobe..."

"Kathryn, I've got a confession to make."

"You don't have to," she protested.

"No, I want to. You deserve an explanation."

She waited.

"I know that I'm a hard person to get to know," I said, "and I know that I'm all over the place emotionally. But I want you to understand that I value our friendship too much to screw it up by messing around with other women."

"Jobe. Stop. You can do whatever you want. It's not like we're going together or anything. I can't very well put constraints on who you see or what you do. Forget about my little outburst the other day. I was just shocked. I thought that... since you weren't seeing me... you weren't seeing anybody. I guess I was wrong. That doesn't mean we still can't be good friends. That is if you're not serious about anybody else..."

She sounded real noble. I almost started to tease her about her martyr-like tone, but thought better of it quickly. I had definitely hurt her the other day. And I definitely regretted it.

"Kathryn, I'm not 'seeing' anyone. I don't expect you to believe anything you don't want to believe but here's the reality. I'm working on a case. One of the suspects is a woman. Some people would say she's an attractive woman. Though I personally don't find her to be. Her more obvious attributes would probably entice your average male. I don't expect most women, especially those that buy into the Cosmo mystique, to get it, but a lot of guys like me are drawn to a relationship for other than those two reasons. However prominent they appear to be. I guess what I'm trying to say is; there are Olive Garden women and there are Trinacria women.

"Anyhow. This gal has taken a fancy to me, and the other day she kissed me. That's what you saw on my lips. I didn't originate the kiss, I didn't promote the kiss, and though I'm fully aware I sound like our former president here, I didn't enjoy the kiss."

"Stop," Kathryn said. "You don't have to tell me all this."

"I do. You may not understand it all, but I have to say it. And I have to tell you this too: The other day, yesterday as a matter of fact, I made a deal with her. I used her to get some information I needed from a person I couldn't have got it from myself. She, because of her 'special' attributes, could. I think the information will help me break open this case. She made me promise to take her to dinner in Seattle in exchange for some extra information she was holding out. I agreed. I'm sorry."

"Jobe," Kathryn said slowly, "Thanks for telling me. I appreciate your honesty. And since we're being honest I admit I'm not happy you're going to another town to have dinner with an attractive woman. But I guess you have to do what you have to do. I can live with that."

"Thanks," I was a little amazed at how the conversation was going.

"Hey, we're just friends anyhow, right?" She laughed ruefully. "Here's to friendship." She held up her glass and knocked back the last half of her wine.

Eugenio chose that moment to make an appearance.

"Kathryn," he said, "Who is-a your new boyfriend?"

"This is Jobe Carson," she said. "And he's just a friend."

"Right. I'm-a happy to meet you," he said, his Sicilian accent adding pleasant extra syllables to the endearing cadence of his speech. "You take-a good care of her, right?"

"Absolutely." I said.

"Good." He flashed me a jaunty smile.

"The penne and the pizza were wonderful," I said. "The best I've ever had. You are an artist."

He glowed with pride.

"Yes," he said. "The coppa and the spinach... that-a was a good combination. You pick-a good. Some people they pick-a the wrong things to put together on a pizza. I won't-a do it. I just say, I'm-a out."

We all laughed. I knew it. A true culinary artist. He went around to some other tables and greeted other regulars. Heather came over and took our plates to wrap the leftovers while Jody put salads on the table. Kathryn and I just savored the romaine and each other. After a while Laura collected out empty salad plates and brought us the best tiramisu I've ever tasted.

"I see Sheila's back to making the tiramisu," Kathryn said.

Whoever this Sheila was, she made a mean dessert. No sooner had the thought formed in my brain than another woman approached the table carrying what looked like a bundle of blankets.

"Hell-o-o," she said to Kathryn, "Eugenio said you had brought in a handsome man... one that had a way with words."

"Is this the new baby, Sheila?" cooed Kathryn.

"Yes..." said Sheila liltingly. Soon they were ooh-ing and aah-ing over the squirming little creature in the bundle. I politely kept my distance. If there was one thing I'd learned from being a single dad, babies grew up to be trouble.

"The tiramisu was fantastic," I finally broke in.

"Why thank you," Sheila said.

The baby made a couple of little squawks.

"Uh oh," she said, "Time to go feed the new boss."

"Thanks for a wonderful evening." I said.

"Our pleasure. We hope we see you again." she said. She gave Kathryn a wink and walked off towards the back.

I winked at Kathryn myself. "I almost forgot. One other thing," I reached into my coat for a newspaper clipping. "I'd like to you to do me a favor. Ever bought a vacu-packer before?"

CHAPTER 59

"Buy a vacu-packer?" Kathryn asked.

"Yeah," I said, "I need to know how easy it would be to get one of these things. Used. I got the idea when was looking through one of those weekly papers and found this ad in the 'Used Appliances for Sale' section. Whoever it is wants to sell their Dee-Luxe Vacu-Packer 2000. Which, coincidentally, is exactly the model I'm looking for."

"Why do you need me?" Kathryn laughed. "Shouldn't a big, manly, private detective like you be able to buy an appliance?"

"But, but," I stuttered, "I don't know nothin' 'bout buying no appliances Miss Kathryn."

She laughed again.

"But seriously," I said. "There's the remote chance the party I want you to buy it from is connected with this case. And they may not sell it to me. They won't know you. Your pretty face hasn't been splashed across the papers recently."

"Great picture of you in the police reports by the way," Kathryn said. "I said to myself, there's a face that should be stamping out license plates."

"Yeah," I replied, "thanks for the vote of 'con'-fidence. Although with my three kids, the thought of living with a bunch of hardened criminals seems mighty attractive."

"I bet you'd be a real hit in the exercise yard with that cute little butt of yours," she said.

"Kathryn!" My eyes widened in mock alarm. "I'm surprised at you."

Just then Eugenio came by the table. He looked first at Kathryn, then at me, and sized up our expressions.

"She's a-hot, yes?" he asked with a friendly leer.

We all laughed.

"I guess it was just the wine," she said, as we got up to leave.

"Oh no," I said, "You're a-hot all right."

All the gals came over and wished us a happy evening, I was not too inebriated to note a few leers exchanged among the womenfolk as well. We bade them all goodbye. Somehow, with the genteel and rustic charm of the place, archaic speech and mannerisms seemed appropriate.

We walked slowly back to my car. I opened the door on Kathryn's side and held her hand as she got in. I drove us to her house. We were mostly silent on the way, basking in the glow of a wonderful evening. When we arrived, I walked her to her door.

She put her key in the lock and clicked it over. Then she turned to face me. I put my hands on her hips and drew her a little closer.

We kissed.

The evening was perfect.

After a blessed eternity we separated. I looked into her eyes and saw what I hoped was pleasure, and understanding.

"Goodnight Kathryn," I said. "Thank you for a wonderful evening."

"Thank you, Jobe," she said softly. "Thank you."

I had turned and made it halfway back to my car before reality reared its ugly head.

"Oh yeah," I said, reaching back into my pocket for the newspaper clipping and returning to the doorway. "Here, I almost forgot to give you this. I've circled the number. Call this person and try to get the vacu-packer. This weekend. We need it by Monday for sure. And try to get a receipt. And get it signed and dated. Tell 'em you need it for taxes or something."

"Yes sir, Mr. Carson, Sir," she said crisply, "I'll do my best. And I'll call you after I get it. If I get it."

"Thank you, Kathryn. I appreciate it. As one of my suspects would say: This will really help me dot all the p's and q's"

"Thanks for a beautiful time Jobe."

"You're welcome," I said, "Thanks for giving me another chance."

I took the long way home. I wasn't ready to face the happy family yet. I had some emotional sorting out to do. And it wouldn't do for the kids to see me in tears.

I didn't know what to do. I loved my wife with all my heart. I couldn't help but feel like I was cheating on her. And yet... Kathryn was a warm and wonderful person who I could really grow to love. In a way far different from any love I'd ever had. The real problem was; the only person I could ever talk to about an ethical dilemma of this magnitude was precisely the person whose absence brought it about: My missing wife.

I looked around and found to my surprise that I was driving on the road where she'd most likely disappeared. A shadowy figure was moving on the edge of the road up ahead. I could see the reflections on the heels of his or her shoes. As I got closer, it became obvious it was a her. I looked in my far sideview mirror. Not a headlight for miles. The road here ran along a little lake on one side and an alder thicket on the other. And there were very few houses. I slowed my vehicle. The woman turned around with a look of sudden panic and headed off the shoulder into the thicket. I stopped the car, grabbed a flashlight from the glove compartment and got out.

"Hey," I yelled out, "Be careful. People have got lost out here."

She didn't turn but ran deeper into the woods. I saw that there was a faint trial that led in the direction of some dim lights in the distance. It looked like a little development alongside the shore of another small lake. I stopped to listen. I could hear the croaks of frogs and the whining chirps of crickets sawing away at their relentless mating chorus. I ran along the trail for a while, soaking in the night air and trying to run out the angst I felt over the evening's emotional turmoil.

I heard a muffled "whoof" up ahead and the sound of something, or someone, crashing into brittle wood. I quickened my pace. It wasn't long before I came up on a figure laid out on the side of the trail. She was lying still, except for the motion of her heaving chest, as her body tried to draw in enough air to sustain her after her exertion. It looked like she'd hit her head on a big branch when she had fallen. As I played the beam of my flashlight around I saw the root that had tripped her glistening on the trail; worn down by numerous encounters with inattentive feet.

She looked so vulnerable lying there. Unconscious to all the world and yet so full of life. I touched her head to see if any blood was coming from her scalp. All I felt was the cool damp of her sweat soaked hair. I ran my fingers down to her neck to check her pulse, which was slowing rapidly as she came back to her resting heart rate. I turned her over and looked at her face.

Then I started to cry. I could see the distant lights of the development through my tears. But no other cars had gone by on the road since I had started my run. No other people to see or hear or notice anything had gone wrong with this gentle woman under my hands. No one to have the slightest clue what had taken place. No one to care whether she would ever get up again. She could die right now, and I could drag her body into the thicket off the side of the trail and no one would ever find her. No one would ever know what had happened on this quiet evening in this isolated place.

Maybe even someday I would forget.

CHAPTER 60

She stirred under my hand. Her eyes opened slowly, then widened in alarm.

"It's okay," I said, "It looks like you tripped. I'm sorry if I scared you. Are you okay?"

"I guess so," she said, twisting her neck a little and moving her limbs to see if anything was broken.

I rose quickly. "Let me help you up," I said, and offered my hand.

"Thanks," she said, but still justifiably wary, ignored it and stood up by herself.

"No problem," I said. "It's not very safe out here at night. Would you like to borrow my flashlight?"

"That's okay," she said, "I don't have far to go." She took a cellphone out of her hip bag and punched a few numbers. "Hello, Honey. I'm just on the other side of the lake. Come looking for me if I'm not home in five minutes."

"Have a good run," I said and turned away as she headed down the trail. I was glad at least that she would make it home.

I went home myself and crawled into bed. I slept badly.

The weekend was filled with all the paraphernalia of fatherhood: Basketball games and horses and cleaning and laundry and all manner of leisurely pursuits that bleed away the daylight hours like a Type A vampire phlebotomist. I'm always amazed how tired I am after a weekend. I guess I try to do too much. Or maybe grocery shopping just drains away my life energy. Supermarkets of the lamia.

I spent part of my time reviewing what I hoped would be the best scenario for Monday morning's inquest. It turned out it was to be Monday. The Sunday papers were full of Knudson's finest. And it was pretty cheesy stuff: How he was going to rid the world of the evil influences of homosexuality. How it was high time people exposed the gay agenda for what it was; an attempt to overthrow the standards of decency that God and the Founding Fathers had established in this great country. How he was sick of "don't ask, don't tell" and it was time somebody told the truth and stood up for it too. His speeches were littered with more sound bites than a national nominating convention. You'd think he was inventing a new medical specialty: audio-orthodontia.

Each article made me madder and madder. He had no business crucifying Fred before he ever came to a trial of his peers. All the evidence wasn't in, and pandering to the press certainly didn't serve the community at large; nominally his charge as an elected public official. I was pretty sure the Founding Fathers had something else in mind when they insisted on the freedoms of expression and religion. They could easily have written a pretty narrow form of Protestantism into the constitution. They certainly had the majority to do so back then. But their wisdom transcended the moment. Having seen the excesses of human religious zeal, they were well aware that one lamb's straight and narrow was another's slaughter chute. And that should any one religious sect come into absolute power, you could kiss democracy goodbye. Farewell personal freedom, say hi to theocracy. And it's attendant fanatical wars. Hello Mullah, hello Father, meet my children: cannon fodder.

Heavy thoughts for a Sunday before a trial. But I needed to steel myself for what I knew would be a delicate and painful confrontation. My immediate goal would be to somehow silence Knudson while presenting the evidence I knew could clear Fred. That wouldn't be easy. Since he, Knudson, was after all the person who was calling the inquest. My next problem would be to make sure I didn't present my evidence too soon. Knudson needed to be pretty far out on his limb before I cut it off. But not too late either. I didn't want him so far I couldn't turn the citizen's panel back in my direction before they fell along with him. My experience is, once a person is committed to the limb of an idea, they tend to hang on to it. And they'll trot out any number of questionable facts and specious arguments to hold on to that prejudice. Even while the ground of reality is rushing up to meet them. Ownership is a very strong force, and whether it be material things or personal ideas, people will defend what they perceive as their property with every effort.

So I needed to move early enough to overcome Knudson's bombast. I knew that as objectionable as he was personally, he could be quite charming in front of a group. He'd unlimber that aw shucks, cornpone likeability of his and have the crowd eating out of his jovial fat hand. "We're just ordinary folks," he'd say, "and this here pre-vert done went on a whacked-out rampage. Thought he'd start his own home chopping network…"

The panel would laugh, mentally slap Knudson on the back, and feel real good about sending Fred to the lethal injection table.

Henderson would be pissed. The hardest part about being a lawyer for the defense is you have to go up second. You can't help but seem a little defensive, which in our culture, is tantamount to admitting guilt. The best thing a defense lawyer has going for him is the jury selection process; that's when he has the chance to get the final decision makers on his side early. Because there he has the opportunity to speak first, and establish his rapport with the jury pool as a whole before any actual jurors are picked. With any luck, they'll remember what a nice guy the lawyer was while he was picking them for the jury, and they'll extend their goodwill to his poor misunderstood client. At least that's what every defense attorney hopes.

There was the beauty of Knudson's plan. At a coroner's inquest, the panel of citizens was selected without all that rigamarole. This wasn't a trial per se. It was just an opportunity to establish if there were enough facts to return an indictment. Of course, then the real trial prosecutors would have the advantage of having an earlier body of citizens pre-condemning the defendant. Not that that really mattered to Knudson. What really mattered was the amount of media attention he could extract from the event.

Well I was hoping he could have a lot of media attention too. Negative. I owed him. And like my mom always used to say: If you're going to smear someone's nose in his own crap, it'll be that much stinkier if you do it with an audience.

Now all I could do was wait. I hoped Kathryn had come up with the vacu-packer. I hoped everything would fall into place as planned. These elaborate set-ups suffered from house of cards syndrome. One misplaced gust of serendipity and the whole thing could come tumbling down.

The phone rang.

"Jobe. Kathryn. I got what you wanted."

"The Dee-Luxe Vacu-Packer?"

"2000."

"Signed receipt?"

"Signed, sealed, and soon to be delivered. Where would you like it?"

"I'd like you to keep it. The farther it stays away from me the better. I'd like you to be able to swear on a stack of bibles that it never left your sight. Bring it to the anteroom off the inquest chambers tomorrow morning. Can you avoid Knudson?"

"I think so. He usually likes to come in the front with a flourish. I don't know that he's ever been in that room."

"Good, I'll try not to leave you there too long. Thanks again. You're the best."

"Thanks Jobe. I'll be there. I just hope I have a job afterwards."

"You will, I'll make sure Knudson thinks you're there under a threat of some sort."

"All right Jobe. I see you tomorrow morning."

"Wish me luck."

"I do," she said, "You'll need it."

I hung up. Tomorrow was the big day. I felt like a teenager going on his first date. I hoped I didn't get a zit.

CHAPTER 61

I was distracted the next morning when I sent the kids off to school. As I finished my preparations, Miranda took my hand.

"Everything will go okay, Daddy," she said. "Remember what Mom used to say: 'Winning a marathon starts in your head.'"

"I know, Miranda," I said as I walked her out to the bus stop. "I think I have the mental toughness. I just hope everything falls into place in the right order. Human beings can be so contrary sometimes."

"I'm sure it'll go just right." She kissed me on the cheek, gave me a big hug and got on the bus. The bus driver gave me a wink and drove off.

I got in my car, headed to the courthouse complex and drove all away around to the back before I found a place to park. I noticed that Kathryn's car was already there. And Henderson's. As I made my way to the courtroom I ran into the crime reporter from the local paper.

"Ready for another steaming stew of horse manure?" he asked.

"Fresh from Knudson to you," I answered. "It's nice of you to print his pronouncements with all the chunks intact. Ever think of writing less uncritically?"

"That's for the editorial department," he laughed, "I'm just a straight reporter. I just fling the muck people squeeze out. I leave it to others to rake it."

"Nice allusion," I replied. "We better get inside before the horseflies attack."

That's when I ran into Henderson. And an annoying delay at the entrance of the courthouse building. I was nervous as a cat by the time we finally made it through the anti-terrorism check-in.

We hustled into the courtroom. A couple of cameras from the local access station were set up on the perimeter. One of the local news stringers for the big stations in Seattle was there gathering up potentially incendiary footage as well. I went over to him.

"Hey Burke, keep your lens trained on Knudson's face," I said. "I guarantee a photogenic explosion."

"You serious, Jobe? You're gonna blow up his honor?"

"Let's just say it's about time someone pricked his ego balloon so the rest of us have room to move in this town," I said.

I looked around and didn't see Knudson anywhere. I went to the back of the room and through the connecting door to the adjoining storage room. Kathryn was there with the vacu-packer. I went up and gave her a hug.

"Ready?" I asked.

"As ready as I'll ever be," she said. "What am I going to have to do?"

"Not much. Follow Henderson's lead. He'll ask you a couple of questions. Just answer them honestly. There'll be a bailiff here in a few minutes. Give him the machine when he asks for it."

I went back to the courtroom. I was happy to see that just about everyone had made it. This was going to be good for business if I pulled it off. The insurance guy Swinson was there. He was sitting next to Elizabeth, who appeared to be chatting him up about his next company party. Mark Wasen was glowering over in one corner. He probably didn't know what to make of the invitation I'd left on his recorder the previous evening. Suzie was on the opposite side of the room, her eyes hidden behind large and unfortunately comical looking sunglasses. She was sitting next to Lulie, who had brought her at my request. There were various other spectators from all walks of life, the kind of people you find slowing down traffic at a car accident— rubber-neckers and pain vultures and People's Court devotees. The people who live off the thrill of experiencing someone else's life secondhand.

Speaking of secondhand, the ever closemouthed Curt was there too. I guess he'd been forced to shut down his store in response to the summons/threat I'd sent to his email. I wonder if he enjoyed the

Mayan clip art I had included on the borders. I noticed Lulie glaring towards the other side of the room and followed her line of sight. There sat Fern. I'm surprised she could get up this early. Never can tell with those ambulance chaser types. Then again, I've heard of people lining up around the block and waiting all night for Jerry Springer tickets. I stroked my head absently where her hoe handle had creased my scalp. She could sell her thrilling story to one of the regional Springer-alikes. I could hear the teaser now: Defending my Grungy Garage from a Masked Man, the true story of Fern Frenello.

There was a general commotion by the opposite door. Flashbulbs started to pop as it opened and the honorable Nelson Knudson strode into the room. Well. It wasn't really a stride. More like a waddle. Call it a stwaddle.

He walked over to the judge's bench and took a seat behind it. Then he grabbed a big gavel and banged it impressively. The room fell silent.

"All rise," called out the bailiff.

Since many of us were still standing this seemed like a superfluous remark. The remaining folk got to their feet while he announced:

"Here begins a Coroner's Inquest into the suspicious circumstances surrounding the untimely demise of one William Flambeau, the honorable Nelson Knudson presiding."

Knudson slammed down his gavel again and bellowed out importantly: "Be seated."

I grabbed a seat on the edge of the room, just off his field of vision. At that point another gentleman came into the room. Nelson started to speak.

"Ladies and Gentlemen, due to the unusual circumstances of this case, and my personal involvement in the investigation thus far, I believe that in all fairness I should recuse myself from presiding over this inquest. I have therefore requested that the assistant coroner take the bench and conduct the proceedings. Are there any objections from counsel?"

Henderson shot me a glance. I shook my head.

"No objections your honor," he said, "I presume defense will have the right to cross-examine and provide witnesses in this 'quasi-legal' inquiry?"

"Absolutely," said Knudson. "We're all just here to find the truth." He then proceeded to have the assistant coroner sworn in as the acting coroner and hearing examiner. As the acting coroner/examiner took his place behind the bench Knudson descended to a table next to the one where Henderson was seated. The citizens' panel who would hear the case, having been selected earlier from the normal jury pool, was also sworn in.

The acting coroner then called Knudson to establish the facts of the inquiry.

"Ladies and Gentlemen," Knudson announced in his most ponderous and impressive voice, "I intend to prove beyond a reasonable doubt that William Flambeau met his gruesome death at the hands of his purported lover and friend, Fred Costner. And that further, Mr. Costner, in an attempt to obscure the details of his malefaction, proceeded to dismember and dehydrate his former object of illicit and perverted lust, and shrink-wrap those portions. To what end we can only recoil from speculating about."

A collective sigh of horror escaped from the crowd.

From me too. I hate it when someone ends a sentence with a preposition.

CHAPTER 62

Knudson proceeded to ask the bailiff to bring out Fred from another anteroom. Fred was sworn in and put on the stand. Allowing this was a tactical move on our part. We certainly had the choice, even in an inquest, to refuse to allow Fred to testify, but Henderson felt it was best if it was out of the way early, and he might do better under direct questioning than cross examination. It was also possible that Fred's pathetic demeanor would engender some sort of sympathy from the assembled panel.

Knudson slammed that pitch right out of the park. So much for tactics. Fred was not so much pathetic as pitiful. He stammered and hemmed and hawed and generally fit the craven profile of a lover-eating, murdering shrinkwrapper. When Knudson asked him about the dehydrator, Fred's lame attempt to say he purchased it from Secondhand City while he was in disguise went over like a pregnant pole-vaulter. The same story of Bill's antics and the homophobia of the store's owner that sounded so convincing in Henderson's office sounded like a dog-ate-my-homework dissembling. Or the finger pointing fabrication normally found with he-did-it-no-he-did-it playground fibbery. Much different than the true tale of prejudice and comeuppance that it seemed like when he explained it to me. By the time Knudson was done with him, even trotting out the video rental record that showed how he had recently rented *Silence of the Lambs*, Fred was a gibbering example of revolting, and at that point, far from gay, human carnage. Knudson asked him one last question.

"Mr. Costner, could you please tell the court whether your partner in sin—"

"Objection, your honor," shouted Henderson, "counsel is pre-judging the witness."

"Sustained," said the examiner.

"My apologies, your honor," Knudson said smoothly, "whether your partner—" he sneered the word, "had a tattoo?"

"Y-yes," said Fred. "Lots of them."

"And did he have a tattoo on his left arm?"

"Y-yes."

"And did he have a tattoo on the inside of his left wrist?"

"Y-yes!" blurted Fred. And then he did a strange thing. He let out a wail and started to cry. And cry. And cry some more. Much to everyone's horror he was soon reduced to a blubbering, sobbing mess. It didn't look good.

"No further questions your honor," Knudson proclaimed triumphantly.

Henderson wisely chose to defer cross-examination to a later time. Fred was accompanied off the stand and to the side of the room where they seated him next to the bailiff. Knudson then took the stand himself. Under the examiner's scripted questioning, he revealed the anonymous phone call that had originally led him to arrest Fred as a material witness, the new focus on the dehydrator and its subsequent revelation of traces of human blood. He then described how his lab assistant had determined not only the origin and type of blood, but that it also contained Coumadin. Since he couldn't actually reveal that he had used privileged medical information to determine that the victim took Coumadin, he testified that a search of Fred's house had turned up prescription bottles, made out to William Flambeau, for such a drug.

"And what did you do at that time, Mr. Knudson?" asked the examiner.

"I watched helplessly while the defendant was released on bail to menace the community," Knudson said righteously. "Since I didn't have a DNA sample to compare the blood to, and since I didn't, for all I knew, even have a dead body, there was nothing else I could do."

There were sighs of understanding from the audience.

"And that's how matters stood till I got a phone call from my sister. Your honor, I'd like to return to my role as prosecutor."

"You are dismissed as a witness, Mr. Knudson. Proceed."

Knudson lifted his bulk from the witness chair and waddled back to his table. He picked up a sheet of paper and studied it for a moment. Then he looked me in the eye and said: "Your honor, the people call Jobe Carson."

I was surprised to say the least. While I expected Knudson to produce the evidence of the severed arm, I didn't dream he would use me to reveal it to the court. I could tell by his smirk that he was really enjoying this. From his twisted point of view, it was poetic justice that he would use me to tie the knot before he slipped the noose around my own client's neck.

"Mr. Carson," he began, "is it true that on last Wednesday evening, November 7th, you were arrested for withholding evidence in a murder case?"

"Yes, but—"

"Fine." He cut me off. "And would you please tell the court what that evidence was?"

"I didn't know it was evidence, and—"

"Please Mr. Carson. Your honor, would you instruct the witness to answer the question directly?"

"Mr. Carson," the examiner said, "though this isn't a court of law in the traditional sense, we nonetheless honor court conventions to maintain the appropriate tenor of justice. Please answer the questions directly."

"Yes, your honor," I said. And then to Knudson: "The supposed evidence was a severed arm."

Various people in the courtroom gasped.

"And how did you come to possess that arm, Mr. Carson?"

"It fell out of a truck one day."

"It fell out of a truck?" His sarcasm was thick enough to stop a toilet.

"Yeah," I explained, "One day I was out using moss killer on my lawn, you know how bad moss gets around here, and this lump falls out of this truck—one of those gypsy trash pickup dealies—because it was barreling through our neighborhood and hit this pothole. I don't know why the county can't fix—"

"Enough!" Knudson barked. "What did you do with this 'lump'?"

"Nothing. It was wrapped in a green Hefty bag, so I threw it over by the garage. Then my dog started gnawing on it, so I shooed him away. Later on, I threw it on a trash heap inside the garage."

"You didn't think to unwrap it?"

"No," I lied.

"So when your daughter told a friend of my niece at school that you had a severed human arm in your garage and that you were using it to solve a murder case she was just making it all up?" He sneered.

"Objection!" shouted Henderson, "Counsel is asking the witness to speculate on hearsay."

"Sustained," said the examiner, "But I think the core of the question is sound Mr. Carson. If you please."

"I have no idea what my daughter said." I equivocated. "Let's just say that at some point I realized it was an arm. But I still wasn't aware of any ongoing murder investigation that I may be obstructing."

"In fact, your honor," Knudson proclaimed and then turned and addressed the courtroom dramatically, "This arm was critical to the investigation into the murder of William Flambeau."

A murmur ran through the crowd. Either they were impressed with the drama of his delivery or his fly was open.

"Mr. Carson," Knudson continued, "When you determined that you actually had a severed human forearm in your possession, did you at any time examine said appendage for identifying characteristics?"

"Only once," I said, "It didn't look too identifiable."

"Why was that?"

"The arm was dehydrated. Shrivelly."

"Like jerky?"

"You might say that."

"And were you able to determine how recently this member had been deprived of its companion body?"

"No," I said, "I didn't want to do all your work for you."

I heard the bright tinkle of Elizabeth's laughter.

"Answer the question," Knudson fumed.

"No. Like I say, it was dehydrated. It was also shrink-wrapped."

"Describe to the court what you mean by shrink-wrapped."

"It was encased in one of those vacu-pack bag things. You know, like on the infomercials. All the air was sucked out of it and it was sealed in plastic."

"And no identifying marks?"

"None that I could tell, the fingertips had been cut off but the callosities on what remained indicated the guy may have been left-handed."

This was obviously a surprise to Knudson. He went back to his table and checked his notes. He pulled out a folder from his briefcase and thumbed through what looked like some photos. Then he looked around the courtroom till his eyes locked on Fred. He seemed to come to a decision.

"Your honor, I know this is irregular. Is the witness Fred Costner still under oath?"

"He is," the examiner said.

"May I ask him a quick question without bringing him back to the stand?"

"You may."

"Mr. Costner. Could you please tell the court whether your former partner was left-handed?"

The courtroom was hushed. Knudson was biting his lip. Fred looked down at his feet. We could barely hear his reply.

"He was," he mumbled, and started to cry.

CHAPTER 63

"Your honor," Knudson continued, expressions of pride and relief competing for room on his face, "I have here a picture of the severed arm in question. The court will note that, far from being dehydrated, it is as plump as if it had been severed yesterday. May I pass copies of the pictures around to the citizens' panel?"

The examiner took one of the pictures and studied it. He swallowed hard. "You may."

Knudson took them around to the panel. He then came up and gave one of them to me.

"Mr. Carson, is this the arm that was in your possession for a week and a half?"

"It's different than it was for most of the time I had it, but it looks like what the police found in my garage." I said.

"Any ideas on how it supposedly changed?"

"I'm guessing that when my dog chewed on the package, he perforated its seal. The police found it lying in a pool of water. It must have reabsorbed enough moisture to return it to its present state."

"Very clever reasoning, Mr. Carson. You might have a future as a detective," he said snidely.

"Thanks for the nice compliment," I said, "You might have a future as a human being."

There were a couple of titters from the crowd.

Knudson smiled fiercely and leaned close to me. "Mr. Carson, could you please tell the court what you see on the inside wrist of the severed forearm?"

"It looks like ink."

"Ink... And that ink appears to be in a pattern of some sort, wouldn't you say?"

277

"I would," I replied slowly.

"And when people have a pattern of ink stained on their flesh, what do we normally call that, Mr. Carson?"

I paused for a moment in thought. Then put an innocent expression on my face. "Crib notes?"

The crowd let out a laugh of tension relief. Knudson waited it out. The red receded slowly from his face. I had to admire him. He was managing to keep his cool.

"What else would one call such a pattern, Mr. Carson?"

"A tattoo." I said.

Knudson let my words sink in to the assembled group. He waited once again until the commotion had subsided.

"A tattoo?" he asked. "What an astonishing coincidence. I seem to remember the defendant's partner having a tattoo on the inside of his left wrist. Huh. No further questions your honor."

"You may step down, Mr. Carson," the examiner said.

Henderson chose not to cross examine me either.

"Your honor," Knudson announced. "In order to maintain the strictest definition of fairness for this inquest, the people would like to call an independent forensic analyst from the Federal Bureau of Investigation. Mr. Kim Putnam."

Kim looked at me as he approached the stand and shrugged his shoulders. He was sworn in by the bailiff.

"Mr. Putnam, would you please tell the court what you have done with the samples the county coroner's office sent to your lab last week?"

"Yes. I ran DNA analyses on them per your request."

"And what were you able to determine?"

"The first sample," Kim said, "after I was able to isolate and remove various hemo factors of obvious animal origin, rendered barely enough human blood to come up with this DNA profile." He handed a readout and a transparency to the examiner, who studied them briefly and then gave them both to Knudson. Knudson placed the transparency on an overhead projector and turned it on.

"This was the sample from the dehydrator's collection well," Knudson announced to the citizen's panel and the courtroom audience.

"The second sample..." Kim shot me a glance and continued, "The second sample was different."

"Different in what way?" asked Knudson.

"Different because I had a clean unadulterated sample and all the tissue I needed."

"This was the sample I personally took from the severed arm." Knudson said to the courtroom at large. He turned back to Kim. "And what was your result?"

Kim handed another transparency to the examiner. Knudson took it from him and started to place it on the screen.

Kim said the next words distinctly: "It matched."

The courtroom exploded. People started excitedly talking to each other. Reporters were yelling across the room. Photographers were jockeying for position to take photos of the matching transparencies and of Knudson. Knudson struck his best campaign pose; his thumbs hooked behind his bulging vest like an antebellum county judge, his carriage proclaiming to all the world that he was just here making sure justice got done. Yep.

One of the reporters bolted for the door, anxious to scoop his competitors. A fast thinking bailiff headed him off and there was a small scuffle between them. The examiner noticed and banged his gavel.

"No one will leave this courtroom!" he bellowed. The crowd settled down a little and looked in his direction. "You will all be seated!" he commanded. "I will have order in this court. Sir!" He spoke directly to the reporter at the door. "Find your seat. We will all remain in this room until the inquest is complete. The forms of justice will be honored!"

Everyone sat down. Occasional whispers passed between some of the audience members, but for the most part the commotion had ceased.

"We will now hear from the defense in this matter," the examiner continued. "Mr. Henderson, have you anything to present on your client's behalf?"

"I do, your honor," Henderson started. "In fact, I assert that by the time we are done here today, my client will be the free man he should have been all along; before a certain overzealous coroner decided to equate a person's sexual orientation with his proclivity for murder.

"Mr. Knudson," he boldly addressed Nelson directly, "although I wouldn't expect a thesaurus to be standard equipment in a coroner's laboratory, I can assure you Homosexuality does not mean the same thing as Homicide."

I could tell by the facial expressions of the citizens on the panel that they didn't quite get that last part. But Knudson was getting red in the face again. He didn't like Henderson's confidence. He was wondering what tricks Steve had up his sleeve. The case looked open and shut at this point. He had won. And yet here was this slimy lawyer challenging him directly, questioning his prejudice and his vocabulary, all in the same sentence.

Henderson addressed the examiner.

"Your honor, I know what I am about to do is somewhat irregular. But sometimes example speaks louder than words. The proof, as they say, is in the pudding. If you would please have a bailiff enter the room behind you and take possession of the appliance he finds within from the person there guarding it. A person whose sight the appliance has not left since it was purchased."

The examiner instructed one of the bailiffs to do so. Henderson turned to the crowd and proclaimed in ringing tones: "The defense calls the Dee-Luxe Vacu-Packer 2000."

CHAPTER 64

The bailiff lugged the big machine into the courtroom. I had gotten up and helped Henderson drag a table over by the citizens' panel. We unplugged the extension cord from the overhead projector and plugged it in to the vacu-packer.

"May it please the court," Henderson began. "This is the vacu-packer that is currently the rage of home grocery budget aficionados everywhere. We have reason to believe, and are certain events will prove, that this is similar to the model used in the shrink-wrapping of the severed arm that has become the focus of this inquiry. If I may demonstrate its capabilities?"

"Proceed," said the examiner.

This was my cue. I reached into the ice chest sitting at my feet and pulled out a half chicken. We'd had a devil of a time getting the chest past the metal detectors and the anti-bomb squad at the courtroom building door. Thank God the superior court judge had come along when he did. That was the first case Henderson had won today. I brought the chicken over to the machine.

"Mr. Carson will now show you the special benefits of the Dee-Luxe Vacu-Packer 2000," Henderson announced, sounding more like a carnival barker than an attorney.

I put the chicken in a special plastic bag, loaded it into the big basin in the vacu-packer and closed the lid. There was a whooshing sound and the smell of slightly ripe chicken wafted out of one end of the machine. A red light started blinking and a melodious chime sounded. I lifted the lid and pulled out a lovely, shrink-wrapped chicken, complete with a bar code and freshness date stamped on the plastic. I handed the chicken to the citizens' panel for review.

"Very impressive," said the examiner sarcastically. "And what is the purpose of this impromptu infomercial, Mr. Henderson?"

"Just this, your honor—"

My cue again. I went back over to the ice chest and pulled out a small leg of lamb. A white rime of fat encased its flank. I placed the leg into the vacu-packer and closed the lid.

"But you—" the examiner started to protest and then fell silent in understanding. Knudson was a little slower on the uptake, he appeared to have fixated on the succulent gustatory potentiality of the leg of lamb. The bell rang, and I lifted out what was soon to be labeled Defense Exhibit A.

"You'll notice," said Henderson as he held the leg up to the panel's scrutiny, "that when Mr. Carson failed to put the severed lamb limb into the plastic bag that the vacu-packer detected no problem and proceeded in its machine-like manner to act as if everything was okay." He turned it over. "Right down to stamping the meat with a bar code and freshness date."

The panel nodded their collective head.

"Sir," Henderson said to the panel member directly in front of him, "the stamp looks a little blurry when it's on flesh doesn't it? Would you be so kind as to characterize this 'bar code' with a different description?"

"Yeah," the citizen said. "It looks like a tattoo."

The crowd erupted once more. Knudson rushed over and nearly yanked the shank from Henderson's grasp. They struggled a bit. Flashbulbs popped. That was one of the pictures that made it into the paper. I took the opportunity to look over the audience. Mark was sitting silently, a look of forced composure on his face. Elizabeth was laughing merrily at the wrestling match between Knudson and Henderson. Lulie had her arm around Suzie, who was crying again, and Fern was just licking her lips. Between her and Knudson I'd be surprised if the lamb found its way home. The examiner called the courtroom back to order.

"Lovely demonstration, Mr. Henderson," he said. "But this court hardly thinks the difference between barcodes and tattoos is at issue here. The DNA evidence is indisputable."

"So it is," murmured Henderson. "But if I may beg the court's forbearance for just a bit? The defense calls Curt Lagnowski."

Mr. Secondhand City himself rose and went slowly up to the witness stand. He was sworn in and took a seat.

"Mr. Lagnowski," Henderson said. "I'd like you to answer just one question: Do you recognize the person in this courtroom who purchased a used dehydrator from you recently?"

"Yep."

"And where is that person?"

"There." He pointed to Fred.

"But I don't understand," Henderson said lightly. "According to Mr. Costner's earlier testimony, he was in disguise."

"I recognized him anyhow."

"How, if I may ask, can you be so sure?"

"Part of the business. Lots of people are in disguise when they deal with me."

"I see. Thank you, Mr. Lagnowski. No further questions your honor."

Knudson approached the stand. "Mr. Lagnowski. Are you certain the dehydrator you sold to the defendant had been used previously?"

"Pretty sure," he said. "It was all put back in its original box and everything, but it didn't look completely new, if you know what I mean."

"But someone could possibly have opened the box up and not necessarily ever actually used the machine to dehydrate anything?"

"Possible," Lagnowski said, "I don't go over the damn things with a magnifying glass."

"No further questions your honor."

Henderson stood up again. "Your honor, would you please instruct the bailiff to summon the person who is in the room from which we just obtained the vacu-packer?"

The examiner paused for a moment while he sorted out Henderson's syntax and then did so. Henderson announced: "The defense calls Miss Kathryn Olson."

Kathryn blinked as she walked into the room. The bailiff took her over to the witness stand and swore her in. When she was seated Henderson launched into an exposition.

"Let the record show that Miss Olson is a hostile witness. As luck would have it, Miss Olson purchased this vacu-packer this weekend. Again, as serendipity often seems to favor those among us who have done the hard work to prepare for it, my secretary was on a similar search for such an appliance and witnessed Miss Olson's acquisition of same. We have brought her here today, under threat of subpoena, to testify to both how easy it easy to purchase used appliances of this sort, and to this machine's provenance."

"Miss Olson, did you purchase this vacu-packer this weekend?"

"Yes."

"Without difficulty?"

"Yes. I don't think one needs a license to buy a used appliance Mr. Henderson."

"It was used?"

"I assume so, though it was neatly packed in its original carton."

"And do you have a receipt for that purchase?"

"I do."

"Would you please give the receipt to the assistant coroner?"

She did so.

"No further questions, your honor."

The examiner studied the receipt with a mystified look. He then glanced over at Knudson. Knudson looked at Kathryn, who shrugged her shoulders. He waved off his right to cross examination.

"I'm not sure where all this is leading, Mr. Henderson," the examiner said.

"Your honor," replied Steve, "the defense would like to call an earlier witness back to the stand."

"As you wish."

"The defense calls the FBI expert Kim Putnam."

CHAPTER 65

Kim walked up to the witness stand. Kathryn had gone over and sat down next to Knudson, murmuring an apology as she did so. He flicked it away like an annoying fly. Good. It looked like he had bought the secretary story. She'd be able to keep her job.

"Mr. Putnam," Henderson started up again. "You testified earlier that the DNA from the dehydrator completely matched the DNA from the severed arm?"

"Yes. It did."

"Indisputably?"

"Indisputably."

"How sure are you that the evidence could not have been tampered with?"

"Reasonably certain."

"And why would that be? Wouldn't it be possible to simply say that the dehydrator sample came from the dehydrator? And actually substitute a different sample that came from the arm itself?"

"Yes. It would."

The courtroom was still.

"It would?" asked Henderson.

"Except for one thing." Kim said.

"What would that be?"

"It would only be possible if both samples were collected at the same time. In this instance that wasn't the case."

"How so?"

"According to the logged entries of the chains of evidence, the sample from the dehydrator was collected well before the sample from the severed arm. In fact, the original sample was sent to my office before the arm was ever discovered, much less a sample collected from it."

Knudson glowed exultantly. Every angle of his posture screamed 'I told you so.'

"So there is no doubt whatsoever that the DNA sample from the dehydrator matched the DNA sample of the severed arm?"

"None whatsoever," Kim said firmly.

"Thank you, Mr. Putnam." Henderson turned around with his shoulders slumped in what appeared to be utter dejection. Knudson puffed up some more. I thought he was going to explode with glee. He leered at me with a big ghoulish grin on his face. He was already salivating for the victory feast. It looked like he could have eaten a big hank of jerkied arm right there. Henderson turned around and walked back to the witness stand.

"Mr. Putnam, could you please tell the court if the DNA readout matches any other samples you have analyzed lately?"

"It does."

"And what would that sample be?"

"I received a sample on Saturday afternoon from FedEx. It was a tissue sample, recently collected. I have the chain of evidence here if you need it."

"And where did that tissue sample come from?"

"It came from the kidney of Joe Frenello."

Fern screamed.

Then she charged. Right at me. Things got rather crazy at that point. Fern ran towards me at top speed. I was surprised at how fast that could be, but when she got the momentum of her juggernaut in motion, God help anyone standing in her way. She knocked over a couple of chairs and thrust aside one reporter, and then she was almost on me. The whole time she was screaming: "I killed him and I'm gonna kill you too. You little bastards are always ruining my life. I'm gonna kill you, I'm gonna kill you—"

I backed away from her and tripped over the stupid ice chest. I kept rolling into a back somersault and got to my feet in time to see her crashing over the ice chest too. Then she surged up from the Styrofoam wreckage and dove into me. Unfortunately, I had run out of room. She crushed me against the judge's bench, slamming my head against its upper edge. I was dazed, thank God, because then she started beating me on the face with the big mallets of her fists.

"I should have killed you the first time you slimy little bastard," she screamed. I turned my head to the side. I could distantly perceive the pandemonium in the rest of the courtroom through my mental fog. Reporters were busting out through the doors. Knudson was yelling at the assistant coroner that this was a travesty of justice and why couldn't he control the courtroom better. Photographers were jostling for position to film either the angry outburst from Knudson or Fern's attack on me. My friend Burke had a lens pointed straight at me, his big TV camera balanced on his shoulder, his right thumb thrust upward in the congratulatory signal that indicated he was getting a good shot. I tried to smile. A couple of bailiffs were headed in my direction. Then all of a sudden the punches to my face stopped. I looked forward and saw Fern being dragged off me by none other than the intrepid Lulie. She had her arms around Fern's throat and was hanging on like a pit bull on a baited bear. When she got Fern clear of me, she let go. Fern turned on her and growled.

"I'll kill you too, you little bitch," she sputtered. Lulie just looked her in the eye and hocked a big ol' loogie right in her face.

"Like hell you will," she said, hauled off, and planted the most vicious uppercut I've ever seen on the point of Fern's jaw. Fern dropped like a ton of jello. She splayed out all over the floor, unconscious, her tongue lolling out of her florid face and her buried muscles quivering with residual adrenalin. She looked like a combination of a boogie man and a giant, overstuffed bean-bag mattress. A beanie bogey.

But a bogey, I couldn't forget, who had nonetheless snuffed the life out of another human being. And then cruelly carved him up, dried him and packed him in freshness dated, easy to store portions. I went and looked down at her grotesque face. I couldn't resist the urge. I kicked her in the side of the head. Lulie came over and gave me a crooked smile. Then she kicked Fern too.

"That one's for Joe," she said.

CHAPTER 66

"But Dad, I still don't understand how you knew it was Fern."

"Simple, Mir, it was the knife."

"The knife?" Kiah snorted. "Was the guy cut up with one of those electric carver thingies?"

"Not that kind of knife, Kiah," I said. "Joe's pocket knife."

They looked at me expectantly.

"It was that first time I went to Fern's house and she tripped over her dog. I went into the one room that must have been Joe's. Remember I told you how neat it was?"

"Yeah," Mir said, "And how the rest of Fern's house was a pig sty."

"A pig sty with occasional attempts at organization." I said. "That's important. Anyhow, when I went into Joe's room I noticed everything perfectly put in place. But one thing jarred my subconscious: The knife on the top of his dresser. I could see him putting it there every night. What I couldn't see was him leaving it there if he went anywhere. I was pretty sure a man like that would always keep his pocket knife with him. It would be a part of him. He'd probably had that knife since he was in the Merchant Marines. Remember what I always say about people being creatures of habit. I doubted very much if he'd left it there voluntarily and gone wandering off without it to escape living with Fern. My suspicions were confirmed later when I talked to Lulie. She went on at some length about his using that same knife to carve her some special napkin rings. Remember?" I looked over at Lulie.

"Damn right I do," she said while she put pieces of pie in front of the kids. We were all gathered around a couple of tables at the café. "I stood right over there and told you all about his whittling."

"But Dad," Miranda persisted. "You told us Joe bowled right-handed. And the severed arm guy was left-handed. You said so yourself."

"I said Joe bowled right-handed, Mir, lots of people do one thing with one hand and other things with another. I write and eat and brush my teeth left-handed, but I play racquetball with my right."

"Not fair." Miranda put a mock pout on her face.

"But I don't get who was shooting at you in that Hyundai." Jack interjected. "I thought you said Fern had a big ol' station wagon."

"And a passing knowledge of the car lot by the Bingo parlor." I said.

"So?"

"Remember the key making machine in her garage? The one Joe must have taken home when the market he worked at closed down for good?"

"Yeah?" Jack still wasn't getting it.

"I'd be willing to bet Fern took a test drive one day and made a copy of that car's key on the machine in her garage. Then she swiped the same car from the lot the day it was closed and used it when she fired a couple of shots at me."

"But why would she shoot at you?"

"Yeah," said Kiah, "That first shot happened before you'd even met any of the suspects."

"That threw me for a while too," I said. "Lulie your meringue is as good as ever. It wasn't until I saw that newspaper article with the picture of me in Fern's garage that I figured she must have recognized me when I was coming out of—or going into—the insurance company's office the day of the first gunshot. The old newspaper article had said I worked on insurance company fraud cases. Maybe she was planning to go to the insurance office to check up on whether she was going to get her money when she saw me. And who knows? Maybe that was the day she took the first test drive in the car. I wouldn't be surprised if there's a record of it somewhere. I'd guess the first shot was a reaction thing. She was excitable, she knew I was going to be on her trail soon, and she panicked. The second shot was probably more planned."

There was a pause while they digested both the information and the wonderful pie.

"But what about the tattoo, Dad? How were you so sure about that?"

"Call it faith in my own intuition, Mir. All my instincts pointed to Fern. When I found out Joe didn't have a tattoo on his left arm I was even more sure. That arm couldn't have a tattoo on it. That's when I remembered about the freshness dating vacu-packer attachment that Elizabeth had explained to me in her back room one day."

A little huffing noise made me look over at Kathryn, who was raising her eyebrows.

"I was investigating." I said.

"Right," she said, making quote marks in the air with her fingers. "Investigating."

"The only thing I was sweating in my boots about," I continued, "was whether the ink would stamp on the leg of lamb at the Coroner's Inquest the way I hoped. I didn't have time to test it beforehand. I was glad I was able to buy a shank with so much white fat on it. By the way Mir, you caused me quite a lot of trouble there—leaving the freezer door open and plumping up the arm just in time for the police to snag it. I've told you a million times to check to make sure you close that door. Now you know why."

"Yeah Mir," Kiah added, "Remember that next time we have a dehydrated severed arm in the garage."

Everyone laughed.

"Dad, there's one little detail I didn't quite get." Kiah must be growing up, he was actually admitting to ignorance. "What was all that stuff with Kathryn in court? When she gave a receipt to establish the machine's—what was the word—provenance?"

"A little bit of insurance, Kiah. It never hurts to pile up the evidence. We might have had to move for a delay if Kim didn't get the DNA analysis done. So we wanted to create reasonable doubt. Kathryn bought the vacu-packer from Fern herself. That was the machine she'd used to seal Joe's fate. It was nice to use it to seal hers as well. Not to mention rubbing Knudson's nose in a little more crap."

"But Dad," Mir asked, "How did Fern manage to put things back in their cartons so well? I thought she was a total slob."

"I don't think she was a total slob Mir. I think she was just a habitual slob. She was capable of intermittent bursts of neatness and organization. It's just that her natural slovenliness would gradually overtake her. She'd run out of organizational gas. It was a great idea to dispose of Joe the way she did. But it was also quite like her to forget to put in a plastic bag one time and accidentally end up having his arm directly freshness dated. Likewise, she was able to pack up the dehydrator pretty good and sell it to Secondhand City. She just didn't clean it thoroughly enough to remove all traces of blood from the collection well. Much to Fred's regret."

"Jobe," it was Kathryn this time. "How could you be so sure Fern would show up for the inquest? I about fell over when I saw her in the audience. And I thought she would explode right there when she saw me."

"Intuition again," I explained. "And logic. If in fact she had been the one that shot at me, I was pretty sure she wouldn't stay away from the inquest. I think the only thing that kept her from blowing up when you came into the room was the way Knudson had the DNA evidence pointed at Fred. We were lucky. It played out perfectly."

"Thanks to Lulie saving your ass." Kiah loved teasing me. "By the way, did you ever figure out who made that anonymous phone call that got Knudson sniffing on Fred's tail in the first place?"

"No, I didn't Kiah," I said. "That's the one mystery I still can't fathom."

"We did it," Suzie said.

I looked at her incredulously. "You did it? Why?"

"Mark saw Fred's name in your notebook when you came out that Friday. He thought it would be funny to get Knudson to throw a wrench in your works."

"Yeah funny," I said. "I don't see why he needs an enlarger, he's a big enough one already."

"What?" asked Suzie.

"Never mind," I said.

"But why was Mark so hung up on returning things, and so neatly?" Jack asked. "I thought for sure it was him because of that."

"I think they were just trying to get top dollar for their product," I said. "Either they wanted to get a full refund from the store where they bought it, or as much money as they could from the likes of Curt at Secondhand City. That a good guess, Suzie?"

"That's right," Suzie said, "Mark used to make me put back every little Chinese inspection sticker and everything."

"But, why?" Jack persisted, "He was rich, right?"

"Correction Jack, his dad was rich. But when his dad disappeared, Mark was suddenly suffering from an acute case of income shortage. Without Dad doling out an allowance, Mark was strapped." I looked over at Suzie again.

"Yeah," she agreed. "We were going around trying to figure what else to sell. We even raided the wine cellar looking for vintage bottles worth some cash."

"Victor's going to be mighty upset when he comes back," I said.

"Comes back?" Everyone asked in chorus.

"From his sea kayaking on the Georgia Straits," I said. "That was just a guess when I said it to Mark that day, but it got me thinking, so I called a private investigator I know up in Nanaimo. He put the word out and a captain of a cruise ship said he thought he saw a guy matching Victor's description tooling around the outer islands. Good thing too. I didn't want to have to trouble Kim for another freebie DNA analysis. I expect Markie will get his allowance back soon."

"And when do we get our money, Daddy?"

"Probably not for a couple of months, Mir my dear, at least from the insurance company. They have to make sure they do all the right paperwork to void Fern's policy on Joe. Interesting sidenote: Officer Greg told me Fern was babbling in her cell. I thought she was pretty smart cutting up Joe and stashing him away the way she did. Turns out she only did it because she thought that somehow it would double what she was getting on her policy."

"Why's that?" Mir asked.

"Joe had both death and dismemberment insurance."

CHAPTER 67

A couple of months passed, and things got back to normal. Fred came through with a big chunk of money for getting him off. As a result, we had a much better Christmas than I had expected and a great New Years with just our little family. Plus Kathryn. I invited her and her mother to share some snacks and champagne with us to ring in the new year. Her mom was having a good day and so did we.

Fern was indicted, tried and convicted for the murder of Joe. I managed to talk Joe's sister into giving Lulie Joe's knife from his personal effects. Joe's sister was happy to do so. She said she still owed Joe for donating one of his kidneys to her. It would be nice to give something to his best friend.

Victor got back into Olympia by the time Hanukkah started and Mark was able to celebrate the New Year at the country club with The Honorable not-quite-as-pompous Knudson. Elizabeth's husband showed up too. Turns out he had been in San Francisco the whole time; engaged in the difficult process of coming out of the closet. He was asking her for a divorce.

And in one of those interesting confluences of events that lead one to believe in a higher power, when he came back, he brought a present for Fred: Bill. One night in San Francisco Elizabeth's husband had been reading a newspaper that focused on gay issues and had come across an account of the Coroner's Inquest involving the falsely presumed dehydration of William Flambeau. Complete with pictures. As luck would have it, he had seen Bill the previous night at a local bar. Elizabeth's husband went back to the bar for a couple of nights until he saw Bill come in again and then approached him with the article and picture. He talked him in coming back to Olympia. Bill was suffering from amnesia. Apparently brought on by a severe blow he took to the head when he was beat up by a gang of who knows who.

Fred was nursing him back to health with a safe home and good food. I hope it didn't include vacu-packed turkey jerky.

CHAPTER 68

Mir and I went out walking the other day. By the lake where her mom had disappeared. We sat on a rock and looked out over the gray water and thought about how lucky we were. We had our health. We had food on the table and a warm place to stay. We had each other. We were starting to put our lives back together. The pain wasn't as bad as it had been. The worst was over.

"Thank you, Mir," I said, and gave her a hug. "Thank you for all you do to make my life wonderful."

"Thank you, Dad," she said. "I know Mom would be proud of you."

"And she'd be really proud of you," I said. I felt a warm serenity wash over me. Her mom would be proud.

We hugged again. "Let's go home and have a big cup of hot strawberry," I said brightly.

I walked back down the trail towards the car. Miranda lagged a little behind—giggling, skipping over the leaves and weaving in and out of the trees with girlish abandon. Then her laughter stopped.

"Dad—" Her voice was cold.

"What?"

"Come look at this."

Her tone sent a chill through my veins. I walked over to where she was standing. While she had been prancing around she'd kicked loose a pile of leaves. Something was poking out from underneath. I reached down and brushed the rest of the leaves aside. It was a shoe. Size 6. Adidas Trailrunner. I remembered the last time I had seen that shoe. When it was being packed in the sports bag my wife took with her to work. On the day she took her long run. I looked at Miranda through the tears suddenly welling in my eyes. She looked at me.

It's never over.

Made in the USA
Columbia, SC
31 May 2022

61151058R00183